THE HAS-BEENS

MIA HAYES

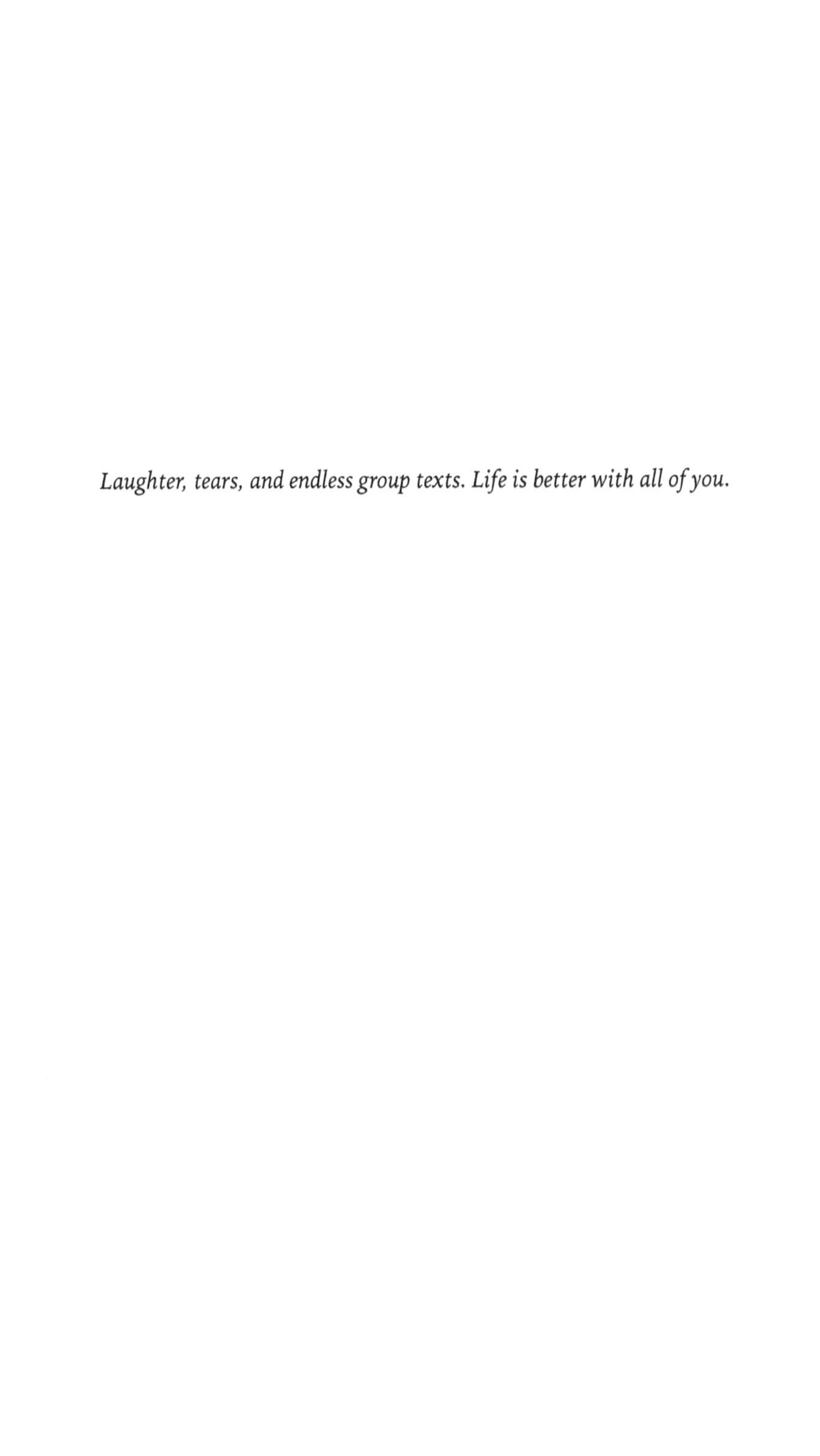

Laughter, tears, and endless group texts. Life is better with all of you.

1

STEPH

When you've known someone since you were ten, you get a good sense of what they're thinking before they say it. Right now, Diana's rigid posture and clasped hands tell me something is bothering her, but it's her wrinkled nose that gives away that she not only dislikes Kristin's invitation but finds it absolutely ridiculous.

"It'll be fun," I say, handing Diana her latte. She pinches her lips together, a sign that it's going to be an uphill battle to change her mind. "Just consider it, Diana," I say. "You may be surprised."

"I really don't think I can." She glances at the door and then back to me with her honey-brown eyes. Instagram models wish they had her naturally flawless hair and gorgeous skin. "This is a busy week for me. I have a client meeting and am speaking on a panel. I have so much to—"

"Your clients won't know if you go out on a Saturday night. No one will give you demerits," I chuckle. Diana's always been a perfectionist. A good girl. I don't think she's ever done anything that would come close to earning her a demerit. "Plus," I say, "Nick has always hinted that he wants to go."

Diana frowns, and her dark beachy waves sway slightly. I

should know better than to spring something like this on her. She takes days, if not weeks, to warm up to new ideas. Always has. Meeting her here, in a still semi-empty coffee shop, was my and Kristin's way of preventing the infamous Diana Shutdown, but the plan is failing fast.

I should have waited for Kristin to bring up the topic, but she's late, and Diana is short on time.

Diana lifts her chin and peers at me like I've grown another head. "Honestly, Steph," she says, enunciating as if speaking to a two-year-old. I hate when she does this to me, but I keep my thoughts to myself. "It sounds miserable."

I expected this. Getting Diana away from her phone and pant suits was going to be an uphill battle. Add in that she isn't a fan of neighborhood parties, and it was bound to be a non-starter. "Look," I say as I launch into my prepared speech, "if I can come out here every year for Amy's Halloween party, you can at least make an appearance. These people are your neighbors."

"I barely know Amy, and I don't socialize beyond book club." Diana drops her voice to an almost whisper. "You know it's going to be a bunch of drunk housewives and their husbands acting like fools."

Diana and Kristin live in a social media-perfect community not far from DC that's full of bored housewives and their golf-playing husbands. It's not my scene at all, but the residents' antics are an endless source of amusement.

I blow into my drink even though it's no longer hot. I'm not really a coffee drinker, so it's more of a prop. Something to do with my hands so that I don't throttle Diana for being so unfun.

"Why is the thought of wearing a costume and having fun with your neighbors so repellant?"

"What I want to know is why you insist on going to this thing every year even though you don't live here."

"There's something fascinating about middle-aged suburbanites throwing down," I say. "And I can't resist a good train wreck."

I don't live here, so really, I have no business going to Amy's party, but Kristin invites me every year, and no one has objected.

Diana checks her phone for the hundredth time. We've only been here ten minutes and she's making it feel like an eternity.

"What's so fascinating?" I ask as she scrolls.

"Work."

"You work too much," I say, even though I probably work as much if not more. This Halloween party is the only party I attend as a guest, not as the host.

Diana sets her phone down and sips from her cup. "Says the woman who throws parties for a living."

Here we go again. "I own three of DC's premier nightclub and concert venues," I say sharply. "I own them, just like you owned your PR firm."

Diana exhales. "You know what I mean: It's not corporate America."

She'll never understand the sacrifices I've made to get where I am. She has never scrubbed toilets and floors, picked up questionable objects with industrial rubber gloves, or found remnants of coke all over tables. But I have, and I do it so that my venues are clean, safe, and comfortable. I have come a long way from working small gigs in Ibiza, but the work will always be grueling, and honestly, Diana couldn't handle it.

"Corporate America—and you—need to relax." I pull her phone so it's in front of me.

Diana's mouth drops slightly open, and she stiffens. Anddd… here comes The Shutdown.

She takes her phone back, swipes it open, and flips it around so I can see her multi-colored calendar.

"See? My schedule is packed. I don't have time for a night of debauchery." Diana's voice is crisp and no-nonsense, and the right corner of her lip twitches. She would be a terrible poker player.

My chance of getting her to come along is plummeting. Time for approach number two. "What about doing it for Kristin?"

Diana sighs and arranges her highlighted brown locks so that they fall perfectly over her shoulders. "Please don't guilt me." She turns her always-attached-to-her phone over in her hand and studies the screen. "Where is she, anyway?"

"She's only five minutes late. Not all of us run on Diana-time."

Diana's chair creaks when she leans forward. "I have things to do—"

"—I saw your calendar—"

"—and I can't wait for Kristin to show up whenever it's convenient for her." Diana rests her elbows on the table and taps her fingers together.

Yup. I've pissed her off, but that doesn't mean she can take it out on Kristin. "Cut her some slack, Diana. You know things haven't been easy for her lately." I cross my arms. Despite my irritation, I'm not ready to give up on Diana going to the party. "We all could use some fun." I pause for dramatic effect. "Kristin and I will take care of the costumes, and all you'll need to do is show up."

Diana cringes. "We aren't twenty anymore, Stephanie." Uh-oh. Full name usage. "We can't just do whatever we want and forget our responsibilities."

Right after college graduation, Kristin, Diana, and I rented a four-bedroom loft with another young woman in DC's Adams Morgan neighborhood. We threw epic parties with coveted invitations. But now, every event I attend with my friends involves passed appetizers and wine.

Life has sucked the crazy, up-all-night fun out of Kristin and Diana.

"It's a Saturday," I say. "If I can take the busiest night of my work week off, you can too."

Diana huffs. "It's not the same."

"You have assistants and a team. Can't one of them step in if a client needs something?"

Diana grunts. "Unlike you, I can't leave my work to the junior staff."

I push my tongue against the roof of my mouth before answering. "Because what I do isn't a real job?"

Redness tints Diana's cheeks. "That's not what I meant, and you know it."

Okay. So, Diana and I aren't two peas in a pod. Hell, we're not even on the same vine most of the time, but I've had enough of her disdain for my life choices. For the past fifteen years, she's implied that I need to: 1. Get a real job; and 2. Grow up. Because in Diana's world you're not successful unless you're raking in money and have a huge house in the suburbs, perfect children, and a husband who dotes on you.

I hate arguing, and I hate arguing with Diana and Kristin the most, so I say nothing. As always.

I am a great sayer of nothing.

Maybe too good.

"Look," I sigh. "I don't want to fight, but Kristin would do it for you. She'd do anything for either of us. Rearrange things. Please," I beg. "It will be more fun with you."

The coffee shop now bustles with activity, and I recognize some of the faces from my years of being Kristin's plus one. Women—because there isn't a man in the place except a barista— sit in groups of two and three with coffee cups grasped in their diamond ring-covered hands. It's a world awash in yoga pants, cashmere wraps, North Face fleeces, and designer bags.

Diana finishes her latte. "I don't know. It sounds like a recipe for disaster."

Okay, she's considering it. I wink. "Or a really great night."

"You're not selling this." Diana presses her phone's volume button, and the screen lights up. She stares at it for a moment before saying, "I'll think about it."

A blossom of hope grows in my heart.

The glass coffee shop door swings open, letting in a furnace blast of unusual October heat. Kristin waves to us as she flip-flop shuffles across the room, and her long honey-blonde ponytail sways from side to side. Lately, every time I see her, she looks thinner and thinner, but today, I'm especially shocked. Her collarbones jut out at sharp angles beneath her navy tank top, and her strategically torn jeans look in danger of falling off, even with a belt cinching the waist.

"I'm sorry I'm late. I... I got caught up on a phone call." Kristin wedges herself into the space between Diana and me. She drops her heavy handbag on the ground and slumps forward.

"Everything okay?" Diana asks.

Kristin nods. "It'll be fine."

"And that tells us you're not okay," I say.

Diana touches Kristin's arm. "What's wrong?"

With her lips pressed tightly together, Kristin waves her hand like she wants us to move on. When neither Diana nor I say anything, Kristin asks, "How are the kids, Diana? Still loving college?"

Diana's twins are freshmen at Princeton and Brown—a personal success for her.

"They're fine. Emily's Parent's Weekend is next weekend and Alex's is the following weekend." She smiles at Kristin. "When's Nicole's?"

"Two weeks ago." Kristin's chin quivers. "We didn't go this year."

Well, that's new. Everything Kristin does is for Nicole— almost too much for Nicole, in my opinion.

It's clear Kristin is upset and doesn't want to talk, so I switch topics. "Diana is going to come to Amy's party."

"Really?" Excitement flashes across Kristin's face. "You'll love it. Her parties are so much fun!"

I've got Diana now. She can't say no without upsetting Kristin who already looks like she may have been crying.

"I fell for Steph's snake-charming ways," she says.

"It'll be like our loft parties." Kristin perks up. Maybe whatever was bothering her isn't too major? "The three of us can be the Pretty Young Things again."

I don't correct her that there were four of us, because we never talk about Jess or how she packed up her room and moved without a good-bye. We never discuss her betrayal.

"The loft parties were fun." Diana actually smiles.

"Imagine it," I say, focusing on the present. "One night of no responsibilities. Your two best friends. Drinks and music and—"

"Gross guys," Diana says. "There are always gross, inappropriate husbands at those types of things."

"Diana!" Kristin says sharply. "They are your neighbors. Besides how would you know?"

"Your stories."

"She's not wrong," I say. "But if you can handle a guy getting a hard-on over sales numbers and his new Tesla, you can handle him wearing a hot dog costume."

"Point taken." Diana's phone dings, and she stares at it while frowning. "I have to run, but I'll talk to Nick tonight." When I start to interrupt, she holds up her hand. "Doesn't mean I'm definitely in, but I'm considering it."

I wave her away. "Go. But I'm going to hound you. On Saturday, the three of us are going to this party, and we're going to have fun."

"This Saturday?" She looks surprised. "You can't be serious! I need to get it on my schedule, Steph. Plus, I have Emily and Alex's Parents' Weekends."

"Amy does it a week before Halloween that way people are

home to hand out candy," I say, even though I did forget. "Emily's thing isn't until next weekend. You'll be fine."

"I can't." Diana rests her hand against her chest. "I have too much going on with work and all."

"Yes, you can," Kristin pleads. "You're the boss. And, trust me, Parents' Weekend is always a disappointment. You will barely see the kids."

"You two are so persistent." Diana stands and looms over us. "I'll think about it, but no guarantees." She grabs her computer bag and her expensive-as-hell handbag, and waves good-bye with her free hand. "I'll text you both tonight."

I flash a smile at Kristin. Diana doesn't know it, but she's coming. She wouldn't leave it open-ended if she wasn't. "I'll be waiting."

After she's gone, I say, "I'll text Emily. You know she'll pester Diana to come."

"Evil," Kristin laughs. "But you're right. Diana won't say no if Emily tells her to go."

As Kristin and Diana's kids have grown older, my role in my relationship with them has evolved into co-conspirator. When Nicole feels smothered by Kristin, I distract Kristin so Nicole can have space. When Alex wanted to go to his first concert, and Diana and Nick refused, I arranged for all of them to be VIP guests. And sweet Emily and I enlist each other in our schemes to get Diana out of her live-to-work rut.

I rest my chin on my hand. "Have you picked out your costume?"

Kristin twists a piece of her ponytail around her finger. "No. I've been distracted."

"By a neighborhood scandal?"

"Not this time." I may not live in the neighborhood, but I know everything going on there. Kristin claims I'm an honorary resident and always invites me to neighborhood parties in the hope that I'll find Mr. Right (aka Mr. Well-off-and-drives-a-Porsche) and settle down.

"What's going on?" I ask.

"I... I don't know." Kristin rubs the back of her neck. Dark circles line her sunken eyes.

A wave of horror hits me. Her drastic weight loss, missing Nicole's parents' weekend, her distractedness.

"Are you sick?"

Kristin eyes grow wide. "No! Why would you think that?"

Relief wells in me, and I gesture at her. "You don't seem yourself."

She twists her hands and exhales loudly. "I think I need a break from life."

This is new. "What's going on? Is everything okay with Tom? With Nicole?"

Kristin tries smiling, but she looks pained. "Everything feels blah. With Nicole gone, Tom and I are stuck in a routine—or maybe it's a ditch. I don't know."

I mull over her words. Kristin has never once mentioned being unhappy in her marriage. In fact, she's always gushing over how lucky she is to have a husband like Tom. "Maybe you need a joint hobby? Or a trip somewhere?" I shrug. "I wish I had better advice, but this is probably more of a Diana thing."

"I don't know if any of that would help. It's like we're operating in two different dimensions." Kristin blinks before looking around the now-full coffee shop and leans closer to me. "Is it too much to want passion? Or excitement? Or to just feel something?"

"Not at all."

"I thought, after Nicole left, we'd find our way back to each other." Kristin looks like she's worried someone is listening. "Diana and Nick are so happy. I want to be like them."

"They're workaholics. I'd hardly call that healthy."

"But they're crazy about each other and have a great marriage."

This is not the time to remind Kristin of all the times Diana told her she shouldn't make Nicole the center of her universe.

"Have you talked to Tom about any of this?" A few months ago, something shifted in Kristin. She went from always smiling and engaged to… well, I don't know what. I know she misses Nicole and wishes she'd come home for more than a few weeks over the summer, but maybe there's something more?

"Tom is… well, he's oblivious. He's happiest just watching TV while I read." She smashes her eyes tightly together before blinking them open. "He keeps saying that we've made it to the nice part of marriage."

"And it's not?"

She rests her chin on her hand. "I'm suffocating, Steph. I don't know who I am anymore. Nicole doesn't need me, and Tom's hit cruise control." Her voice hitches. "I wish I could be more like you."

I raise my eyebrows. For the past twenty-five years, Kristin has done nothing but try to make me more like her. She has never understood my life choices. "I think you're having a mid-life crisis."

She traces a line across the wooden tabletop. "I think you may be right."

2

———

KRISTIN

As soon as I'm in my car, I blast the air conditioning and check my phone. Joe hasn't texted or called since this morning when he messaged that he hoped I had a great day. And that's fine. Really it is. After all, we're just friends.

And yet, I can't stop the disappointment welling in me as I stare at the darkened phone.

I shift my car into reverse and navigate out of the tight parking lot and onto Main Street past cute rows of brightly colored shops. A few women with babies and toddlers walk along the sidewalk, stopping to greet each other.

When Tom and I decided to move to here for the great schools, a family-focused community, and big houses, I knew Nicole would have an amazing childhood with unlimited opportunities. I've never regretted our decision—even with all the craziness and scandals that seem to happen regularly.

The drive from downtown to my house is short, and I park on my empty driveway. A twinge of sadness hits, but I push it away. Tom likes to joke that I'm a "lady of leisure" now that Nicole is away at school, but he doesn't understand that my life is very full.

I have lunches with friends and tennis lessons and, of course, the club's Junior Committee. Volunteering is a full-time job.

I have so many things except the one that makes me happiest: being a mom.

My house smells like lemons, and everything shines because the housecleaner came while I was out. When Nicole was little, I'd tell her we had cleaning fairies, and she was convinced Tinker Bell and her friends arrived every Thursday at our house with buckets and brooms.

She was so cute.

There are no signs of life in my silent house. No tail-wagging dog—Tom took him to work—or daughter blasting music in her room. It's just me and my thoughts, which is the worst thing for me right now.

The tea kettle sits on the stove. I fill it and find my second favorite mug with the phrase, "Sparkle On," written across it in glitter. Nicole and I found it one day while shopping at the craft store, and she had to have it. But like everything else she had when she went off to college, she's left it behind.

The only bright spot in my life is Joe. His daily texts and calls lift the monotony of my life, but he has been radio-silent all day and hasn't even replied to my texts.

Has something happened to him? Or is he busy with work? Does it matter? I can't possibly keep texting him without a reply; it seems desperate.

Outside the kitchen window, a cardinal perches on a nearly bare tree branch. It stares at the window as if watching me. Does the bird see what Steph had seen? That I'm spiraling into middle-aged malaise?

"Why can't I be happy?" I ask the bird. "What's wrong with me?"

The bird cocks its head as if listening.

"I'm fine, you say?" A never-ending grayness has settled over me. "I'm not fine. I know I'm not fine."

The bird flits off as if my sadness is too much for it.

When the kettle whistles, I pour the steaming liquid over my tea bag. The water turns pale green, and I wait as it deepens before tossing the bag into the sink. I should throw it in the garbage, but since there's no one to argue with me about it, I don't bother.

It's twelve-thirty on a Monday, and other than seeing Steph and Diana, I have no plans today. Tom is working late which means I'll order dinner in and Netflix binge, but that feels depressing.

I settle onto a pink velvet side chair, balance my tea on the wide arm, and turn on an HGTV rerun. It's my pathetic effort to not think. The designers are arguing about how to best remodel a family room. The colors the guy likes are safe and predictable, but the female designer wants to go bold.

"Pick the woman designer," I say to the TV. "Take the loud wallpaper and run with it."

Tom and I always watch remodeling shows at night and have discussed redoing the kitchen again. Maybe I should ask him about it? It would give me something other than my loneliness to think about.

Ding.

Like a greedy child taking extra candy from the bowl, I pick up my phone. A giant picture of a sandwich fills the screen, and a tiny glimmer of light breaks through the grayness.

—*Think I can eat this whole thing*—

I laugh out loud. It looks like one of those cartoon subs. —*No*—

—*Bet?*—

A smile stretches across my face. —*lunch tomorrow if I'm right*—

Three dots appear.

I wait.

—*how bout we just make it a date*—

My heart sputters. —*okay. The normal?*—

I've known Joe and his wife, Thalia, for years. We all moved into the neighborhood around the same time and have watched each other's kids grow up. In fact, for a moment in tenth grade, Nicole dated their son, Tyler. But recently, Thalia has drifted away from our group of friends with no explanation.

—*I'll see you around 11:45*—

A few months ago, Joe and I bumped into each other at the grocery store and rekindled our friendship. Now, we have lunch once or twice a week. Sometimes we talk about the kids, but mostly I listen to him discuss his job and dreams about the life he wants after his youngest heads off to college next year. I've told him a little about Tom's indifference, and Joe says living with Thalia is like having a roommate. Unfortunately, I understand all too well.

I text Joe a thumbs up emoji and open my laptop. I promised the Junior Committee that I'd reach out to some local businesses about donating to our annual silent auction.

I should call Thalia, just to check in on her. Joe said she's been under a ton of stress at work and snappish, but what would I say? She doesn't play tennis, and I never see her at the club anymore. Plus, she doesn't participate in our friend group's text chains anymore.

As I'm holding my phone, it rings.

"Hey, Steph. What's up?"

"Diana is in! Emily came through and bullied her into hit." Steph takes a big breath. "I just sent you some costume ideas."

"Gotta love Em." I force excitement into my voice.

"We don't have much time, so we need to move. I can get one-day Prime shipping which gets everything here by Thursday end of business. It's risky, but it can be done."

"Hold on." I switch my phone to speaker and open my email. I wrinkle my brow. "Sexy fairytale characters? Diana will never go for that."

"I'm just going to order it, and she'll have to wear it because she won't have anything else." Steph giggles. "Do you think she'll prefer Busty Little Mermaid or Daddy's Little Girl Red Riding Hood? I'm taking Dominatrix Snow White."

I laugh. "Diana is going to die if you put her in one of those."

"Her fault for not picking her own costume."

I swirl my tea. "We should raid Nicole's costume closet. She has some gorgeous ones." From sixth grade on, Nicole was obsessed with anime, and she and I spent hours making and sewing costumes for various ComicCons. We even turned our second guest room into a costume closet for her.

Steph blows into the phone. "Ohhh, I want Nicole's closet!"

"I can guarantee there is no Dominatrix Snow White in there."

"Boo."

Jealousy pings at me. I wish I had the guts to wear Steph's costume of choice. "I've gotta run," I say even though I have nothing to do. "But it's a no-go on the fairytale costumes. I'll find something for Diana and me."

Steph groans. "Fine, but it better be something other than a sexy cat."

"I promise."

"Talk to you later."

I hang up and leave the TV on before climbing the stairs to Nicole's costume room. There has to be something in her stash. Outside her half-empty bedroom, I pause. Nicole moved into an off-campus apartment last summer and took most of her things with her. Trophies and awards still litter her shelves, but everything else that made the room uniquely Nicole's has been packed up and trucked three hours south to Virginia Tech.

My throat constricts.

My daughter rarely comes home anymore, and she no longer needs me. Yes, Nicole answers my daily texts, but she only reluctantly takes my calls. And forget about Facetime. She's always too busy.

I exhale loudly. No one told me how bad losing my daughter would hurt—I've lost the most important part of myself; one that can't be replaced. Maybe I'm weird. After all, Diana hasn't had a problem with the twins going off to college. Then again, Diana handles everything in life with grace.

I exit the room, walk down the hallway, and stop in the costume room doorway.

"Can I be Princess Peach?" Eleven-year-old Nicole sat sprawled on floor next to my sewing table with a collection of manga books scattered around her. Her blonde hair was done in two neat French braids, and she wore her field hockey uniform.

"Show me a picture." She held the book up, and I nodded. "We can make that."

My sewing machine hasn't been touched in at least two years, and honestly, I avoid this room. The happy memories hurt too much.

I run my hand over the costumes Nicole left behind, searching for a connection to her. I pluck the Princess Peach costume off the hanger and ball it against my chest. We spent hours working on it together. Hours laughing and having fun.

Does none of it matter to Nicole anymore?

Tears burn my eyes.

Do I matter anymore?

The cat tail isn't right. Not at all. I contort in front of the mirror and glance over my shoulder. The tail dangles precariously from the black leotard I'm wearing.

"Damn. This won't work." I frown and swat at the deflated tail before tugging the bodysuit off. Steph was right: it's too safe and only slightly sexy. I set it aside as a possibility for Diana.

A stray blonde hair dangles in front of my left eye, and I tuck it behind my ear. None of the costumes feel right. I've discarded six, deeming them either too bland or too wild. If Nicole were here, she'd pull something stunning together.

I stare at myself, zeroing in on my problem areas. My stomach isn't as flat as it could be, and my thighs have a hint of cellulite. My boobs could be perkier. Honestly, I could use a Mommy Makeover, but Tom would never go for it. He claims to like me how I am.

Buzz. Buzz. Buzz.

I pounce on the phone, and a smile tugs at my lips. "Hello?"

"Hey, K. What are you doing?"

A deep sense of warmth wraps around me, and my shoulders relax.

"Standing in Nicole's costume room, trying not to cry." I should lie but there are no secrets between us. That is our rule, and I live by it.

"I'm sorry. Is there anything I can do?"

I smile wider. Joe just gets me. "Not really."

He blows into the phone. "I'm sorry to do this, but I need to cancel tomorrow. Maybe next week?"

I struggle to hide my disappointment. "Sure." My heart sinks, which is ridiculous. Why am I so upset about not getting to see Joe? It's silly. "Just let me know when."

"I will." He pauses. "You're still going to Amy's party, right?"

"Of course! Are you?"

"Yeah. Thalia doesn't want to, but I wouldn't miss it." His tone is slightly playful. "What's your costume?"

"I don't know." I steal Steph's line: "Maybe a dominatrix Snow White."

Joe chuckles. "I can think of about a dozen guys who would love that."

"Only a dozen?"

"You're being greedy."

I grin. "Am I?"

"Hey," a deep voice says from the doorway. "What are you doing with all that?"

Shit. I fumble the phone before hitting the 'end call' button. How long has Tom been standing there? "Just talking to Steph about the Halloween party."

"It didn't sound like Steph."

Please don't let him hear my pounding heart. "She's convinced Diana to go to Amy's party Thursday, and she wants me to be a dominatrix Snow White."

I pause and pray Tom believes me.

"That sounds…" He eyes me with surprise. "Steph is always getting you to do weird things." Tom runs a hand through his short, graying hair. He doesn't eye me hungrily even though I look kind of cute. "Do you want grab some lunch? I have a two-hour break."

Lunch? Most husbands with a two-hour mid-day break would want something other than lunch. I force myself to smile as I change into my jeans. "I thought you were working late?"

"My meeting got canceled." Tom's monotone voice reminds me of his khaki pants and ill-fitted dress shirt: boring. He has a closet full of beautiful shirts and slacks that I've bought, but he always wears the same bland clothes and casual athletic shoes. He's a sixty-five-year-old man trapped in a forty-five-year-old body.

"We could go to Max's," he says, naming one of the two restaurants he likes.

"Sure." I spin around and wait for him to compliment how I look. Instead, he stares past me, and I fight the words stinging my tongue.

"This is the best part of being empty nesters. We don't have to work around Nicole's activities." Tom leans against the door-frame. "It's nice being able to do whatever we want."

"Was it really that awful?" Pressure builds in my chest. "Nicole's activities gave our lives structure."

Tom frowns. "It wasn't awful, but you know… it's not like we ever got to do anything we wanted."

"Like go to Max's in the middle of a workday?" I brace myself against the bed. "Because we could have done that while she was at school. We could have done so many things while she still lived here, but you never wanted to."

"I guess I never thought about it." Tom steps into the room. "You always seemed so busy with the PTO and lunches and all the other stay-at-home mom stuff you did."

"You wanted me to do all that, remember?" I cross my arms. "You insisted that I stay home with Nicole."

"And it was absolutely the right thing for our family." Confusion flashes across Tom's face. "Are you okay?"

"No," I snap. "I'm not okay." I sweep my arms wide. "This hurts. And all you do is talk about how being an empty nester is so great." Tears burn my eyes. "It's not great for me. I hate it."

"You hate it?"

"Yes!"

Tom crosses across the room and pulls me against his chest. Once, being in his arms was comforting. Now, it is a painful memory of how life had once been. He presses his hand against the back of my head and kisses my hair. "Why didn't you say something sooner?"

I lift my head and meet his eyes. "I've been screaming, Tom. I've been screaming."

3

———

DIANA

"**N**umber thirty-six!"

I check the piece of paper in my left hand even though I know I'm number forty-two, and then I glance at my phone in my right hand. My colorful calendar is a masterpiece—even if Steph made fun of it. Emily calls my phone my brain, and she isn't wrong. I'd be lost without it.

On Saturday, against my better judgement, I've penciled in the Halloween party because Steph and Kristin enlisted Emily into their scheme. When she called and begged me to go, if only to share stories about the other moms with her, how could I say no?

"Number thirty-eight!"

—*Diana, call me*—pops up on my screen. I swipe it away. I've avoided my mom all day, but if I don't call her back now, she'll guilt-trip me forever. Hopefully, the sandwich shop noise will give the appearance that I'm busy.

"Hi, Mama!" I say, keeping my voice upbeat. "Is everything okay?"

"Why has it taken you hours to call me back?" she asks without a greeting. She always speaks to me in Hungarian, and

20

it's a deep family shame that neither Emily nor Alex understands the language.

The crowd around me thins. "I'm working, Mama. I've been tied up on an issue. I'm sorry I didn't call earlier, but I am calling now."

"Have you prepared Thanksgiving yet? Your cousins are coming this year."

Thanksgiving. Every year, I host my large extended family because Mama likes showing off my large house and success to her sister and her family. The two of them are so competitive that it makes me thankful I'm an only child.

The worst part, however, is that Mama makes me feel like an incompetent hostess. Nick, bless him, cooks the meal since I can barely make spaghetti, but my parents expect the presentation to be formal and precise. There's no room for imperfection. Nick and I must have the perfect marriage, the kids need to excel in every area, and my home must be pristine.

If one thing is out of place, I'll never hear the end of it.

"I'm on it." My number is called. "My lunch order is ready. I'll call you after work."

I hang up and with the paper bag clenched in my hand walk back to the office. I need to focus on work. FireSpot is coming in this afternoon to discuss their congressional hearing, and I want to run through my notes one more time before they come in.

"Diana, Senator Dyson called for you." My assistant Claire looks up at me as I pass her cubicle. She's fresh out of college and in desperate need of a professional wardrobe. It pains me that I can't say anything because of 'personal dress preference' or whatever HR calls it these days.

I furrow my brows. "Why didn't you call me immediately?"

Claire shrugs. "I thought he would?"

"No." I hold out my phone. "That's your job. You put him through to me."

"Ummm… he didn't say to."

"Claire, if someone like Senator Dyson is looking for me, it's your job to find me. Understand?"

"Ummm… okay?"

She's not going to last long if she keeps letting things like this happen.

I stride into my corner office, drop my lunch on my desk, and sit down. As I nibble my sandwich, I ring Senator Dyson's assistant (who doesn't answer), and scroll through my FireSpot PowerPoint presentation. Everything looks perfect.

C-SPAN plays on one of the TVs across the room. Senator Dyson stands on the steps of the Capitol, and I turn the volume up.

"There is no place in this country for terrorism—and make no mistake—organizations like Clean Water Now are thinly-disguised environmental terrorist groups."

A picture of a young blonde woman speaking to a group of protestors on the Capitol steps fills my screen. Police hover on the edge of the protest.

I flip off the TV. Well, now I know why he wanted to speak to me.

"Diana, babe, you've got to see this from our point of view." Aidan Maddox leans forward, arms resting on the mahogany meeting room table, and smiles like he's trying to disarm me. "We can't see the win for us here."

I resist wrinkling my lips and instead plaster a pleasant smile on my face. In my twenty-plus years of doing crisis communications, I've never meet anyone as pompous as Aidan. The fact that FireSpot sent a lowly junior executive to meet with me is all I need to know about how seriously they're taking their current situation.

"Aidan, love," I say smoothly. "If FireSpot doesn't come out swinging, you're going to get eaten alive by the media. FireSpot sold millions of consumers' information to a firm that's been linked to Russia. The optics aren't great."

"Fuck the optics." Aidan waves his hand. "What I want to know is how you're going to make this go away."

I close my eyes briefly to gather myself. "I can't make this go away if FireSpot won't admit a tiny sliver of wrong-doing." I glance around the room at my team. All eyes are on me. FireSpot is our largest account and the one that keeps the lights on. "Where's Therese? Or Mark?"

Aidan bristles. "I'm fully capable of making these decisions."

I chuckle. "Forgive me, Aidan, but… well, I'm used to dealing with the C-level execs on these types of issues."

"And forgive me, Diana, but I'm used to working with doers. Are you a doer, Diana? A visionary? Because that's what FireSpot needs. Someone fresh who has innovative ideas."

Despite the annoyance growing in my gut, I sip from the water glass in front of me. It's always best to pause and reflect before speaking in these types of situations. Finally, I answer. "I've been in this business over twenty years. I've seen this type of situation play out time and again. You're being called before a congressional committee. That's serious."

Aidan slaps his hands on the table and smirks. "Twenty years of doing something the same way is a long time. Maybe too long." When he nods, his hoodie string sways. I'd love to wrap it around his neck. "Are your results ever different?"

This isn't how the conversation was supposed to go. I have a PowerPoint and detailed plan on how to handle this crisis. I've made strategic calls to prominent journalists promising inter-views with top-level FireSpot execs.

"What are you saying, Aidan? Are you here to fire us?"

Aidan shrugs. "You tell me, Diana. The ball's in your court, but I think, perhaps, it's time to hand the reigns off to someone with more exciting ideas."

"Exciting?" I snort. "You realize crisis communications isn't about disrupting the norm or whatever bullshit you tech bros like to preach. It's about getting ahead of a story and fixing your image." I lean closer to the table and lay my hands on the cool surface. "If you know better, then I suggest you handle this alone."

Aidan clenches his jaw. "Diana, your old way—your twenty-plus years-old way—is done. It's time for fresh blood." He points down the table at one of my junior team members, Hailey. "Like her. Why can't she handle the account? She's hot, and I'm sure there's something exciting going on in her brain. Right, sweetheart?"

Hailey's eyes grow wide. "I—I—"

"Do not *ever* speak about anyone on my staff like that," I say evenly, despite wanting to leap over the table and throttle Aidan. "Hailey is a Georgetown graduate and a valued member of my team. She does not exist for your visual appreciation."

"Says the woman whose time has passed." Aidan settles back against his chair and crosses his arms. "Admit it, Diana, your age isn't helping you. You're stuck in the 2000s."

My face grows hot. I will not lose it in front of my team. I can't afford to. I'm supposed to be level-headed and calm all the time. "I think you should go, Aidan. I'll follow up with Therese."

"Therese is no longer with FireSpot." Aidan cocks his head. "Didn't you get the memo? The C-Suite got cleaned."

"Mark, too?"

Aidan nods, and his grin grows.

I blink and hold back my surprise. Therese and Mark have been my contacts for three years. How did no one fill me in on this? "Is that why you're here today? FireSpot had to bring in the JV team?" Someone gasps, but I keep on. "Because Aidan, that's what you are: JV. You have maybe five years of work experience. You're nowhere near ready to handle a massive PR team or crisis."

Aidan scowls. "Tell that to my new boss, Tessa." When I give no reaction—because who the hell is Tessa?—Aidan smirks. "The board wanted fresher blood. People with new ideas. That's not you."

"Are you firing us?" I shift so that my shoulders are square to his. "Are you making me jump through hoops for your amusement? Or did you come here to find a solution to your substantial problem?"

Aidan pushes away from the table and stands. The two younger—if that's possible—guys with him gather their notes and stand also. Like Aiden, they wear jeans, hoodies, and sneakers. "I'd hoped we could come to an understanding, but I guess it's true what they say: you can't teach an old dog new tricks."

Someone chuckles, but I don't break focus. "You're making a huge mistake, Aidan. FireSpot needs representation now more than ever."

He curls his finger over his shoulder and motions for his lackeys to follow him. "Oh, we have representation ready to go."

I raise my eyebrows as I stand. "Really? Who?"

"Beast Communications."

At the far end of the table, Hailey and another junior person whisper. I glare at them, and they stop.

"Are you serious? They've been in business for less than a year. Katie and Aubrey are nice young women, but they have minimal experience. Neither have ever led a campaign like this."

Aidan slings his backpack over his shoulder. "They're fresh. They have new ideas. And they're hungry. All the things you're not."

He yanks the conference room door open, and he and his team exit. I don't bother to follow them. What the hell? What the ever-living hell? I steady myself with a deep breath before turning toward my team.

"So, that didn't go as expected," I say. "But now we can double down on our other accounts."

Liz, JKP's operations officer, peers up at me and frowns. She knows better than to say anything in front of the team, but no doubt she has thoughts. She always does.

"Alright." I dust my hands together. "Sam, I need you to close out the FireSpot account immediately. All work is finished. If we get media inquiries, forward them to Aidan." I pause. "Better yet, put out a press release with his contact info in it. I want to wash my hands of him."

Sam scribbles a few notes, and I turn my attention to Hailey, the account executive. "I need an assessment of your other accounts by this afternoon. I want everything—work done, project status, revenue, et cetera."

Hailey nods, but I can tell from the way she holds her shoulders, she's panicked. FireSpot was her biggest account. Without them, she doesn't have enough work to support her team.

"Hail, no need to worry yet, okay?" I say. "I'm going to figure this out."

She glances at her hands.

"What is it?" I ask.

Hailey refuses to meet my gaze. "What if he's right? What if our way isn't working anymore? Should we be trying something different?"

Mutiny from Aidan is one thing; from my staff, it's something else. "Is that what you really think?" When she doesn't answer, I probe further. "What's this really about?"

"Beast offered me a position. A VP spot working on FireSpot."

My face burns. "You knew about this and didn't say anything?"

"I didn't want to burn bridges."

"You wanted to hedge your bets." I ball my hands before relaxing my fingers. "You should take their offer because there's no longer a position for you here."

"Diana," Hailey says. "It's not like that. I just wanted—"

"To blackmail me into a better job title?" I shake my head.

"Sorry, but your position has been eliminated. Gather your things." I glance at Liz. "Escort her out. She's not allowed on her computer."

"Can you give us a minute?" Liz says to the staff. "I want to talk to Diana."

As they file out, I calm the rage flooding through me. How dare Aiden come into my firm and disrespect me? How dare Hailey jump ship when I've been nothing but accommodating with her mental health days and missed deadlines?

I pace the room. *Pause when agitated. Pause when agitated.*

Aiden thinks my twenty-plus years is a detriment, but he needs institutional knowledge. And Hailey—what was she thinking? She knew this was coming and said nothing. That isn't how a VP operates, and she's going to find that out fast.

I fall into my chair and rest my head on my palm. Why are young people so unwilling to work? They all want titles, but also a remote situation, more vacation days, and no after-hours calls. Do they understand the work we do? Crises don't happen on a neat schedule.

The conference door swings open, and Liz enters... followed by our CEO Meghan Cross and a woman I don't recognize.

"Well, that was a disaster," I say. My blood pressure has lowered, and my thoughts are clear. "I can't wait to see how Fire-Spot survives this one."

"It's a mess," Liz says. "They're going to be eaten alive, and Beast is not positioned to handle something like this."

"Liz, can we have a moment alone with Diana?" Meghan asks, taking the seat across from me. The other woman sits next to her.

As Liz gathers her things, I run through a dozen potential clients—including Senator Dyson—and prepare to launch into my plan to land a new client or two to cover FireSpot.

I drum my fingernails on the table. "I can onboard Senator Dyson this week, and I heard rumblings of trouble over at Laude. We'll be back to full billing within two weeks."

"Diana," Meghan says. "You've built an amazing firm which is why we acquired it, but your contract is up."

I nod. A year ago, I sold Clarke Communications to JKP, and in addition to a huge payday, I was made managing partner. "I know, but can we negotiate a new contract later? We need to figure out our FireSpot issue."

The woman sets a pile of papers on the table. "I'm Sarah Millkin, the new head of HR." She taps the papers. "We've collected numerous complaints about you."

I blink, trying to understand. "From FireSpot?"

"From staff and clients," Meghan says. She folds her hands on the table and frowns. "I hate having to say this, but you're not a good fit culturally for JKP."

My head buzzes, and it feels like someone has covered my ears. "What are you saying?"

"We need FireSpot."

"But not me?" My heart hammers against my ribs. I shove my chair back and stand. Pause and reflect. Pause and reflect. "How am I not a good fit? Is it something I can work on?"

Sarah shakes her head. "Unfortunately, we feel it's your style, and we can't afford to lose more clients and staff while you adjust."

I keep my jaw from dropping open. "I'm being let go because I don't coddle adults? Is that what you're saying?"

Meghan shakes her head. "There's a difference in coddling and creating a workplace where everyone feels safe and included."

"They don't do their jobs!" My heart thunders. "They take endless vacations and expect me to act as their therapist and mother. PR professionals need thick skins."

Sarah pushes a few papers at me. "This is the terms of your severance. Since you've already received a sizable payment when JKP bought Clarke Communications, we're offering six months' salary and health benefits. We will allow you to control the narrative of your departure as long you're not derogatory toward JKP, our staff, or clients."

I stand frozen. All my life, I've done exactly what has been expected of me: top schools, amazing kids, a strong marriage, and a thriving business. I've never lost.

"There's no other way?" I ask.

"I'm afraid not," Meghan says. "We'd like you to stay on through the end of the month to hand off accounts."

I snort. "No. I'm done. Today." I gather my computer and notepad. "Have fun being warm and fuzzy and getting results for your clients." I walk toward the conference room door. "Have my office boxed and sent to me."

The walk to the elevator is excruciating. I pass Hailey sitting at her desk and focused on her laptop, Claire keeps her back turned, and Liz stands in her office doorway, looking confused. She starts toward me, but I wave her away. I can't do good-byes right now.

I jab the elevator button and wait. There are whispers, and some sound smug, like they know what's happened and are happy about it.

Maybe Aiden is right. Maybe I am a dinosaur.

4

STEPH

Something always goes wrong.

But it's okay because I expect it. After twenty-plus years in the nightclub industry, I've learned a few lessons, which is why I've survived when so many others have failed.

Rule number one: the unexpected creeps up on you if you're not ready for it and can send you spinning into an abyss.

Rule number two: always be ready for the unexpected.

Half of my staff is currently missing, but I'm not worried. My employees are loyal and hard workers, and I've never had a night when I couldn't open due to staffing issues.

Bright overhead lights illuminate the dance floor and expose all the gritty parts of the room. Paper wristbands, empty water bottles, and an errant credit card litter the floor. I shake my head. LUSH opens in five hours and there's an insane amount of work to be done.

But everything is going to be okay, just like it always is.

"Is anyone going to sweep?" I shout. "The floor's a mess and it needs to be power washed too."

Across the room, Layla grabs a push broom and hurries toward me. "I've got it."

She isn't wearing her uniform, which isn't a big deal since I'm not a tyrant, but Layla has on a leather jacket, black booties, light-wash jeans, and her long, dark hair hangs in bouncy curls down her back. It isn't a manual labor outfit.

From my pocket, I produce a hair elastic. "Tie it back. It's a work hazard."

Layla plucks the elastic from my palm. "Thanks."

I motion for her to follow me toward the bar. Of the younger staff, she is my favorite. Layla always pitches in, never complains, and hustles. She will go far if the industry doesn't burn her out first.

I shove a stool aside and lean against the bar where Jean-Luc polishes glasses. "Hey," I say. "Do you have everything you need?"

"No." He closes his heavy-lidded eyes briefly and gives a very French half-shrug. "No one has given me lemons." Jean-Luc's voice is like velvet, not that any customer can ever hear it over the music. But his voice matches his beautiful face, and the first time we met, I knew he'd be a fantastic bartender even if he didn't know gin from vodka. People like pretty, and Jean-Luc is pretty.

"Lemons?" I rest my hand on the polished bar top. Soon, it will be covered in spilled drinks, paper napkins, and questionable substances. "Who's supposed to bring you lemons?"

Layla pushes the broom in short, neat strokes around the bar. "Sammy is on stock."

"And he's gone missing?" I ask.

"I think..." Layla glances at the entrance. "Maybe..." She stares at the door again. "I don't—"

"Why are you staring at the door?" I ask.

"Maybe Sammy is a special friend?" Jean-Luc teases.

Unlike every other young woman and man who works for me, Layla is completely immune to Jean-Luc's charming ways, and she scowls. "Sammy is a dumbass who can't find lemons."

"Okay. Enough. I need everyone out here. Now." I take the broom from Layla. "I've got this. You go find them."

Jean-Luc continues readying the bar, and Layla disappears into the back where the performers' green room is, along with the stock room. SuzySoCal's crew buzzes around the stage setting up for her set, but even with them and a few of my employees, the club feels empty.

I drag the broom across the floor, creating piles of dust. I'll have Sammy finish scooping it up as a punishment. Then he can power wash.

My phone dings, and I pull it from my back pocket.

—*Who's ready to party? I can't wait!*— Kristin has animated her text so it jumps around the screen.

—*I'm rethinking*—Diana responds

Damn it. What happened? Diana had agreed.

—*No take-backsies*—I type and shove my phone into my pocket.

My employees have magically appeared and move in a type of synchronized choreography that happens when everyone knows their part. Layla catches my attention and gives me a thumbs-up.

Rule number three: don't be afraid to delegate.

"Right back where I started." I push a pile of crushed water bottles and cigarette butts toward the stage. "Shouldn't the owner be immune from such injustices?"

A guy on stage shrugs at me. "Hell, if I know. I'm just a roadie."

As the owner, you'd think I'd no longer have to do basic tasks, but no, I'm still working the line, still cleaning puke off the floors, and apparently, still sweeping.

If I had known my life would be this glamorous, I may have stayed in Ibiza.

"Come to Blitz's foam party tonight!" I shoved a flier at a group of young Americans standing near a restaurant entrance. Every day between 6 p.m. and 11 p.m., I canvassed Ibiza's streets trying to drum up business. "Girls get in free, and it's insane. You have to come."

"What happens at a foam party?" a chisel-jawed guy asked. He was about my age, over six feet tall, and tan from all the Ibiza sun. Not my usual type, but cute enough.

I winked at him. "Anything that you want to happen."

"What if I want you to happen?" he volleyed his shot. One of his friends laughed and another shoved his arm. The three girls with him looked bored.

"Why don't you come tonight and find me. I'll be there." I sounded flirty, but I had no intention of ever seeing this guy again. He'd probably want some vacation romance, and I'd seen that play out enough times to know how it ended.

"How will I find you?" he asked, grinning at me.

I tossed my sun-kissed brown hair over my shoulder. "I'll be the one dancing with the girls you wish would dance with you."

"Hello?" a woman's chirpy voice calls from across the room.

A blast of speaker feedback screeches across the club, and I spin around, kicking the pile of debris I just swept. "Jesus!" I shout at the roadies. "What are you guys doing?"

"Sorry," the lead roadie says. "We're having some technical difficulties."

"Hello?"

A woman stands in the doorway, holding a cloth shopping bag. Her dark hair hangs in a loose braid over her shoulder and contrasts with her emerald-green jacket.

"Can I help you?" I ask. "We don't open for a few more hours." The woman doesn't look like a SuzySoCal fan, but who knows these days?

"I'm looking for Layla." The woman is too far away for me to make out her features.

I glance around and don't see Layla. "I think she just ran to the back." I bend to pick a water bottle off the ground. "She'll be out in a minute," I say. "If you can't wait, you can text her."

The woman holds up her phone. "Already doing it."

From the stage, SuzySoCal's roadie shouts, "Steph! Where's the breaker? I think we killed the outlet."

I sigh. "What the hell did you plug into it?"

"Just the normal. I swear." He wipes his forehead with the back of his hand. "Nothing fancy."

"The breaker box is in the staff room."

"Thanks."

The woman smiles when I turn back toward her. "Sorry," I say. "It gets crazy before a show."

"It's okay." She tilts her head slightly to the right like she's studying me. Then, with deliberate steps, she moves closer, stopping just a few feet from me. "Steph?"

The woman's voice sends my mind tumbling through a string of confusing, blurred images: bodies crowded around a stage, the VIP room, guys laughing.

And Jess.

I blink.

"Jess?" Her hair is longer now, and she's thinner, but it's Jess.

"I had no idea you worked with Layla." She looks confused. "I thought you moved to Europe."

"I did, but I came back." I cross my arms to fight the tightness in my chest. "Why... why are you here?"

The hesitant smile that forms on Jess's lips sends me speeding twenty-three years into the past.

"Come with me, Steph!" Jessica smiled and climbed on the subwoofer dominating the space in front of the makeshift stage. "They'll let us backstage. I promise."

Blink. I'm at LUSH, not some seedy DC warehouse rave. All those things are years in the past. Done.

But Jess is standing right here. Right now. I've dreamed of having this chance, but now... why won't my mouth work?

"Steph?" Jess tilts her head and studies my face. "I didn't know. I can go. I'm so sorry. I didn't mean to—"

"Why are you here, Jess?" I don't hide my confusion. "Why are you standing in my club asking for Layla?"

She holds out the cloth shopping bag. "I brought Layla's key and uniform. She locked herself out of her apartment."

Her voice bounces around my brain, colliding with the solid wall I've erected over the years.

"Hey, Mom!" Layla emerges from the backroom. She stares at us, but there's no flicker of knowledge that she understands the situation. "Thanks for bringing my stuff."

Mom? Jess is Layla's mom? What the hell? Stay calm. Don't let them see how rattled you are.

Jess gives Layla the bag. "You're welcome."

"Oh! I'm sorry!" Layla clutches the bag. "Mom, this is Steph Torres, my boss. Steph, this is my mom, Jessica Stevens."

"Nice to meet you." Jess extends her hand like she's never met me before.

I wish I could pretend to not know her. I wish I could forget everything she did.

I shove my hands in my pockets and nod curtly. "Layla, go change. We've got a ton to do; we need to hustle."

Before I turn away, Jess's eyes meet mine. Maybe I'm delusional, but hurt and confusion radiates from my former friend.

"This is going to be the best night ever!" Jess stood on the stage and offered me her hand. "Trust me, Steph!"

Never again.

I stand before the floor-to-ceiling window of my office and watch the crawl of the night traffic and people below. Life blurs into red brake lights as cars roll to a stop, and a steady autumn rain touches the windows and races downward.

The shock of seeing Jess hasn't worn off—but why? It's been nearly twenty-three years.

Jessica freaking Stevens is Layla's mom. What are the odds?

Downstairs, the opening act's set sends bass vibrations through the building. Normally, I'd be on the floor, monitoring things, but tonight, I left Layla in charge. I need some space to think.

The VIP room. Guys laughing. And Jess. Always Jess, telling me it would be okay.

Except it wasn't. At least not in the moment. It is okay now because everything has worked out. But back then, it wasn't okay.

Calm down. I take a deep breath. *You are right where you're supposed to be.*

A little of the tension in my shoulders eases, but one thought runs through my mind: how do you let go of hurt that you didn't know you still had?

I consider ignoring my ringing phone, but all that will accomplish is having to call Kristin back later.

"Hey," I say. "What's going on?" I will not tell her about Jess. Not yet. Maybe not ever.

"I think I found a few costumes for us in Nicole's closet." Kristin's normal perky cheerleader voice is flat. At some point I need to suggest therapy, but I want Diana in on that.

"Great! What are they?"

"Diana's going to be an elf princess. I found Nicole's costume makeup stash, and I'm a pro at applying liquid latex."

The thought of Diana wearing latex takes my mind off Jess. "I'm sure you are."

Kristin ignores me. "You want something sexy, right?"

"Isn't that the point of Halloween?" I ask.

"That's what I thought." She snorts. "Nicole went through an anime phase, and I still have the schoolgirl outfits. We'd have to really do up your eyes though."

"That should be Diana's costume," I say. "She's the one with the big eyes and glossy hair."

"No," Kristin answers. "It's too provocative for her."

"I'm going to order the Dominatrix Snow White," I say. "It will be here in time."

Kristin sighs. "Are you trying to antagonize my neighbors?"

"Maybe." I know Kristin's neighborhood friends have complained about their husbands ogling me. I don't try to stand out, but I don't exactly blend in with their cute, tiny blonde wives who all wear the same suburban uniform. I'm five-nine, naturally thin—but curvy—and what those assholes call "exotic-looking." I wear fitted tee-shirts, jeans, black boots, and a leather jacket pretty much all year long.

Kristin's housewife friends call me 'edgy' and apparently, their husbands aren't safe around me—which is ridiculous. On a nightly basis, I'm surrounded by a bevy of young, attractive people who hit on me constantly. These women fail to understand that I don't need a middle-aged, punchy man to rock my world. I'm doing that on my own.

"You can't wear that costume." Panic peppers Kristin's voice. "You know that right?"

"Watch me." I turn my chair so that I face the door again. "But hey, there's a show going on, and I've gotta run. Can we talk later?"

"Oh! I didn't know," Kristin says. "I'm sorry to bother you."

"I'll call you tomorrow to game plan."

I hang up. Hiding in my office forever isn't an option. I need to face Layla, and I can't hold her parentage against her.

Fluorescent lights flicker in the vacant stairwell down to the main floor, and I pop my earplugs in as I near backstage. When I was younger, I didn't worry about my hearing, but like carbs and blood pressure, it's been added to my growing list of concerns.

The group of unfamiliar young women sit in the green room, laughing.

"Hi!" I say. "Are you with Suzy or the opening act?"

All five turn to look at me.

"Um, hi?" A young woman wearing a leather skirt and crop top eyes me dismissively.

The others don't bother looking up. I have enough experience to know groupies when I see them. And groupies are the worst. They think they're special. Chosen. They actually dream of having relationships with the performers.

"I'll ask again," I say with my arms crossed. "Who are you with?"

A young woman with ironic, over-sized glasses stares up at me. She tucks a piece of mousey blonde hair behind her ear. "Okay, grandma."

These little…"You need to leave. All of you."

They ignore me. In the old days, I'd grab them by the arms and toss them into the alley, but we can't do that anymore. Lawsuits and whatnot.

Layla sticks her head in the doorway. "Steph! I've been looking for you everywhere. Suzy is refusing to go on if we don't find her mandarin oranges ASAP."

"That diva bitch," I mutter. "Send Sammy to CVS. They always have bad fruit." I jerk my head at the group of women. "Get rid of them. Bring in Marcus and Jose. I don't care how you do it but get them out of here. And put them on The List."

"Seriously?" Layla's eyes are wide. "The List? For all clubs?"

"All of them. I don't want to ever see these lovely young women again." I skirt around Layla and into the hallway. "Hey." I turn around. "Can you run the floor with Mary on Saturday? I have a Halloween party in the suburbs to go to."

"I'd love to!"

I planned on having Stevie help Mary, but right now, I need to prove to myself that I'm not going to punish Layla because she's Jess's daughter.

"A party in the suburbs?" Layla asks, trotting along side of me as I walk toward the front of house. "Why would you go to that?"

I stop short of the main floor door. "I go every year. It's fun in its own way." I shove the door open, and music overwhelms me. "I think of it as research," I shout. "For when I throw geriatric Gen X raves."

Layla laughs, but the sound is lost to the music. She watches the stage where the opening act is finishing up. How did I not notice her resemblance to Jess? They have the same eyes, the same hair, the same mouth.

She leans close to me and shouts into my ear. "You should do it! Throw a Gen X flashback rave. You'd make bank."

"You think so?" I shout back.

Layla nods.

I jerk my head toward the bar, and she follows me. It's a little quieter here, but not much. Luckily, one thing I've learned in clubs is lip reading.

"If you're interested in doing a Gen X thing," Layla says. "I'm happy to research it. I like oldies and acts."

"Oldies?"

She blushes. "Vintage?"

"Better," I say. A thought nibbles at me, and I bat it away twice before letting it take hold. "Why don't you come with me? We can drive out together, and you can stealthily take notes on what would make forty-something suburbanites leave their cozy bubbles of blandness and come into the District. We can get something on the books for March or April."

"Could be fun, but I thought you wanted me to help run the floor?" Disappointment crosses her face. Running the floor is a promotion—one she wants badly.

It's not her fault who her mom is. It's not. She's still Layla. Plus, if she was Emily or Nicole, I'd be her fun Aunt Steph, and I would make sure she had all the training she needs to succeed in this business.

"Layla? How would you like to put on the Gen X rave?"

Her hazel eyes grow wide. "Produce it?"

"I think, with some guidance, you would do a great job."

"Yes!" She can't hold back her smile. "It will be amazing, Steph. A huge revenue generator. I promise. I'll book the best DJs and do all the research and work with marketing—"

I can do this. I can separate Layla from Jess. "Let's just get through the Halloween party, okay?"

5

DIANA

Ice cubes clink against a glass. Nick stands in the butler's pantry eyeballing gin as he pours. He doesn't often drink, but there are two old-fashioned glasses on the white granite counter in front of him.

I didn't call him immediately after being fired. Actually, I haven't told him I was fired, just that FireSpot severed our contract. The most pathetic part is that I drove around for hours, until it was the end of the business day, so that I wouldn't be home too early.

How am I supposed to tell Nick, the man who believes in me more than anyone, that I've failed?

"You and Liz get anywhere on next steps?" Nick asks as he stirs the drinks. He glances at the clock. "It's nearly eight."

I drop my bag on the counter and kick my shoes across the gleaming hardwood floor toward the coat closet. Normally, I'm a stickler for putting everything in its appropriate place, but not today.

I take the gin and tonic and sip liberally. It burns in just the right way.

"What's going on?" Nick asks. "Why did FireSpot fire you?"

I exhale and sip again. I can't hide this forever. If I were my client, I'd instruct myself to rip off the Band-Aid.

"FireSpot dumped JKP, but JKP fired me." My chin quivers. I've never uttered such defeat-laden words before, and it makes my throat tense. "My contract is done, and so am I."

I hurry across the great room so Nick can't see the tears glistening in my eyes. Throw pillows in various shades of pale blue and green neatly decorate the cream sofas flanking the sleek, modern fireplace, and I toss two on the ground and curl onto the deep sofa, bringing my knees to my chest. My skirt rides up, but I don't care.

"I don't have a job anymore," I say.

Nick stops in front of me, his glass clenched in his hand. He draws his brows together but seems calm. "What exactly happened?"

I close my eyes and with the hand not holding the gin and tonic, rub my temple. "FireSpot cleaned their C-Suite and replaced them with some Gen Z'ers who think they can ignore a congressional hearing request."

Nick sits next to me so that my knees touch his forearm. "JKP fired you for telling them that?"

Even though gin and tonic is a sipping drink, I pound the rest of mine.

"Apparently, they've been gathering complaints about me for not being warm and fuzzy enough with staff and clients and never told me." I rest my head against the back of the couch and let the warmth of the gin spread through me. "Would you call me cold?"

"Not toward your family or friends." Nick plucks the empty glass from my hand and sets it on the concrete coffee table. I should care that he isn't using a coaster, but I can't. Not now. "However, when you work, you're a beast."

"I'll take that as a compliment." I rub my hands over my face, not caring if I smear my makeup. "I get things done. I make things happen. I get results."

"You expect perfection."

"And professionalism." I press my lips together. "What is wrong with young people? Why do I have to be their boss, therapist, and mother? I mean, give me a break! Mental health days? I never used anything like that."

Nick shakes his head slightly. "That didn't go well, remember?"

Right after Alex and Emily were born, I had spent months thinking I had a weird postpartum heart condition, but my doctors insisted my heart was strong and healthy. Finally, after one particularly trying day when I was trying to balance tending to two babies—and Mama's unhelpful help—with working full-time, I melted down while at the park.

As Alex and Emily grabbed fistfuls of sand and tried to mouth them, I had watched the other mothers. They smiled and redirected and seemed much more suited for motherhood than me. I panicked every time the kids didn't hit a milestone exactly on time, and I could barely hold my eyes open most days, let alone act perky and excited to change diaper blowouts times two.

From where Mama sat on a bench, she called my name. She had moved in with us to help with the babies, and while I was thankful she helped with meals, her presence was getting harder and harder to tolerate. Nick had suggested the night before that we let Mama know we were okay now and didn't need constant help.

"Diana," Mama barked. "They're eating sand."

The babies sat on each side of me, facing each other. Emily had pulled her sunhat so that it nearly covered her eyes, and Alex had drool all over his overalls. As for me? I sat in the sand with my legs tucked under the skirt of the pale green dress I had worn to my ten o'clock meeting that morning.

I grasped Alex's hand and emptied it of sand. Then I fixed Emily's hat. Near us, a mother gleefully pushed her son in the bucket swing and a small group of women stood near the climbing structure. Occasionally, one would leave the group to retrieve a child, but mostly the other mothers stood around visiting.

"Diana," Mama said again. "They're going to get too hot. Put them in the shade."

It was maybe seventy-five degrees and downright pleasant.

I scooped up my babies, placing one on each hip and walked toward the group of women. There was shade under the structure, and I set Emily and Alex down there. On the bench, Mama continued knitting and surveying the playground. She often reminded me that she had made do with less when I had been a baby, and that Alex and Emily didn't need all the fancy car seats, bouncers, and carriers that Nick and I had bought.

The other moms were discussing some sort of snack that their kids loved. Mama insisted on making Alex and Emily's food, and I never argued with her. After all, it was what she had fed me. But listening to these women go on about puffed snap peas made me wonder if I was missing out on something.

Nicole was nearly two years older than Alex and Emily, and Kristin and I occasionally arranged playdates on the weekends, but we never discussed treats. Actually, every conversation we had was about something that had happened years ago, and I was beginning to wonder if we were growing apart. I worked all day; she stayed home.

As I watched these women, a deep ache grew in my heart. My entire life had been spent doing everything I could to make my parents proud, to the point where I had given up friendships and sacrificed my social life. Nick had been my first and only boyfriend, and other than Kristin and Steph, I had never had many friends.

One of the women waved a bag of puffed snap peas at her child who came running, and the friends laughed. I inched closer to them. I wanted these women to notice me, and I wanted to talk about snap peas.

I smiled awkwardly at the friends. "Hi," I said. "I'm Diana."

"Tamra," the woman nearest me answered. She pointed at her friends. "This is Mindy and Lacey."

The other two women smiled politely.

"How old are your babies?" Mindy asked.

"Six months."

"Diana!" Mama shouted. "We need to go."

I didn't want to go. I wanted to stay and talk to the women. I turned slightly toward Mama who had packed up her knitting and stood at the double stroller.

"Come," she ordered.

"Your nanny is bossy," Tamra said. "I would never tolerate that."

I stared at my mom. With her cardigan sweater, sensible shoes, and knee socks, she looked out of place, and maybe a little... foreign?

I laughed. "Oh, maybe. But she keeps me on track."

Mindy nodded. "I understand completely. I'd be lost without my nanny."

The all-to-familiar sensation of my throat constricting choked back my next lie. Alex cried, and I pick him up. He had tipped over and face planted in the sand. I dusted him off and placed him on my hip.

"Your nanny looks angry." Tamra frowned.

Mama stood with her arms crossed and a stern look on her face. "Diana, come."

I tensed. The playground swayed around me, and I staggered.

"Watch out!" someone yelled as I fell to my knees, cradling Alex against my chest.

I narrowly missed crushing Emily when I rolled onto my back. The sun flickered, and my chest tightened. I was dying from a heart attack at age twenty-seven.

Mindy knelt next to me. "You need Xanax."

"What?" I blinked at her.

"Xanax. My anxiety isn't bad now that I take it."

I shook my head, pushed up to standing, and grabbed the babies. "I don't need drugs."

Mama had stomped over to us and snatched Emily from me. "They need dinner."

"I know." I brushed the sand off my dress.

"Then stop socializing and come."

I tried to find a steady breathing pattern, but the world swayed. Two hours later, I woke up in the hospital with a concussion and a knot on my head from hitting it on the play structure.

The attending ER doctor suggested I see a psychiatrist, and at Nick's insistence, I did the following day—after work. I was given a diagnosis of generalized anxiety and a prescription for Xanax.

I never went back to that playground, and Mama didn't move out for another year. But when she did, I stopped taking the drug. More importantly, I never missed a day of work.

Now, sitting on the sofa and feeling miserable, a silence settles between Nick and me. He shifts slightly. He's a successful litigator and an expert at seeing all angles. "Can I offer my perspective?"

"Of course."

He laces his fingers and stretches his arms overhead, giving me a peek at his toned abs. He always does this when he's preparing to deliver bad news.

"Being devilishly handsome won't make the truth more palatable," I say. At forty-five, Nick is in the best shape of his life. A few years ago, he was diagnosed with what we refer to as a "liver issue." He mostly stopped drinking, started exercising, and became focused on nutrition. Now, he occasionally has a bourbon or gin and tonic, but for the most part, Nick prioritizes his health, and it shows.

"The world is changing. Younger employees want more work-life balance, and they're willing to take lower salaries for more work flexibility."

I huff. "They're a bunch of babies who need constant hand-holding and praise."

"Maybe so, but we've got to adapt or—"

"We get fired." I stand and face Nick. At five-foot-nine, I can almost look my husband in the eyes. Sometimes when I wear heels, I am slightly taller, but unlike most guys, Nick doesn't care. I touch his slightly graying beard scruff and flash a smile he can't resist.

"What?" Nick grabs my hips and pulls me closer. When he holds me like this, nothing bothers me, and yet, all the emotions I've repressed today bubble up. I choke back the sob wedged in my throat.

"Dinner?" I turn toward the kitchen to hide my face. Since the kids left for college, we rarely cook—that is, Nick rarely cooks anymore. I never have. "Thai takeout?"

He catches my face in his hands and kisses me. "I love you," he says. "And I believe in you. You have incredible experience." His warm lips linger on my forehead. "If you want, you can start a new firm. You've done it before, and you can do it again."

"I know," I laugh nervously. "And I love you for that."

Nick dabs the corners of my eyes with his fingertips. "You know it's okay to have setbacks, right?"

Not once in my life have I failed. Not once. Until today.

The sob I've been holding back, escapes, but I cut off the next one. "I feel like a loser. How do I tell the kids?" My stomach churns. "Or my mom?"

"Be direct. Isn't that what you'd tell a client?"

I close my eyes. "Sounds better when I'm giving the advice."

"Helen will understand."

"Will she, though?" I love my mother. I do. And I appreciate the sacrifices my parents made when our family moved to the U.S., but everything I've done in my life has been to please them, and to this day—even with all my personal and professional successes—I still haven't met their expectations.

And now I've been fired.

When I sold my firm to JKP, I received a sizable payment, and my mom loved showing her friends the write-up that ran in a few industry publications. Realistically, I don't need to work, and Nick and the kids joked that I could retire. I could become a lady of leisure, they had said, and spend my days gossiping about HOA rules, having tennis pro romances, and going to barre classes.

It sounded miserable at the time, and it sounds even more miserable now.

"Oh!" I say, hoping to change the conversation. "I almost forgot. We're going to Amy's Halloween party—but only because Steph told Emily, and Emily of course, begged me to go."

Nick falls onto the sofa and pulls me with him. He wraps his left arm round me. "After all these years, we're finally going to the infamous Halloween party? Hmmm."

I twist and look at him. "Hmmm what?"

Nick tips over and takes me with him. "Please say you'll dress as a sexy princess."

I push up on my elbow. "Out of everything that's happened today, Nicholas, you've chosen this moment to share your fetish for sexy princesses?"

"The mermaid is hot." Nick smiles impishly and holds his phone over his face so he can read it. "I bet something like that exists."

"Are you looking that up?" I gape at him. "Be careful, that's your work phone."

"If I found one, would you wear it?" Nick makes puppy dog eyes. "For me?"

There has never been anyone for me other than Nick, and there never will be. If he wants me to wear a sexy mermaid costume, why not? "Maybe?"

He types on his phone. "I'll take that as a yes."

"Nick?"

"Yeah?" He lays the phone on his flat stomach, and I push upright.

"Do you really want to go?" I have spent the past twelve years avoiding all neighborhood social events, except book club, as much as possible. I never volunteered as room parent, never attended a single Junior Committee meeting, and I've never been to a girls' night. "It's not exactly our scene."

Nick rights himself. "We don't have a scene unless it involves boardrooms." He shrugs. "Maybe it's time we branch out. Have more work-life balance, like the youngsters say."

The idea of careless fun sounds dangerous. "I don't know. People take videos and post them all over social media."

"Just don't wear anything offensive and we'll be fine." Nick rubs my arm. "Let's go, and if it's awful, we can leave, but I think we should give a try."

The gin has started to hit me hard and even though I'm angry, heartbroken, and embarrassed about being fired, I giggle. "Okay, but I won't wear anything too sexy. Kristin said I can borrow a costume from Nicole's stash." I shift so I can straddle Nick's legs. The musk of his aftershave fills my nose, and my nerves tingle. I'll never understand how other women fall out of love with their husbands. Loving Nick is effortless. "Can you handle a tasteful, sexy mermaid?"

"Can you handle this?" Nick lifts his T-shirt a little and runs his hand over the hint of his exposed abs.

I push gently against his chest. Nick grabs my hand and pulls me onto him. I dip my head near his and let my hair tickle his face before moving it out of the way.

"Can I practice my vampire skills?" Nick tries to nibble my neck and I squeal.

"Am I going to die or join the undead?"

Nick playfully snaps his teeth at me. "That's to be determined."

6

KRISTIN

"I'm so happy we get to have coffee two days in a row!" I release Diana from my hug. It's after ten-thirty and the yoga and barre crowd have started rolling into the coffee shop. I'm still in my slightly sweaty clothes, and I'm surprised Diana didn't cringe when I hugged her.

"It's a treat," she says with her nothing-is-wrong fake smile. It's a look I've only seen her wear occasionally, and it's one that alarms me. Very few things bother Diana.

I try crinkling my smooth, Botoxed forehead. "I'm surprised you're available given how busy you are at work."

Her faux smile grows. "You and Steph always chastise me for working too much, and now you're complaining because I'm taking time to see you?" Her laugh is high and tinkly, and completely fake. "I can't win!"

Something is definitely up with Diana. "Yeah. No. Don't even try that." I wag my finger at her. "I know what you're doing, and I also know you would never take a random Wednesday morning off to hang out at a coffee shop."

"Let's get our drinks." Diana tilts her head toward the growing line.

50

"Is there something going on?" I step into line and turn to face Diana.

Behind us, Kelly Martin and a few younger women spill in through the door. Like me, they're dressed in athletic clothes and have post-workout, perfectly mussed hair. As Steph has pointed out on more than one occasion, there's a daytime dress code for my neighbors: yoga pants, coordinating top, and a designer bag.

I give a small non-committal wave to Kelly's group and pray they don't try to talk to me while Diana is around. She claims I switch personalities when I'm with my other friends.

"What can I get you?" the barista asks. Her diminutive size gives her the appearance of a middle-schooler, but her nose piercing and wrist tattoo mark her as being over eighteen. I shudder. If Nicole ever did that to her body…

I study the chalkboard menu on the wall. I don't know why. I always get the same thing.

"Go ahead," I say to Diana.

"A skinny latte, please." She reaches into her bag.

"Anything else?" The barista's monotone voice feels out of place in the cozy coffee shop.

"That's it."

"Cool." The barista turns toward the beanie clad guy from yesterday who is now making drinks. "One Skinny Bitch."

"Excuse me?" Diana says lightly. "I ordered a skinny latte, not"—she waves her hand and frowns—"whatever it is you just shouted."

"Riiiight." The barista drags out the word. "Every lady in here drinks skinny lattes. That's why it's the Skinny Bitch."

Diana sets her wallet on the counter, so she can talk with her hands. I cringe. Whenever she talks with her hands, things are about to take a turn for the worse.

"Can't you just call it a skinny latte?" she asks, holding up her index finger briefly before pinching it against her thumb like she's telling the barista to shut up. It's a gesture I watched her mom make when we were growing up, and it means Diana is annoyed.

The barista runs her tongue over her teeth. "I could, but I didn't."

No one has noticed the conflict yet—which is good. "Diana," I whisper. "Just get the Skinny Bitch. It's funny."

"It's insulting." Diana purses her lips. "What happened to 'the customer is always right'? When I worked in service that was the golden rule."

"We've evolved," the barista says with her hands on her hips.

Diana's mouth drops open, and I try laughing to diffuse the awkwardness. "Evolution," I fake giggle. "That's funny!"

Diana clearly does not find it funny, and as she taps her credit card against the reader, she asks, "Do you think your boss would appreciate you talking to customers like this?"

"Diana," I say, looking at the line behind us. "People are waiting, and they're starting to stare."

The barista raises her eyebrows, and my heart pounds.

Oh no. Please do not challenge Diana. Please.

"What's funny?" Diana asks as she slides her card back into her wallet.

"I am the boss. This is my coffee shop."

"You own this place?" Diana asks, sounding more like a challenge than a question.

"Uh-huh."

"By yourself?"

The barista holds up her arms with fingers splayed wide. "Surprise!"

"One Skinny Bitch," beanie clad guy says, handing Diana her drink.

"Well, congratulations," Diana says. She seems both impressed and annoyed. "You're clearly doing something right since it's always busy here." Diana pops the top off her drink to let the steam swirl out. "But maybe you should rename your drinks. 'Skinny Bitch' is insulting."

I touch her arm. "Diana—"

"Seriously?" The barista chuckles. "You're like, literally, the only person who's ever complained. The ladies think it's funny. So, no. I'm not changing the name, but maybe you should order something different next time. Like the 'Lady Who Lunches,' which is a chai latte. The yoga and barre crowd love those."

"I am not the yoga and barre crowd. I have a job," Diana snaps, stepping aside for me to order.

A twinge of disloyalty ran through me. "One Skinny Bitch," I whisper. "Extra hot, please."

The barista laughs, but Diana has retreated to our table and doesn't hear me.

As I wait, I study the groups of women gathered around the tables. Kelly Martin and her friends sit in the middle of the room. Their designer bags that double as gym bags are thrown haphazardly on the floor. Libby Dwyer is crowded into a corner with a woman—who I don't know—holding a toddler. And few younger moms with babies in strollers have staked out the perimeter. That was me and my friends not that long ago, and in a few years, these women will be on the PTO, running the Junior Committee, and driving carpool and I'll… I'll being doing what exactly?

"Kristin!"

I nearly rip my drink from beanie guy's hands and join Diana at a window table. Late morning sunlight creates a halo around her as she studies her phone intently, scrolling and swiping.

"What was that about?" I ask, taking my seat. "You bit that poor girl's head off."

Diana sets her phone down and blows on her steaming drink. "First, tell me what's going on with you."

As the other patrons' conversations and laughter fill the room, my heart pounds and I shift in my seat. This isn't a conversation to have in public. "What did Steph tell you?"

Diana focuses her deep brown eyes on my face and raises her eyebrows. "Nothing. But now *you're* going to."

I walked right into that. "It's nothing really. Just... I don't know. It's nothing."

"Liar." Diana adjusts her perfect posture and touches her pearl necklace. "I know you, and I know something is wrong."

I dip my head and rub the area just above my eyebrows. Telling Steph how I feel about my marriage was easy because Steph never judges, but Diana... she doesn't judge exactly, but her world is black and white.

"You can talk to me," Diana says.

I glance around the room to see if anyone is listening, but the other patrons are all lost in their own conversations. "Tom came home early yesterday while I was trying on costumes and overheard me speaking to Joe Nillson on the phone."

Diana doesn't hide her confusion. She knows Thalia from our book club but has never met Joe. "Why were you talking to Thalia's husband? Is something wrong with her?"

This part is easy. "No. Thalia is fine, I guess."

"So why were you talking to Joe?" She narrows her eyes. "Kristin, what did Tom hear? Were you... acting inappropriately?"

I touch my finger to my lips. "Shhh. I don't want anyone to know."

She gapes at me.

I cast my eyes downward. "We were only talking about sandwiches or something."

"Two Skinny Bitches for Kelly!" the barista gleefully shouts.

Diana rolls her eyes. "That young woman is a glowing example of what's wrong with Gen Z." She taps the tabletop with her petal-pink manicured finger. "I need more information about Joe. I don't understand why you were talking to him about sandwiches or why Tom overhearing you is an issue."

I've already confessed to Steph my marital discontent and if

Diana pressures her, Steph will spill her guts. She always does. My only option is to come clean.

"I'm having issues with Tom right now, and my conversation with Joe was borderline flirty." I keep my voice low, and Diana leans closer to hear me. "But I wiggled out of it with Tom."

"We'll come back to the unhappy part, but the fact that you had to cover your conversation should be a sign you shouldn't be talking to Joe." Diana crosses her arms. "Do not lose your soul to middle-aged malaise."

"Do you think—"

"That you're flirting with a married man? Yes, I do." She rolls a pearl between her fingers. Diana always plays with her necklaces when she's thinking. "You know it's wrong."

The lump in my throat swells. I knew, unlike Steph, Diana wouldn't see nuance. Joe's my friend, but if I'm honest, I also know Diana's right. Still, Joe and I have never taken anything past silly one-off comments.

"Kristin?" Kelly Martin says as she hurries toward us. Her Louis Vuitton bag dangles off her arm, and she eyes Diana. They vaguely know each other. "Diana, right?" Diana nods, and Kelly continues. "Did I interrupt something?"

"Not at all!" I stand to hug Kelly. "How have you been?"

"Really busy, but will I see you tomorrow for wreath-making? We can catch up then."

I force myself to act like the biggest tragedy of my life has just happened. "Oh, I'm not going this time. I hate missing girls' night, but life obligations. You know?"

Diana smirks. "You should go. It sounds fun."

Kelly adjusts her huge handbag over her shoulder. "Come for a drink? You can even bring Diana."

"I'm busy with work." Diana taps out a message on her phone. "Sorry."

I wish I could get Kelly to leave, but there's really no polite way to do it.

"Did you hear about John Simmons?" Kelly asks.

And this is why Diana thinks most of our neighbors are ditzy gossips. I nod solemnly, playing the game I'm supposed to. "I can't believe it. Honestly, I hope it's a mistake for Michelle and the kids' sakes. I heard they may lose the house if it's true."

"No!" Kelly widens her eyes. "I can't even imagine the stress Michelle is under." She sighs dramatically. "I guess she won't be coming tomorrow. I mean, I wouldn't under the circumstances." There is something so wrong about how Kelly says this—like she is almost gleeful.

"Sounds like she has other things on her mind," Diana says without looking up from her phone. I doubt Diana knows anything about John and Michelle.

"Oh, I've gotta run," Kelly says. "The girls from my yoga class are waiting." She hugs me again.

Once Kelly is well out of earshot, Diana rolls her eyes. "She's vapid."

Across the shop, Kelly and her friends hug and kiss goodbye even though they'll see each other at the school bus stop pick-up in a few hours.

My phone dings, and I glance at it.

Joe.

Okay. Stay calm. Diana will notice if you act oddly. "Do you want to go to the wreath making party?" I ask her while reading my message.

—lunch? At my office?—

*—when—*My heart pounds, but I pretend like this is a normal text.

Diana stacks my empty cup in hers. "Zero interest."

—12?—

She isn't bothered by my texting and politely hasn't asked who it is.

*—yes—*I set my phone face side down.

"They're not all terrible," I say, trying to focus on my and

Diana's conversation and not let my excitement of seeing Joe show. "You like the book club ladies, after all."

Diana wipes imaginary crumbs off the table and shoves her balled napkin in her empty cup. "They have substance, and the discussions are interesting."

"I love you, Diana, but you can be too blunt—which I like, but these other women don't." Why isn't my phone vibrating? "Sometimes you need to pretend to like things you don't."

"I'll never understand why you do that."

"Because it makes life easier when you fit in." The coffee shop is mostly empty now, and my voice carries. I drop my head and whisper. "I can't stand Kelly. She had an affair and got pregnant, and her now-husband left his lovely wife and kids to marry her." To this day, it still infuriates me. "Kelly thinks she's amazing for having accomplished so much in such a short period of time."

"Okay. One, I didn't know that. And two, you really don't like her?"

"Not at all. Mary, the ex-wife, was a friend. Do you remember her?"

"No."

A flicker of regret hits me. I despise what Kelly did to Mary, and yet here I am flirting with Joe and planning a lunch meet-up while Thalia runs their home. I am better than Kelly. I'm one hundred percent better than backstabbing, husband-stealing Kelly.

And yet, I can't wait to see Joe.

"Don't let these despicable women influence who you are." Diana leans forward so that the space between us narrows. "Just because they turn a blind eye to infidelity doesn't make it okay, and you shouldn't surround yourself with terrible people."

"Isn't it your job to represent reprehensible people?" I raise my eyebrows. "Think of it like that. These ladies are just clients I need to deal with."

Diana rolls her eyes. "That's a sad analogy, but it makes sense."

"Okay, then." I heft my bag off the ground. "I've got to run. Lots of errands."

Diana daintily hangs her bag off her forearm. "I can tell you're avoiding the conversation, but we're going to talk about all of this later."

I pull my keys from my bag. "Of course. Just let me know when you're available."

Diana twitches. "Yeah. I'll text you."

It only takes twenty minutes to drive to Edgington, but it feels like an eternity.

Edgington has a cute downtown area with a mix of retail and office space, and Joe works in one of the quaint buildings near the parking garage. Normally, we meet at Bigelow's for lunch, but today Joe suggested eating at Ivory, a more upscale place at the far end of downtown.

Shoppers mill about on the sidewalk as I rush past. After leaving the coffee shop, I hurried home, rinsed off, fixed my hair, and put on a cute outfit, but I forgot my lipstick. Outside Ivory, I dig in my bag until I find a nice neutral color, and while looking in my phone's camera, I swipe the lipstick across my lips. Satisfied with my appearance, I enter the restaurant.

"Can I help you?" the hostess asks.

"I'm meeting a friend. Joe Nillson." My voice sounds breathy, like I just ran up a flight of stairs.

"Mr. Nillson is already seated. Follow me."

It's just after twelve, and the restaurant overflows with the suit-wearing crowd—which is why my breathiness, nerves, and obsession about my appearance are ridiculous. Joe and I aren't doing anything illicit. We're two friends meeting for lunch in a busy restaurant where anyone can see us.

If we didn't want to be seen together, we would go closer to DC. Not that I've thought about it. I haven't. Well, only once or twice.

Snippets of conversations float past me as I follow the host to the back of the restaurant. Most of the diners seem to be co-workers, and their conversations revolve around deals and clients. Joe works in government contracting, like nearly everyone else in Northern Virginia, and I'm sure he's sat through many meals here. In fact, he probably knows at least a dozen people here right now.

We aren't hiding, and we aren't doing anything wrong. It's just lunch.

Joe is typing on his phone and doesn't look up until I stop next to the table. He beams at me and places his phone face down on the table.

"There you are! I was beginning to think you stood me up." His blue eyes twinkle, and he stands and pulls me into a tight hug.

He would not do this if we were doing something wrong.

Still, my pulse thunders in my ears, and I inhale deeply to rid myself of the breathiness. "Why would I stand you up?"

Joe pulls out my seat. "Maybe you realized I'm just a poor slob who isn't worth your time?"

With his perfectly trimmed five o'clock shadow, dress shirt, and slim fit pants, Joe is anything but a slob. In fact, I wish Tom took a tenth of the interest Joe did in his appearance. Instead, I can't remember the last time Tom put on a pair of jeans that fit properly or a dress shirt and pants.

"Sorry. I was with Diana having coffee." I flash a smile that lands between sweet and flirty. "She called and asked to meet, but I still have no idea why." I frown at the realization. "It was so weird. She never makes coffee plans on a random Wednesday morning."

Joe places his forearms on the table. His sleeves are rolled up, exposing his large and very expensive watch.

"People do weird things." He scans the QR code on the table. "Are you hungry? This place is pretty good. They have giant salads if that's what you want."

I rarely eat around Joe. How can I when my stomach is always a mess of emotions?

"Which salad do you like?" I want to sound calm, but my voice is an octave too high. Can he see how nervous I am?

My heart skips when he lifts his gaze from his phone and meets my eyes. "I've never had one." He glances at the menu. "Thalia likes the blackened salmon and greens, though."

He's brought Thalia here? "Well, I think I'm in the mood for something more substantial." I need something that isn't a salad, but still light. Something Thalia wouldn't order. "The sea scallops sound good."

"They're delicious," Joe says. "Actually, I think I'll get them too."

The waiter brings water to the table and takes our drink orders—cava for me and a bourbon neat for Joe. When we're alone again, Joe settles back in his chair but keeps his forearms on the table.

"Can I ask your advice?" His blue eyes captivate me, and I can't look away.

"Of course."

"Thalia wants to quit the club, but I think she's wrong." Joe shakes his head. "She says now that the kids are mostly grown and she never goes to the pool, we should quit. But I still like to golf with the guys."

"Hmmm… that's hard," I say. And really it is. "She never goes up anymore, but you love golf." I pause. "I don't know, it seems a little selfish—especially since the kids can use the pool when they're home during the summer."

"Exactly." The waiter sets our drinks and a basket of bread on the table. Joe selects a brown roll and tears it in two. "It's like she doesn't want me to have a social life because she's decided to not have one."

"Is everything okay with her?" I ask before taking a sip of cava.

Joe half-shrugs. "I don't know. She barely talks to me anymore. It's like once the kids started flying the nest, she decided she didn't have to try. She works, comes home, does kid stuff, and ignores me."

"I can relate to that." This is why I love being around Joe. He understands how it feels to be neglected by your spouse. "Tom thinks we get to coast through life now, and I can't get him to do anything other than watch Netflix every night."

Joe winks, and my heart flutters. "Maybe we should switch partners. They can be boring and miserable together and we can have fun."

My heart races, but I can't respond because the waiter appears with our food. I take a tiny, polite bite of my scallops. "Delicious."

Joe nods. "Thalia never appreciates when I bring her here."

A dark shard of pettiness takes a hold of my heart. "Just like Tom doesn't appreciate any of the meals I make. He just eats and plops down in front of the TV."

Joe sips his bourbon. "Like I said, we should spouse-swap." His deep laugh makes my heart trill. "I'd love a home cooked meal for once."

"And I'd love to feel like my efforts were appreciated."

"I appreciate you, K." Joe's kind eyes meet mine. "You're the best thing I have in my life right now."

Heat flushes my cheeks. If Diana heard this conversation, she'd flail me. "You keep me sane." I glance at the white tablecloth. "Diana and Steph don't understand what it's like to be in a marriage like mine, but you do. You get it."

Joe nods. "Unfortunately for both of us."

Our conversation veers into his workday and a client he's trying to land. I listen intently and give feedback where I can. We eat too quickly, and I want to order dessert so I can spend more time with Joe, but he has to get back to the office.

We stroll down Main Street until reaching Joe's office building. He tugs at my hand, and the butterflies in my stomach swarm. He's never really touched me before. "Hey," he says. "I'll text you later, okay?"

In a stupor, I nod.

He drops my hand, places a peck on my cheek, and heads inside.

I stand still, trying to process what just happened. He held my hand. Was our lunch a date? And the joke about them switching spouses—what did that mean?

Is Diana right? Am I crossing a line?

7

DIANA

"Sweetheart? Hey. I brought you some tea."

I swim through a haze of consciousness and flutter my eyes open. Nick's blurry figure stands next to the bed, and sunlight pours through the open curtains. A yawn roars out of me. "I'm so sleepy."

"It's almost ten." Nick sets the mug on the bedside table.

"Ten?" I shoot upright and squint at my phone, searching for confirmation of the time. "I overslept. What's wrong with me?"

Nick brushes his warm lips across my forehead. "Nothing. You just need sleep." He sits on the edge of the bed, and I move to make more room. "Your brain needs a rest."

The past two days come rushing back. KPL, FireSpot, and Kristin's slippery slope all collide into one mashed up memory of misery. I sigh. "I'm okay."

"Please don't lie; I know you're not."

My insides jitter like I've had too much caffeine. "I'm just off balance is all. I'll work through it." Nick is dressed in a suit, but he said it's nearly ten. "Why are you still home? Don't you have a big case coming up?"

I'm intentionally vague because Nick and I rarely discuss our clients. Sleeping with one of DC's top litigators has its down-sides, and if our clients don't overlap, we're often on opposing sides.

He pats my thigh. "I'm worried about you."

"That's sweet, but I promise I'm okay." I nudge my foot against his hip so that he stands, and I swing my legs off the side of the bed. "You don't need to worry."

Nick is the only person who knows about my anxiety diagnosis.

"But I do worry." He follows me into the master bathroom. "Maybe you should see about having your prescription refilled or even seeing a therapist. Just for now."

I take my toothbrush off the holder and keep my gaze fixed on him in the mirror as I vigorously scrub my teeth. I spit out the foamy mess. "I'm managing."

"Are you?" The corners of his mouth turn down. "Because you drank a lot the other night—and again last night." After seeing Kristin at the coffee shop, I came home, picked at some Thai left-overs, and opened a bottle of wine. By the time Nick got home, I had finished it and started another.

It's the most I've had to drink all year.

I spit into the sink again and run my tongue over my clean teeth. "Yesterday was a one-off. Promise." I turn around. In his navy suite and light blue dress shirt, Nick looks ready to take on the world. Meanwhile, I'm wearing sweats and a ratty tank top. I pat his chest. "You look nice."

"Stop changing the topic."

Damn litigator. "I swear, I'm fine. Upset, but fine. I think that's understandable."

"Last night, you mentioned something about Kristin and seemed upset. Is everything okay with her?"

Alcohol makes my lips loose which is why I'm normally a one-glass-only drinker. Was anything she told me off the record? "There are some things."

"Like?" Nick and Tom have always been friendly, but not friends, so there's no risk in Nick saying something. Plus, my husband is discreet and good at keeping secrets.

"I'm concerned. Kristin is hanging around Joe Nillson—without his wife, Thalia, who is in my book club—and she doesn't see how inappropriate it is."

Like me, Nick works with morally gray situations. "Is she having an affair?"

I shrug. "More like she wants to, but is insisting Joe is just a friend."

"Joe Nillson isn't just friends with any woman."

I tilt my head. Nick doesn't hang out with guys in our neighborhood, so the fact that he has an opinion on Joe is strange. "What do you know?"

"Tom pointed him out once when he and Kristin invited us to have dinner at the club—I think Nicole was dating his son?"

I nod.

"And in the five minutes I watched him, the man was all over three different women standing at the bar." He shakes his head in disgust. "Guys only do that if they're looking for... an easy score."

My dislike for Joe hits a new level. I've seen this play out numerous times with my clients, and it has never ended well. Nick's confirmation of Joe's smarminess is all I need to know that Kristin is endangering her marriage.

Nick shakes his head. "You've got to talk to her."

"I know." I brush out my hair. "If I can't stop Kristin from self-destructing, I need to protect Nicole as much as possible."

"Absolutely." Nick turns on the shower for me, and I strip off my pajamas. His eyes linger on my breasts. "You're making it hard to leave, but I have to head into the office for a few hours."

The water is almost the right temperature when I test it with my foot. "You'll be home for dinner?"

"Probably early. Around three."

"Okay. Love you." I step into the shower and the wall sprayers massage my shoulders. When I glance back, Nick's gone. I flip on the overhead rain shower head and let the water wash over me. As the water circles the drain, I press my hand against the cool tiled wall and try to steady my racing heartbeat.

I can't remember the last time I've had nothing on my calendar—not even a doctor's appointment. My inbox probably only holds spam, and I have no idea how I'm going to occupy myself until three.

I want Nick to be wrong about my anxiety, but I struggle to draw a deep breath and sink to my knees as tears mix with the water and run down my face.

Anxiety is a beast, and its grasp grows tighter with each passing moment.

Who am I without a job?

Who am I if I'm not the boss?

Who am I if I'm not winning?

Who am I now?

—Diana. You need to call me. Immediately.—

—Diana. This is an emergency. Call me now.—

There were two newer messages, too.

—Diana. We need to discuss Thanksgiving.—

—Call me immediately.—

The uncomfortable band around my lungs squeezes tighter, and a clammy sweat dampens my hairline, sending shivers through my body. What kind of daughter avoids her mother?

An ungrateful one.

I spin around in my desk chair. One of the reasons Nick and I chose this house was for the two main floor offices. Technically, Nick's is the former front room, but since no one ever uses a front room, we had it converted into a second office with French doors and built-in shelving.

Even though Nick's office is newer, I like mine better. There's a bank of floor-to-ceiling windows that overlook the expansive back lawn, and I've placed my desk along the side wall so I can see the both the door and look out the windows. Across from my desk is a cream sofa with a chaise, and Nick hung two TVs on the wall so I can watch multiple channels at once, which is helpful if I have multiple clients making the news.

When the kids were little, this was my private retreat, and they knew not to bother me when I closed the door. And let's be honest, what mom doesn't need alone time occasionally?

"Okay," I say, opening my laptop and pulling up my JKP separation agreement. I haven't signed it yet and am waiting for my lawyer to go over it. I scanned it briefly before sending it over to my lawyer, Cheryl, but don't remember many details. "Is there a non-compete clause?"

Sure enough, there is. If I sign the agreement, I can't work for myself or anyone else in the crisis field for a year from signing.

I fire off an email to Cheryl, telling her I want that struck. And more money. It's unlikely JKP will agree, but I have leverage: I don't need their severance package, and they need me to not poach their clients. Six months' salary isn't worth not being able to work for a year.

My phone dings again and out of habit, I reach for it.

—When will Alex and Emily be home?—

"I surrender," I say, glancing up at the ceiling. "Whatever it is that I've done, I apologize."

The only way to avoid Mama is to punt, so I text *—in a meeting—* and hope it buys me some time.

How has Kristin done this all day, every day, for over twenty years?

Kristin. I need to call her and force her to her senses.

The phone only rings once before she answers. "Hello?"

"Hey," I say. "How are you?"

"Are you calling to scold me?"

"No, I'm just concerned." Outside the window, three deer stop and graze next to the winterized pool. "Have you thought about anything I said?"

"Yes," Kristin says with what sounds like a mouth full of food. "And I think you're wrong."

"Are you eating?"

"A salad. You called in the middle of my lunch." She swallows loudly. "Look, I appreciate your concern, but men and women can be friends." The hesitancy in her voice betrays her doubt.

"But you're—" My phone beeps, and I pull it from my ear to see the screen. "Hey, Alex is Facetiming. Can I call you back?"

"Sure."

My children, like most younger people, prefer video calls. I didn't like it at first, but now I love seeing Alex and Emily's faces when they call. I prop my phone up, so I have my hands free. "Hi, honey! What's going on?" Alex holds the phone so that my angle is up his left nostril. "I can't see your face."

"Mom." Alex rights the phone. His hair is too shaggy and in desperate need of a cut, which is emphasized by his over-the-ear headphones that force random pieces to stick up. "Is it a good time?"

My priority, no matter what I'm doing, has always been my family. In the past, I've stepped out of press conferences for Nick and the kids' calls. "Of course. Is everything okay?"

Alex drops his phone, and for a moment, I'm looking at the ceiling. When he picks it up, his red-rimmed eyes shatter me. "Honey? What's wrong?"

He draws a shaky breath. "I don't think Princeton is right for me."

"What?" I couldn't have heard him right. We've worked so hard for the past eighteen years to get him and Emily into college. And not just any colleges. Princeton and Brown. Alex has dreamed about going there since he started pre-K.

"I want to drop out. I hate it here."

He's joking. "Excuse me?"

"It's not like I thought. It's so… I don't know." He twists his hands together. "I want to do something meaningful with my life, and Princeton isn't it."

I brace my hands against the glass desktop. Its coolness helps ground me. "Did you fail a test? Because that's not unusual during the first semester. It happens." I smile to ease some of his apprehension. "And you love Princeton. It's the only school you've ever wanted to go to."

"I don't love it, though." Alex glances to the left. "I'm tired of tests and essays and planning my perfect life." He pauses as if he's trying to be dramatic, which makes me wonder how much of this is rehearsed.

Pause when unsure or agitated. "If you don't want to go to an Ivy, just say so. Dad and I will understand. You know that, right? We want you to be happy."

"That's the thing… I don't want to go to any college." Alex turns his face so I can't see his eyes. "I want to travel and work. Maybe take a gap year."

What is he talking about? My phone buzzes again, but I ignore it. "Alex, you're going to disappoint your grandparents. They've worked hard and sacrificed to make this life for us, and we owe it to them to be successful."

"Mom." Alex waves his hand, and the camera jumps around. "Don't you get tired of Gigi always telling you what to do?"

I tug on the ends of my hair, a bad habit left over from childhood. "What do you mean?"

"Mom. C'mon." Alex's image steadies. "Every time Gigi doesn't like how you're doing something, you change and do what she wants."

I close my eyes and try to slow my pounding in my chest.

"She's my mom, and she wants what's best for me." I open my eyes. "Just like how I want what's best for you." Alex's camera faces the ceiling again. "Honey, she can be a lot, I know, but she means well. If she's bothering you at school, I'll handle it. You just focus on your classes and making friends, okay?"

Alex pops back onto the screen. "You know you're like Gigi, right? The way you need to control everything?"

Heat rushes up my spine and across my neck. "Where is this coming from? All I've ever done is make things easier for you to be successful."

"Maybe I don't need your help anymore." He has the phone at a weird angle, but it looks like his chin quivers. "Next Tuesday is the last day to withdraw. I've already gotten all the signatures. You'll get most of the money back."

I shake my head to dislodge the awful words he's filled it with. "This isn't about money; it's about your future."

Alex's golden-brown eyes flash. "I want to work and see the world. That's my future."

Clearly, something's happened. Why else would he be even considering this? My breath shakes. "Please, just finish the semester. We can discuss spring semester at Thanksgiving."

"Mom, I'm making a plan, and you need to let me live the life I want—not the one you and Gigi planned for me."

"You have so much potential. Do not do this. I'm begging you."

"How is this different than Emily with her undecided major?"

My two children couldn't be more different. "You will stay at Princeton. That's final."

"Dad says—"

"What did Dad say?" Did Nick go behind my back and okay this?

Alex bites his lip. "Nothing. I'm just tired of chasing your dream. Why don't you understand?"

Blood pounds in my temples, and my throat aches. How is it

possible that my valedictorian, baseball-team-captain son suddenly lacks ambition? How does he not understand the opportunity he wants to throw away?

I swallow to wet my parched mouth. "Please, Alex, please don't be difficult. Finish the semester so you at least have the credits."

"I'm not being difficult!" Alex shouts, and I flinch. He never raises his voice. "I'm also not you! I want more from life than to just work all the time. I want to live!"

"Stop it," I whisper as the band around my chest tightens. I can't draw a deep breath and hunch forward. "Alex, why don't you come home this weekend, and..." I can barely speak. "We can." I gasp. "Discuss with Dad."

"Mom? Are you okay?"

I set my head down on my desk, and the room spins.

"Mom!"

My chest constricts and nausea washes over me. Icy heat races along my spine and spreads across my neck and chest. "Call 9-1-1," I gasp. "Something's wrong."

8

KRISTIN

I write the text, delete it, and write it again. Is it because I don't know how I feel about the Joe situation that I can't figure out what to say?

I set my phone on the white quartz counter and attack the pile of carrots next to the sink. Tonight, I'm making a proper home-cooked meal—probably out of guilt—and I've planned after-dinner drinks at the club for Tom and me. Something to get us out of our Netflix rut.

As I slice the carrots, I replay my brief conversation with Diana. Thank God, Alex called when he did.

I'll never understand how Diana's personal world is so black and white, when professionally, she deals in various degrees of gray. There's no way the politicians she represents are the generous family people she portrays them as.

But maybe she's right, and I have no business talking to Joe. Maybe.

The front door creaks open, and I set the carrots aside and dry my hands. "Tom?"

Henry, our elderly golden lab, saunters into the kitchen and plops down at my feet. He was one of Nicole's Christmas presents when she was ten, but Henry has always been Tom's dog. The man takes him everywhere, including work.

Tom wanders into the kitchen wearing joggers and a Rolling Stones T-shirt. "Hey."

"Did you go to work like that?" I ask.

Tom runs his hand through his thinning brown hair. "What's wrong with this?"

I don't want to have this argument, again. "Nothing." I pick up a carrot and the butcher's knife and slice the carrots into perfectly round pieces. "I'm making steaks, mashed red potatoes, and glazed carrots." I stop chopping. "There's a salad too."

"Cool." Tom clicks his tongue. "Henry, let's go rest our eyes before dinner."

I spin around with my hands on my hips. "You're going to take a nap while I cook dinner?" Fire builds in my chest. "Don't you want to know about my day or let me ask about yours?"

"My day was boring. It was just me and Henry in the office." Tom reaches around me, grabs a carrot slice, and pops it in his mouth. "It's a ghost town now that the junior staff can work remotely."

"No meetings?"

Tom shakes his head. "The most exciting thing I did was toss a few treats in the air for Henry." He reaches down and pat's the dog's head. "The old boy can still catch." He takes another carrot. "What did you do today?"

I inhale. What had I done? Went to Barre. Avoided Diana. Wished Joe would reach out, but he hadn't. Oh, and I texted Nicole a hundred times about Thanksgiving and am still waiting for a response.

"Nothing, really. I'm trying to find out when Nicole will be home for Thanksgiving." I throw a pat of butter in a grill pan. "Have you spoken to her?"

"Not yet." Tom has his phone out and his fingers fly over the keyboard. I add the steaks to the hot pan and place the carrots in a different skillet. As I cook, Tom stands behind me. Since he doesn't say anything, I don't try to engage him. What's the point?

"She'll be home Wednesday night."

I stop stirring the carrots and turn around. "She answered you?"

Tom holds up his phone with the screen facing me. "Yes, why?"

I clench my jaw to hold back my ridiculous tears. Tom sends one message, and Nicole immediately responds, but she couldn't answer me all day? "Is she avoiding me?" I ask. "Have I done something to upset her?"

"Hon, I doubt she's avoiding you." Tom puts his phone on the counter. "I probably got her at the right time."

"She had all day to respond, and she didn't." Hurt builds in me. "I feel like she's intentionally pulling away from me."

Tom shrugs. "Maybe she needs space."

"From her mother?" I scoff. I spit out the next words. "Why would you suggest that?"

"Because you're constantly calling and texting her." The steaks sizzle. "You going to get those?" Tom points. "I think they're burning."

I shove the skillet to a cool burner and stir the carrots. "You act like being interested in our daughter's life is a crime."

Tom's eyes grow wide. "Why are you snapping at me? You asked a question, and I answered you."

The smoldering fire inside me ignites. "You do nothing, Tom. That's the problem." I raise my voice. "You do nothing, and you get all the rewards."

"I do plenty, Kristin." He jerks his head to the right. "How do you think we afford all this?"

A sob rumbles out of me. "I am the one who made Nicole's childhood magical." I point a finger at myself. "I'm the one who was always there while you traveled for work. Me. Not you!" My knees buckle, and I lean against the counter. Henry licks my fingers, and I push him away. "I'm her mother, and she acts like I'm intruding on her life."

When Tom touches my arm, I recoil. Unlike when Joe held my hand, there are no sparks, just Tom's unwelcome hand touching my arm.

"Kids grow up, and Nicole's asserting her independence." Tom stares at me like he wants me to agree, but he's being nonchalant. "It's normal," he says. "And it means you did something right."

"This isn't her asserting her independence. She's literally avoiding me." I bury my face in my hands to hide my tears.

Tom gently pulls my hands away. "Nicole can't be your everything, Kristin. It's unfair to ask that of her."

The emptiness that's been swirling around me, grows. "But she *is* my everything."

"That's the problem." Tom squeezes my hand, but I feel nothing. Not comfort or disdain. Just nothing. "You need to find something to fill your time. Something more than yoga and lunches with your friends. You like kids—maybe volunteer at the elementary school."

"I wanted more kids, but you said no!" I tear my hand away from him. "And I wanted to have a nice dinner and a cocktail at the club tonight, but you've ruined it!"

Tom gapes at me. "I don't understand what this conversation is about, or why you're mad at me."

I can't stop the irrational swirl of rage growing in me. I want to. I do, but the words just keep coming out. "All you do is eat and watch TV. You're stuck in a rut, and you're dragging me into it."

"We didn't have more kids because we agreed not to." Confusion settles across Tom's face. "And I thought you liked our routine?"

"No, Tom," I say, storming toward the stairs. "You like your routine, and you like the life I created for you." I spin around. "But now, I want something different."

"Kristin, wait." Tom follows me. "I think we have some things to unpack here."

"Enjoy your dinner, Tom. I'm sure Henry will make the perfect dining companion."

Rage courses through my body. I sit on my floor with my back against my bed's upholstered footboard, trying to calm the anger festering inside me.

Why am I so angry? Am I mad that Nicole answers Tom, or am I mad that Tom doesn't want more from our marriage? Is it both?

I was unfair to Tom. I know it, but I can't bring myself to go down and apologize. He didn't do anything wrong, and he didn't deserve to be screamed at, but in the moment, I felt possessed by an angry, irritated gremlin.

Honestly, everything Tom does annoys me.

My ragged reflection in the full-length wall mirror steals my breath.

When did I become... old? I drag my fingers through my hair to tame it, but it's no good. My shine has dulled, and I'm no longer the pretty mom the other mothers emulated. I was always pulled together, loving, and willing to do whatever it took to make Nicole happy. But look at me now. My hair is a mess, I'm still wearing my athleisure clothes, and there are fine lines around my eyes and mouth.

Past me would be horrified that I've devolved into this.

"Mommy? Can you help me make a cake for Daddy's birthday?" Seven-year-old Nicole stood in the kitchen with her kitty-cat apron already tied around her waist. A cookbook sat open to a page with a picture of a German chocolate cake, and Nicole had moved the heavy stand mixer all by herself to the island.

"Oh, sweetheart, you're such a good girl!" I studied the recipe. "Let's see, I think we have all these ingredients." I didn't have the heart to tell her

Tom hated German chocolate cake. I let Nicole grease the pans while I sifted and mixed.

When we put the cake in the oven, I told her to run upstairs to get her field hockey clothes on. Once she was out of sight, I dumped the cake in the garbage.

"Ready!" she said, beaming at me with her missing tooth smile.

"Let me get my keys." I hurried her toward the door so she wouldn't notice I'd turned the oven off.

Normally, I waited at her practice and cheered along the sideline with the other moms, but on this day, I hurried to the bakery, bought a gorgeous chocolate cake, and ran home to put it in the now cold oven before returning to Nicole's practice.

When we arrived home, she ran straight to the oven and peered inside.

"Mommy! Look what we made!"

I lifted the gorgeously decorated cake from the oven. "Daddy is going to love this! You did such a good job!"

Nicole giggled. "I'm a good baker."

"Yes, you are."

For twenty-one years, my life has been making my family happy. But now I'm a retired mom. How did I get here? How did I become a shell of myself?

Is there any way back to what I once was?

Tom didn't try to stop me from going out. I had hoped, when I told him I was going for a drive, he'd follow me to the car or at least ask me to talk. He did neither. Instead, he barely looked up from the Vietnam documentary blaring from the TV.

I've been driving aimlessly for an hour, but at the next turn, I pull into a well-lit but empty parking lot tucked behind the medical complex near my house. My car is hidden from the road.

"What's wrong with me?" I say out loud and move my seat

farther from the steering wheel. "My life isn't bad, so why can't I appreciate what I have?"

In the cupholder, my silenced phone lights up. Finally, Tom is showing some interest in where I am. Or did his documentary end, and he just realized I'm not home?

—goodnight, K. Lunch again soon?—

My lungs expand, and some of the anger I'm holding stills.

—I'm out driving. Fight with Tom. Could use some company—

Joe and I have never met this late at night, and I hold my breath, hoping I haven't overstepped.

—where?—

I take a full breath.

—behind the tall medical building on Foxbriar—

—I'll be right there—

I stare blankly out the car window. Joe is willing to come to me in the middle of the night while Tom can't be bothered to look up from his show. That speaks volumes.

<hr>

Even though it's late, Joe is immaculately dressed in jeans and a sweater. He's even wrapped a gray patterned scarf around his neck. "Hey," he says softly. "What happened?"

I shake my head, hoping to hold back my tears, but it's no use. "Nicole wouldn't answer my texts or calls, but she immediately responded to Tom." I hope my face isn't blotchy. "And I had planned a nice meal for us, but he could care less."

Joe folds his arms against his chest and leans against my SUV. "I know you know this, but Tom doesn't appreciate you." His eyes meet mine, and I melt a little. "And Nicole's watched him treat you like that. She's learned from him."

"Nicole appreciates me… I think." I settle against the car next to Joe. Cool, October air rushes over me, and I shiver. "Tom, however, takes me for granted. What will he do if one day I'm not there anymore?"

Joe stares up at the sky. The parking lot lights make it hard to see the stars. "What do you mean?"

The irrational anger bubbles up again. "I don't know, exactly, but I'm tired of being the only one trying. He makes zero effort."

"You deserve more than that, Kristin. You deserve to be happy and to not be treated like the scenery."

He quarter-turns his body and opens his arms. My heart aches from both Nicole and Tom's indifference, and I do deserve more. I've spent twenty-two years being a wife and mother, and no one has ever thanked me. In fact, I always planned my own Mother's Day brunches because Tom can't organize himself enough to do it.

I turn slightly toward Joe, who reaches out and wraps me in his arms. I sag against him as years of neglect press down on me. Joe's arms tighten around me, and he rests his chin on the top of my head.

"I've got you, sweetheart," Joe whispers into my hair. "I've got you."

Why can't Tom give me this? Is it so hard to be compassionate? I told him what was hurting me and yet, Tom refused to help me feel better.

I place my hand on Joe's chest and move my head so that my cheek presses against him. His steady heartbeat slows my anger. "Thank you," I say with a sniff. "I think I just needed to vent, and Diana doesn't get it. Her marriage is perfect."

Joe leans to the side and peers down at me. "Never feel bad about standing up to people who are making you feel bad."

Even though I want him to hold me forever, I break my physical connection with Joe. When I step back, the wind swirls between us, and I immediately long for him to wrap me in his arms again. I gently touch his chest.

"I should go. You should too. Thalia probably wonders where you went so late at night."

Joe scoffs. "She goes to bed at eight. She says she's exhausted, but what exactly does she do all day besides work part-time?"

I half-shrug. "I have no idea. We haven't really talked since she stopped coming to the club."

"Exactly." Joe squeezes my hand, setting off fireworks along every nerve in my body. "She doesn't do anything, just like Tom."

I drop Joe's hand. "I have to go, but I wish I could stay a little longer."

"Me too." His eyes hold a sense of desire I haven't seen from Tom in years, and my pulse quickens. "Stay?" Joe asks. "For a little longer? Or meet me tomorrow?"

If I stay, everything will change between us.

"I can't." But can he see how much I want to?

"Can I see you soon?"

"Soon." I spin around before I change my mind. "I promise."

"Keeping you to it, Kristin." Joe's deep voice fills my ears, and a smile stretches across my lips. "I'm not letting you get away so easily next time."

My head spins as I climb into my car and for a second, I consider getting out to see if Joe would do the same. He would, of course—which was why I need to drive home.

Diana is right. I'm careening down a slippery slope. But if I'm honest, do I want to get off?

9

STEPH

6 is a snarl of traffic. Normally, it wouldn't bother me, and I'd turn on a new song from a performer wanting to book my venues and zone out. But today, being in my head is dangerous because all I can think about is Jess. And Layla. And possibly having to tell Diana and Kristin about everything.

A black motorcycle zips between my car and the one next to me, cuts in front of me, and speeds off. When I lived in Ibiza, I had a teal-blue scooter and loved zooming around the island. It didn't seem like the death wish it does here with semi-trucks and aggressive drivers. In Ibiza, I'd speed up one-lane mountain roads with no guardrails, and I frequently drove home after a night of partying and drinking.

I was twenty-five, and my reckless lifestyle was hedonistic. Now, I wonder if all the drugs and drinks and boys and girls were a way of getting over what Jess did.

An impatient silver Audi SUV passes on my left, drives up the shoulder, and exits the road.

"How am I going to explain Layla to Kristin and Diana?" I wonder aloud.

Jess seemed unfazed when she saw me, while I was shaken. I

tap my hand on the steering wheel. Everything was in the past, like it should be. "Why do I care anymore?"

My phone rings, and Kristin's name pops up on the car screen as I exit the freeway.

"Hey," I say. "What's up?"

"Are you home? Or at one of the clubs?" she asks.

"I'm actually headed home from a vendor meeting. Why?"

Kristin will take the news about Jess worse than Diana. After all, it was her dad who saved my life when he bailed me out and represented me in court. My parents couldn't afford an attorney and being a young woman with Torres as a last name didn't set the odds in my favor. But Mr. Danvers miraculously managed to get all the charges dismissed and in exchange, I promised to leave DC and end my friendship with Kristin.

He even gave me money for a plane ticket and first month's rent.

During college, Jess and I had dreamed about partying in Ibiza, but I didn't go there first. With my only-used-once passport grasped tightly in my hand, I backpacked across Europe, stopping first in Amsterdam, then Berlin, and finally Barcelona.

My parents immigrated from Madrid before I was born, and I speak Spanish fluently which made assimilating in Ibiza easier. My plan was to party and forget, but as my funds dwindled, I found a job and for the next ten years, I worked non-stop to forget Jess and my life in DC. I rarely spoke to Kristin and Diana until Facebook infiltrated everyone's lives.

I thought I was happy, but was I?

"Is it okay if I come over?" Kristin asks, tearing me from my thoughts. "I'm in DC."

Kristin never leaves the ten-mile radius of her neighborhood. "Is everything okay?"

"Yeah." There's hint of sadness to her voice "I just thought I'd visit."

I don't buy it. "Traffic is a beast. You know the door code. Go ahead and let yourself in."

After twenty-plus years of not thinking about Jess, I now need to. I have to think of what to say to my friends. I have to think of what to say to Layla. And I have to think of what to say to Jess if I ever see her again.

I need to think about the one night that completely changed my life.

A fire burns steadily in the gas fireplace, and Kristin sits cross-legged on a dark green floor pillow as I unpack the Thai takeout we ordered. I hadn't planned on having company today and have nothing in my fridge except Coke Zero and beer.

Outside, heavy grayness licks the loft's windows as a steady drizzle dampens DC. On days like this, I wish I lived somewhere with year-round sun again, but I've built my adult life here and here is where I'll stay.

"Are you going to eat?" I ask. Kristin ordered lunch for us, but she doesn't seem interested in eating. She's always been thin, but she almost looks sickly. "Have you lost weight?"

She's walked over to the island and eyes the food with resignation. "I haven't had much of an appetite. Tom, Nicole. You know. All of it."

"Eat this." I push a paper plate of drunken noodles toward her. "A little goes a long way." I fill my plate with some of everything, motion for her to follow me, and sit cross-legged on the floor next to the coffee table.

"You do have a dining table," Kristin says. "And real plates."

"Why would I use either of those?" I take a bite of yellow curry, savoring the spicy goodness. "Want to tell me why you're here?"

"I wanted to go to the Portrait Gallery." Her voice trembles slightly. "I've been meaning to go for a while."

She's such a terrible liar.

"Anyone newly dead been added?" I ask. I'm not big on museums, something Kristin has always chided me for, but I don't see the point of scribbles and toilets and labeling weird stuff art.

Kristin pushes at a minuscule piece of noddle around her plate. "I didn't go. I called you instead."

Well, at least she's being honest about that.

I yawn and fix my messy topknot. I was at LUSH until five in the morning and haven't showered yet, but I looked presentable enough for my meeting. "Well, now that you're here, what's going on?"

She sets her chopsticks down and looks wistful. "Do you remember when we moved into our first place? That first day?"

"Of course." I head to the fridge for drinks. "How could I forget that logistical disaster?"

None of us had considered the difficulty of moving from our on-campus apartment to our loft without transportation. Diana had come up with the idea to use taxis, and we, along with Jess, had crammed our lives into the yellow cabs.

"I never thought you'd come back to DC."

I keep my back to her. Over the years, the three of us have danced around the topic of what happened with Jess. It's like we made a silent pact to let that mess that fade into the past.

"In all fairness, I didn't think I'd come back either." Years of late nights and long days took a toll on me in Ibiza, and most of my friends left years ago to start families and be so-called "responsible adults." Even though I ran two clubs for the Oliviet family, I wanted my own club, and I couldn't do that in Ibiza. The buy-in was too high, and no one wanted to back a woman running a club—even though I was highly qualified.

I open my fridge and scan its emptiness. "Beer, Coke Zero, or water?"

"Coke, please." Kristin stands and walks across the polished concrete floor to the windows. I join her and below us, typical DC weekday traffic snarls its way past my building.

"Let's eat," I say, taking her hand and tugging her back to the low coffee table. "The food's getting cold, and while cold noodles taste great, I'm not a fan of cold curry." I shove noodles into my mouth and slurp. Kristin, however, daintily nibbles at a piece. "In Asia, they don't nibble, they slurp," I say.

"I'm not in Asia." She fidgets with her chopsticks. "Can I ask you something?"

I brace myself. This could go two ways: a full confession about Joe... or... No. She doesn't know about Jess and Layla. Not yet. "Sure."

"Do you have regrets?" Kristin traces her finger through the beads of condensation her can of Coke Zero has left on the table.

"Regrets like, 'I wish I had gotten married and had kids?' or regrets like 'I did too many drugs and may end up with dementia?'" Jess pops into my mind, and I swat her away.

Sadness lies behind Kristin's eyes. "I don't know," she says. "General regrets, I guess."

I stop eating. "Do you?"

Over the course of our long friendship, I've acted as Kristin's sounding board numerous times, and I can't think of anything other than her so-called friendship with Joe that she'd consider regrettable.

She leans against the base of my cognac leather sofa. "Life's funny, isn't it? I believed I'd be a powerful executive somewhere and I was only just a mom." She pauses. "And you were so boy crazy—"

"I'm not anymore?" I'm not one to share the details of my sex life with others, but I have brought plenty of guys around over the years.

"I'm just surprised you never found The One."

I hate when she and Diana start on my lack of a life partner. "I am my One. And you should be your One, too."

"Are you fulfilled?"

I study Kristin. She looks like hell. She sounds like hell. And she's acting defeated. "What exactly is going on Kristin? What aren't you saying?"

"Should I have married Tom?"

Time stops for a beat as I process her words.

And another beat.

She's not saying it, but she's having an affair.

"Diana said you had doubts on your wedding day, but I thought you were happy now?" I missed both Kristin and Diana's weddings—which is one of my life regrets. "Don't you love being Nicole's mom and all the wonderful suburban things you do?" I roll my eyes, trying to ease some of the tension hanging over us. "You and Diana dream of me becoming just like you."

Kristin pulls her legs to her chest and wraps her arms around them. She exhales shakily. I knew she was struggling, but this is more than I anticipated.

"I wonder if I set a good example for Nicole. Should I have had a job outside the home? Something just for me?" She stares up at me with watery eyes. "Diana has such a great relationship with Nick and the kids. Yes, she's a workaholic, but maybe she was right when she told me to go back to work after Nicole started school."

This is an interesting twist. "Nicole is a wonderful young woman," I say. "And you've raised her to be independent and strong." I take another bite of my near-cold curry. "Who knows, maybe I can still persuade her to join me in the debauchery of the nightclub industry."

"No," Kristin says, curtly. "You barely survived the dens of drugs and sex, and I'm not letting my daughter go anywhere near that."

"I think I'm doing fairly well for myself—and have you

forgotten that you're the one who introduced me to those very dens?" I push my half-finished plate toward the middle of the square coffee table.

"Have you forgotten what happened with Jess?"

My heart drops, and it takes me a moment to gain my balance. "Why are you mentioning her?"

Outside, rain now pommels the windows as the wind picks up.

"Because she's the reason you left, and she's the reason Diana and I didn't see you for years." Her voice rises, unleashing years of pent-up anger. "If it weren't for Facebook's invention and cell-phones, you would have become some random girl we grew up with."

My ears ring as I attempt to force unwanted memories from my brain. But I can't. Jess let me take the fall for her, and she moved out of our loft without a goodbye or an apology. And none of us heard from her again.

Until she walked into my club.

"I need to tell you something," I say.

Kristin tilts her head. "What?"

LUSH's ringtone sets off my phone, and I jump up to grab it off the never-used dining room table. "I need to get this."

It's Layla.

"Hey," I say. "Is everything okay?"

"Sammy called off sick, and we don't have enough people to pull someone from the floor for stock." She pauses. "And the kitchen app is down."

It's always something. "Alright. I'll be right there."

Kristin curls up on the couch and pulls a blanket over her legs. "Everything okay?"

I shake my head. "Catastrophe at LUSH. Want to come?"

Kristin shoves back the blanket and studies her suburban-approved ripped skinny jeans and loose sweater. "Am I dressed okay? I don't want to look too momsy."

"We're not open yet." I slip on my black motorcycle jacket. "And you look fine." I grab my car keys from a basket on the countertop. "Coming?"

Kristin studies the warehouse with a look of wonder. "No offense, but this doesn't look glamorous at all."

"I tell you and Diana that all the time." Around us, my staff hurries through the opening routine. "There's nothing glamorous about this job unless you like cleaning up puke and dealing with high customers and diva performers."

"Then why are you still doing it?"

"Despite all that, it's fun and I'm damn good at it." I stride across the floor toward the bar where a small group of my employees are gathered. Kristin trails behind.

I spot Layla pulling a keg on a dolly toward the bar. Every so often, she stops and directs one of the other staffers. My team respects her, and I appreciate how seriously she takes her job, but how is Jess okay with Layla working here? If I had young adult kids, and I knew what I know, there's no way I'd let my child work in nightlife despite what I said to Kristin about Nicole.

"Layla," I say as we near her. "Any update on the kitchen app?"

"It's not good. Either we don't serve food tonight, or we take orders the old-fashioned way." She shakes her head. "We're already short-staffed, so unless you pull from performer hospitality or social media, I don't know how we can do it."

Tonight's act is an up-and-coming DJ. He has a huge following in Europe and is gaining some traction here. Our numbers show a full house. If we can't serve food, people will be pissed.

"Leave Jake on hospitality and Charlotte on social. Put everyone else on kitchen. We don't need six people on a guy who hasn't cracked the top 100 on iTunes yet."

"Okay." She yanks at the dolly. "Let me give this to Jean-Luc, and I'll work on that." She must notice Kristin behind me because she adds, "Hi! I'm Layla."

"Nice to meet you. I'm Kristin, Steph's friend."

Layla nods and gets back to work. I motion for Kristin to follow me as I head toward my office. I need to find a tech-support person to fix the kitchen app or tonight is going to be chaos. And chaos isn't how I run my clubs.

"You're welcome to hang out and watch me work," I say to Kristin. "But if you want to call an Uber and go, I won't be offended. I'm going to be on hold with tech support for the next three hours."

"Steph?"

I stop walking and turn around. "Yeah?"

Kristin stares at Layla and lifts her index finger. "Why does she look familiar?"

A chill runs through me. Since I never realized how much Layla resembles Jess, it didn't occur to me that Kristin would see it. "I don't know."

Kristin opens her mouth slightly and side-eyes me. "You don't see it? Really?"

"I have no idea what you're talking about." Don't say it. Please don't say it. "But I hope you like her because she's coming with me to the Halloween party."

"What? You invited her? Why?"

I nod. "We're doing research on what middle-aged suburban-ites consider fun for a 90s-themed event I'm letting her promote."

Kristin crosses her arms. "Are you crazy? Why would you bring a twenty-five-year-old as your plus one?"

"She's probably twenty-two." Somehow, I've dodged the Jess-Layla connection. "And I am truly considering doing a throw-back party for Gen Xers. It was Layla's idea, and I'm testing her out."

"People are going to talk." Kristin follows me backstage and toward the stairs leading to my office.

"So? Your neighbors gossip about everything. That's nothing new."

"Fine. But she needs to blend in. You coming is one thing. You inviting your stunning employee is something else."

I jog up the stairs. "Oh my god. Stop worrying about what everyone else thinks. So what if Layla is young and cute? Most of the husbands ogle anything that they're not married to."

"Don't be horrible." Kristin stops mid-flight. "You don't know what it's like to be married. Eye candy is a welcome reprieve sometimes."

I wait for her on the landing. "Is Joe eye candy? You should show me his picture."

Kristin's cheeks flush. "He's my friend. Just like you are."

I pull my phone from my back pocket. "What's his last name?"

"Nillson."

I find him quickly. He's in his late forties, graying, with a too-straight nose and a tan he probably picked up by playing golf daily. Not my type at all. "He's attractive if you like middle-aged dads."

Kristin stares at the ceiling. "You know what? I think I'm going to get an Uber. It's getting late, and Tom may start to worry about me."

I can tell she needs space and a topic change. "What time do you want me over tomorrow?"

"Four-thirty? Or five? The party starts at seven-thirty, but I thought we could hang out first."

"Diana's still coming, right?" I haven't spoken to her since I had Emily bully her into coming.

"She said she was." Kristin quarter-turns on the step. "You really don't think Layla looks familiar?"

My heart pounds, and my lips lie. "No."

"Huh." She half-shrugs. "Okay, I'll see you tomorrow."

I head to my office, close the door, and lean against it. I shouldn't bring Layla, but if I rescind my offer, she'll be devastated, and I can't do that to her. My best hope is that her costume disguises her resemblance to Jess.

10

———

DIANA

"Alex saw me melt down, didn't he?" I rub crusty sleep from my eyes. The medicine the hospital gave me made me calm down, but it also made me sleep.

"Yes." Nick has turned me into a human burrito and placed me on the couch. He rubs my shin through the blankets. "He's worried about you. We both are."

When the paramedics arrived, I had managed to unlock the front door and was sitting on the stairs, trying not to topple over. They took my vitals and decided to transport me to the hospital. I had been strapped to a gurney and loaded into the ambulance while my nosey neighbors watched.

If I hadn't been panicked about having a heart attack, I would have been mortified.

"I'm worried about Alex." I yawn. "At a minimum, he needs to finish the semester."

"We can talk about that later." Nick pats my leg. "Let's talk about what happened."

"There's nothing to discuss. My nerves of steel failed me, and it won't happen again."

Nick tilts his head and studies my face. "Here's my take," he says. "You need to take Xanax and see a therapist." I start to object, but he cuts me off. "For now. Not forever. You're under a tremendous amount of stress, and it will help. It did last time."

"No wonder JKP fired me; I'm the only crisis expert who buckles under pressure."

Nick's gaze softens. "Sweetheart, it's easier to deal with other people's crises than your own."

This is true. I can save the careers of politicians knee-deep in scandal and prevent unsavory stories from hitting the media, but I'm too invested in Alex's life to be objective.

Silence settles between us, and Nick shifts slightly. "Maybe this is just Alex's path for now," he finally says. "College will always be there."

Despite my best attempt to remain calm, my brain swims. This can't be happening. Not all at once, anyway. First JKP and now Alex.

"So, following his bliss is worth wasting his youth? He's headed toward a lifetime of gig jobs." I frown. "Do you know how many lost and lazy millennials I deal with regularly? He's going to end up just like them if we don't nudge him toward something better."

"He's not lazy." Nick rubs the back of his neck. "That's not a word I'd ever use to describe Alex."

Blood pounds in my temples. I can't believe what I'm hearing. "He could be a CEO by the time he's thirty if he wanted."

"That's the thing." Nick tries taking my hand, but I shove it under the blanket. "He doesn't want it. It's not his dream."

I clench my jaw. I'm not controlling Alex. If anything, I am too easy on him. I always made sure his homework was done. I followed-up with his teachers. I kept his life running so that all he had to do is focus on school, sports, and volunteer work.

The only explanation is that he's ungrateful.

"He's wasting his golden opportunity." I loosen my tight jaw. "Children are supposed to follow their parents' advice."

"My advice," Nick says slowly, "is to let him figure this out. The most successful people often have wavy paths."

Every inch of my body has been pulled taut, ready to snap. "My parents are going to be devastated."

Nick scoffs. "When have either of your parents approved of anything you've done?" He stares at me in disbelief. "Hell, Diana, you could be the first woman president, and they'd still think it wasn't enough."

"They've always wanted the best for me—just like I do for Alex."

"Diana—"

"Don't 'Diana' me. I know what I'm talking about. Kids need to be guided. And that's what I'm doing. Guiding him to make the best life choices."

"You need some water." Nick's trying to reset the conversation. "The doctor said you need to hydrate."

I sit up and let the blanket puddle around my hips. "I don't need water. I need my son to see things clearly." I blink rapidly to hold back my tears. "This is a disaster."

"It doesn't need to be."

"Please don't fight me. Please." I'm going to explode. How can Nick and I not see eye to eye on this?

Nick places his hand on my arm, and I pause. "Babe, you've been under so much stress. I've given you a pass because of how busy you were with work, but I know the kids leaving has you more upset than you're letting on. Add in being fired and Alex's decision, and well... you've been a tinderbox for a while now."

"I have everything under control," I say evenly. And I do. I'll talk sense into Alex.

"You don't have everything under control, and it's not the end of the world."

Nick is too calm. Almost like he's had more time to process everything.

"When did he tell you?" I ask.

My husband sits on the coffee table. His face is soft, not at all hard like it is when he's dug in on something—so there's hope. "Yesterday. Right before he told you. I wanted him to wait until we were together."

"You didn't call me immediately?" His betrayal hits me hard. "How could you not tell me?"

"I didn't have time, plus I don't think this is as big of an issue as you do." This, coming from my husband, is laughable. Since I've known him, he's done nothing but work his ass off to make partner at his law firm. "Some kids just need more time to figure things out."

"Alex has always known what he wants to do."

Nick presses his lips together. "Has he? Or has he always done what we wanted?"

"What's this?" I asked, looking up from my laptop.

Sixteen-year-old Alex stood across from me with a paper clenched in his hand. "Guess who's number one in his class of 600?"

"You?" I leaped off the bar stool and snatched the paper from him. His report card was a steady line of A-pluses and at the top, under his cumulative GPA was his class rank. Number one. Last year he slipped to number two behind Henry Comling, but now Alex was back on top.

I jumped up and down before grabbing his hand and pulling him into a hug. "I am so proud of you."

Like everything else he did, Alex wasn't overly emotional about his ranking, and he shrugged. "Thanks, but I still haven't made starting pitcher. I need that if I'm going to get into an Ivy."

"You will." I released him. "You just have to work harder, like you did with your grades, and keep up your volunteer work."

"I will."

I snapped a picture of his report card. "I'm sending this to Gigi. She's going to be thrilled."

Alex headed toward the garage door.

"Where are you going?" I asked. "Dad will be home soon, and I want to eat as a family."

"I need to practice my pitches. I'll be in the backyard."

I watched him out the window for a few minutes. He precisely threw the baseball against the bounce back, and I marveled at his commitment. Emily worked hard, but Alex excelled.

My son has never been a quitter—especially when faced with a challenge.

"I need time to process this," I say. I fuss with the blanket. "I've spent eighteen years envisioning Alex doing amazing things, and it's vanished with no warning."

"That's his point. It's your dream, not his." Nick reaches out and squeezes my hand. "Want me to start the shower for you?"

I nod. "Nick?"

"Yeah?"

"Are you really okay with this?"

He sighs. "Not really, but he's our son and I want him to be his own person." He bobbles his head from right to left as if thinking. "Alex is going to follow this path whether we like it or not, so let's do what we can to help him be successful."

"My mom is going to be furious. She's—"

"Sweetheart, for Alex's sake, let's put his wants before Helen's."

I was never allowed to choose what I wanted to do with my life, and while everything has turned out better than I imagined, I sometimes wish I had followed my own dreams and worked for the non-profit I had interned with in college. My parents believed it didn't pay enough and lacked prestige. Being the dutiful daughter that I am, I rejected the non-profit's job offer and took a well-paying, but boring job in PR.

"If we press too hard, we could alienate Alex." Nick holds my gaze. "Part of being a parent is knowing when to let go."

I exhale loudly. "I'm not ready, and how do we know he is?" What Nick is asking goes against every sane part of my brain. "What if he fails?"

"Then we help him get back up. We're his safety net."

I don't know how to fail, so how I'm supposed to help Alex if he does? In fact, I'm spectacularly awful at failing—as my panic attacks shows.

And yet, on some level, what Nick is saying makes sense.

"Okay," I say slowly. "I'll try it your way. But…"

"What?"

"Can you tell my mom?"

11

KRISTIN

I have glasses, wine, and Hollywood Fashion tape ready to go, but no snacks and we should eat something if we're going to drink tonight.

I poke through my refrigerator and find red grapes and some questionable cheese. I haven't bothered to grocery shop this week. There's no point since Tom prefers to eat out, and I haven't had an appetite.

"Where did I put the small charcuterie board?" I ask myself as I walk across the gleaming all-white kitchen to the pantry. When we remodeled several years ago, I had custom shelves put into the pantry complete with appliance garages and cute organizers. Tom thought it was overboard, but I've been told more than once that my color-coded pantry is enviable.

I sort through the different charcuterie boards until I find the small, wooden one with the gold inlay.

My front door alarm chimes. "Hey!" Steph calls. "I'm here!"

"In the kitchen!" I emerge from the pantry as she saunters into the kitchen.

Steph is dressed exactly like she was yesterday except her

messy bun has been transformed into sleek beachy waves. She is stunning when she tries.

"Do you have the costumes?" Steph slips off her jacket, lays it over a bar stool, and sits on the one next to it.

"They're in Nicole's costume room."

Despite her best efforts, Steph's Dominatrix Snow White costume has not arrived, so she's relying on me to make her sexy —in an age-appropriate way, of course. Although Steph never really does age appropriate. Not with clothes, or men, or life. It's like she's permanently stuck in her twenties—but with more money, a nicer car, and a better loft.

I'm insanely jealous.

The front door opens, and the sound of Diana's heels clacking against the wood floors greets us before she does. Her light pink skirt suit with a crisp white button-up blouse and impossibly high floral-printed heels is a stark contrast to Steph's all-black ensemble.

I arrange the grapes and cheese on the board. I've purposely skipped adding crackers because no one wants to be bloated in a costume. "Here we go!" I say, pushing the board toward my friends. "I know it's not much, but we need something in our stomachs."

"I had a large salad for lunch," Diana says. "I think I'm okay."

"Think?" Steph raises an eyebrow. "How do you not know if you're hungry or not?"

"I log everything in my food app, and I'm nearly at my caloric limit today, so I need to refrain from eating high-caloric foods like cheese."

"Since when do you do track your food?" Steph asks.

"Since maintaining my weight has become more and more difficult." She sits next to Steph at the island. "You can't tell me you haven't noticed the same thing?" She eyes me for a moment. "Well, not you Kristin. You need every last bit of cheese."

"Sounds delightful." Steph cuts off a piece of Manchego and chews with exaggeration. "Mmmm... so... good."

I reach for the bottle of Medoc. "Anyone?"

Diana raises her hand. "Just a small pour."

I pour a tiny bit into her glass, and she gives me a strange look. "What?" I ask. "That's a small pour."

She sighs. "A small pour is code for I need all the wine."

"Work?" I fill her glass two-thirds of the way up. I know Steph and I had to coerce her into coming tonight, but she seems... sad more than put-out. "Is everything okay?"

Steph takes the wine bottle and pours a glass for herself and then one for me. "Yeah. You seem off."

Diana folds her hands in her lap. Honestly, she looks like she may burst into tears. "This is embarrassing." She keeps her eyes downcast. "I had a panic attack the other day, and the ambulance came, and now I have an as-needed prescription for Xanax."

"That was you? Why didn't call me?" Alarm knots in my stomach. The neighborhood message board lit up yesterday with thoughts and prayers for whoever had been wheeled from their home. If I knew it was Diana, I would have been with her in a heartbeat.

"Embarrassingly, yes."

"Because of work?" Steph asks. "Or something else?"

"It's a lot." Diana appears pulled together, like she always does—but, oddly, she hasn't reached for her phone once.

"Are you sure that's all?" I ask. "You seem sad."

Diana lifts her glass to her lips and knocks back half the wine in a gulp. She swallows, sets her glass down, and smiles tightly. "I'm no longer employed by JKP."

Shock ripples across Steph's face, and I try to hide my surprise. "You quit?" I say. "Why?"

"No." Diana exhales. "I was fired. I was unceremoniously escorted from the building after a meeting with our largest client, who has gone off the rails." She absent-mindedly pops a grape in her mouth. "Apparently, I'm not a good fit for JKP's culture."

Our coffee meetups this week suddenly make sense. "When did this happen?"

"Tuesday. It's been a long week." She shifts uncomfortably on the barstool and opens her mouth like she's going to say something else but stops. "We should get ready. I can't wait to see what you've picked out for us, Kristin."

I decide not to press, and Steph must think the same because she says, "It better be sexy."

I grin. "I think you're going to love what I found for both of you!"

Diana eyes me suspiciously. "God help us."

Diana sorts through the costumes I've draped over the bed. She acted like the panic attack was a non-event, but she does not melt down. Diana is the calmest person I know, and if she had to go to the hospital for a panic attack, something is terribly wrong.

I study her for a moment, and guilt settles into my brain. I've been so consumed by my self-made problems that I overlooked Diana's unusual behavior. What kind of friend am I?

"What do you think?" Steph poses with her hand on her hip and her other one high over her head. "It's not short enough, is it?"

"Your butt cheeks are almost hanging out." Diana fidgets with the skirt of the witch costume she's wearing.

"Then it's not short enough." Steph yanks the skirt higher. "Find anything you like?" she asks Diana

"Maybe this?" Diana holds up an elaborate fae costume. Nicole and I spent hours working on it; the beautiful wings make it one of my favorites. I'd wear it, but it doesn't hang right.

Steph studies the costume. "You could make that work. You have the legs."

Diana is a few inches taller than Nicole, and the costume will sit right above her mid-thigh. "You should try it on," I say. "Make sure it fits okay."

"Nothing else looks right," Diana says. "It has to work, or I'm going in that." She points at her pink suit neatly folded on my sewing table. "I could pretend I'm an accountant."

Steph pushes her boobs together and knots the bottom of her costume so that it resembles a bra. "This isn't nearly slutty enough."

"I hate that word." I wrinkle my nose. "It's degrading."

To my surprise, Diana says, "Emily says it's a word women can reclaim and change the meaning of." She's so matter of fact that I almost forget about her panic attack confession. "Like bitch. Everyone's a bad bitch or a boss bitch or a bitch babe, now."

"That's just as bad."

"I one hundred percent agree," Diana says. "Which is why that Skinny Bitch drink is so insulting."

I'm not opening that can of worms again. "What do you think?" I admire my figure in the mirror. The witch costume hangs a little loose, but it doesn't look terrible. I turn to see my butt. "I look cute, right?"

"Not sexy enough." Steph grabs the fabric around my waist, pinching it, and pulling it up to show more of my thigh. "That's better."

"Except that's not how if fits." I push her hands away and the costume falls loose again.

"Belt it or something." Steph wears one of Nicole's Sailor Moon outfits. She studies herself in the mirror. "What do you think? Will this be appropriately sexy?"

"Oh, I think your sidekick will be sexy enough for both of you." I put my hands on my hips. "Have you told Diana?"

Diana tugs the fae tunic over her head. "Sidekick?"

"Layla," Steph says, digging through clothing racks. "She works for me, and she's helping me plan a geriatric Gen X night. I thought it would good to bring her to take notes on what excites old suburbanites."

"Hey!" I point at Diana and myself. "You're talking about us."

Steph rolls her eyes. "Exactly. Your definition of fun is different from mine."

"You're bringing Layla to make fun of us?" Diana pinches her lips together. "So nice of you." She's too consumed by this new info to notice just how short the costume is.

Steph finds a sash and holds it out to me. "You'll like Layla, okay? She's my best employee, and she'll blend in."

"She's twenty-two," I say. "Unless she's wearing a hag's costume, she's going to look like someone's college daughter who crashed our adults-only party."

Since meeting Layla yesterday, I've struggled to place why she looks familiar. I even asked Nicole if she knew a Layla from high school or her sorority. To my surprise, Nicole immediately texted me back. She didn't know any Laylas.

So why do I feel like I've met a twenty-two-year-old before?

Nick's ringtone blares from Diana's phone. She scoops it off my sewing machine table and steps into the hallway. "Hey," she says when she returns. "Is it okay if I run home? Nick is struggling with his makeup." She's already stripping off the fae costume. "Text when you're on your way to do my makeup."

"Start with this," I say, handing her a box of theater makeup. "Really focus on your eyes and I'll do the rest."

"Dark?"

"Use the blues and greens," I say. "And some glitter."

"I understand the assignment."

I wait until the front door shuts and exclaim, "She had a panic attack!"

"I know." Steph pulls on her thigh-high boots. They look

perfect with her costume. "I'm worried about her." She flips her hair when she stands up. "She's acting like it's no big deal, but Diana does not fall apart like this."

"Should I reach out to Nick?" I rehang the discarded costumes. "I feel like there's something she's not telling us, and we never keep secrets from each other."

"Everyone has secrets." A strange look flits across Steph's face. "Including you."

My throat constricts. "I don't have any secrets."

"I don't believe you." Steph runs her fingers through the ends of her dark hair until it looks perfectly bouncy. I'd kill for hair like hers. "How friendly are you and Joe exactly?"

I lay an armful of costumes over the top of a clothing rack. "We flirt, but it's innocent and never goes anywhere."

"Yet."

"Ever." I select a discarded costume and hang it while keeping my back to Steph. "But sometimes I wish it would."

Steph sighs. "Let's have some wine and talk. When's Tom getting home?"

I turn around. "He took Henry to the dog park, so who knows? Soon maybe?"

"Then we better talk fast." Steph narrows her eyes. "And you better not leave anything out."

Disappointment clouds Steph's eyes. Should I not have told her everything?

"You're having an affair. An emotional one." She glances out the windows and back at me. "Or is it physical, and you're lying? Because you've been hanging out with Joe and have never mentioned him to Diana or me which makes me think you're lying."

"I'm…" I press my lips together and glance toward the foyer. We're sitting in the family room in our costumes, drinking more wine, and analyzing my options. The sound of the keypad unlocking the front door interrupts me, and I lower my voice. "You know how Diana is."

Steph nods. "Judgy, but you also know you're doing wrong."

Henry bounces into the family room, his tail wagging. He stops next to Steph and nudges her knee until she pets him.

"Hey, Steph!" Tom says. Like always, he's dressed in joggers and sneakers, and his fleece vest covers a long-sleeve T-shirt. "You ready for tonight?"

"When am I not ready for a good party?"

Tom plants a chaste kiss on my cheek. There are no fireworks. No excitement. It's a kiss out of habit. That's all.

"Are these your costumes?" he asks.

Steph finishes her glass of wine. "I wanted to be a dominatrix Snow White, but Kristin turned me into a naughty schoolgirl instead." She wiggles her eyebrows. "It's honestly worse if you think about it."

"I thought you were using Nicole's costumes?" Tom stares at Steph's costume. "I can't remember her having anything like that."

"This is one of hers." Steph places her feet on the coffee table and tugs the costume skirt down so she doesn't flash Tom. "Isn't it amazing what a little imagination can do?"

You'd never know Steph and I were discussing the breakdown of my marriage just moments earlier. If only I could switch gears as easily as her.

"Tom," I say. "Steph and I don't want to eat so much that we're bloated, but we have leftover curry in the fridge."

"I'm good." He flops onto the chair across from Steph. Henry leaves Steph and arranges himself at Tom's feet. Tom's gaze lands on me. "You're a witch?"

"The White Witch. I only do good deeds." I wink at him, but he ignores me. "Your vampire costume is on the bed. You should go get ready so we're not late." Tom's the same thing every year. Unlike me and my friends, he has no problem making zero effort.

My phone buzzes, and I pretend to not hear it. It buzzes again.

"You going to get that?" Tom asks. He's flipped on the TV.

Steph catches my eye and frowns before pointing at the phone.

See? I want to scream. *See how little he cares?*

I don't need to flip the phone over to know Joe's name is on the screen, but when I see it, a smile snakes across my face. I glance up at Steph, who purses her lips at me.

—hey. See you tonight?—

I walk into the kitchen and lean against the island. From here, I can keep an eye on Tom.

—can't wait— Two simple words that hold a tremendous amount of weight.

—me too—

Steph joins me in the kitchen. "Is it him?"

"Yes."

Tom is too engrossed in his show to notice our hushed conversation.

Steph swipes the phone from my hand, runs into the pantry, and shuts herself inside.

With Tom sitting nearby, I can't bang on the door or make too loud of a noise. "Steph," I whisper. "Give me back my phone!"

I tap the door with my fingertips and wait. Finally, Steph opens the door and tosses my phone at me. "You lied. You two are more than flirty."

"Steph, I swear, nothing has happened between us. We're just friends."

"Good, because I told him to piss off."

My stomach churns, and I frantically open my text messages.

—Do not contact Kristin again—

"Why did you do that?" My voice shakes.

"Think hard, Kristin. Think about how you—not Joe—will be responsible for hurting people you love. Think about what you're willing to lose—because you will lose something. It may be your family, or it could be your moral compass. Neither are easy to get back."

12

———

STEPH

Diana is not happy. She keeps pulling on her pointy ears. "Are you sure I don't look like a trampy elf?"

"For the hundredth time, you look amazing," I say. "You did an amazing job with your eye makeup, and if you're photographed, no one will be able to ID you."

Nick lays his hand on her bare thigh. "She's right. You look incredible—even if you're not a sexy princess."

Diana's flushes, and I decide not to pursue that line of conversation. There are some things about your friends and their husbands that you do not need to know.

Kristin glances backward, over her shoulder, which would be fine if she wasn't driving.

"Careful," Tom shouts, and Kristin slams on the brakes, narrowly missing the Audi in front of us.

With the car stopped, Kristin turns around and looks back at Diana again, completely unfazed by our near accident. "It's going to be fine and if it isn't, you can leave."

Kristin turns onto Amy's street. Every spot is taken, and she turns the next corner and parks half-way down the block. "There

108

are more people than normal," she says excitedly. "It's only seven-thirty, and parking is already tough."

"Then we're in for a great time," I say, getting out of the car. Pounding music is audible even from here.

We follow a small group of what I think are goth doctors to the entrance. Bass thumps heavily, and it does feel like I'm outside a club. About ten feet from the door, I stop. "Hey, I need to wait for Layla. You guys go ahead."

"Who's Layla?" Nick asks. It's odd to see him in a chest-exposing vampire costume with fake blood dripping from his mouth. Nick's always had a little bit of a party boy in him, and I hope he brings it out tonight and wraps Diana up in it.

Kristin huffs. "Layla is Steph's child-employee who's here to take notes on the party,"

"Why?"

"Work stuff," I say.

Tom wanders off to talk to someone dressed as a CVS receipt, leaving the rest of standing on the walkway.

Diana tugs at her skimpy skirt again. I can't tell her, but she looks a tiny bit like a trampy elf. It's completely appropriate for Halloween and even though she doesn't think so, she's pulling it off.

"Stop messing with your costume." Kristin adjusts Diana's hair. "You're going to ruin it." As she talks, Kristin scans the crowds of people passing us. She was irate over my text to Joe, but she couldn't say anything in the moment. I, however, have no doubt I'm going to meet the infamous Joe tonight. Or rather, he's going to meet me because I have a few things to say to him.

Across the street, Layla gets out of her Uber. "Layla's here," I say. "Be nice."

She strides confidently across the street in a black catsuit. Cat ears are perched atop her dark, wavy hair, and she's drawn whiskers and a cat nose on her face. Oh, and did I mention, there's not a single misplaced lump anywhere on her body?

She stops just short of our group, and I hold my breath. She looks just like Jess, and if Diana doesn't notice it, Kristin will say something.

"Hi!" Layla zeroes in on me. "Your costume is killer!"

"Thanks! Kristin made it." I spin, and my skirt flares. It's much shorter than Diana's, something I pointed out when we got to her house, but this didn't comfort Diana.

"Hi, Layla." Diana extends her hand. "I'm Diana. It's nice to meet you."

"It's nice to meet you too," Layla says before turning to Kristin. "We met the other day, right? Kristin?"

"Yes, at LUSH." Kristin tilts her head. "Have you worked there long?"

Layla looks at me before speaking. "Like a year?"

"Should we go in?" Diana asks, and I immediately beeline to the door and beckon Layla to follow me. I need to keep her away from Kristin.

As we walk, I'm suddenly aware of how much older we are than Layla. At work, I'm surrounded by young people and her youth doesn't stand out, but here, surrounded by middle-aged Gen Xers, she seems like she's barely out of high school—which, honestly, she is.

I've aged. We all have. I just haven't been paying attention.

At the door, Amy has a fake bouncer. She likes the appearance of exclusivity even though everyone in the neighborhood is invited. He waves each of us through but stops Layla. "You here with your mom?"

I bristle. "Oh, come on," I say. "Do we look old enough to have a daughter her age?"

He shrugs and steps aside.

The thumping music grows louder when we part the heavy, black curtain separating the main room from the hallway. Strobe lights flash at regular intervals, and groups of costumed party-goers mill about with drinks in hand.

"The dance floor is downstairs," I shout at Layla. "That's where you should hang out. Get a feel for the vibe and what music sticks."

"Drinks?" Nick shouts at Layla and me before turning and doing the same to Diana.

We form a chain with Layla and snake through the crowd to the basement. All the women have on sexy costumes: sexy ghosts, sexy angels, sexy pumpkins. The men's costumes skew toward the grotesque: severed heads, fake blood, and bruises. But the one thing they all have in common is their age. Layla is a minimum twenty years younger than everyone.

She takes a video of the crowd, probably for later reference, before shoving her way to the bar next to me.

"You look cute!" Layla shouts.

"Thank you. I borrowed it from Kristin's daughter and made a few alterations." I hold out my phone. "Can you snap a picture of me?"

I pose, leaning a little forward to better show off my cleavage and smile.

"How's this?" Layla shows me the screen.

I look damn good. "Perfect." I glance at Diana and Kristin who are having an animated conversation about something even though Kristin keeps glancing around the room.

Nick shouts something, but it's lost in the noise. On the dance floor, a group of women shuffle politely to early 2000s rap. They step and clap off-beat to the song while wearing skimpy costumes, and their husbands—at least I hope the men are their husbands—watch from the perimeter and laugh.

I grab Layla's arm and pull her closer to me so that she can hear me. "What do you think?"

She shrugs. "The DJ is good, but I can throw a better party than this."

I nod. "When you don't get out much, this is what happens. The bar is pretty low."

A gaggle of drunk women lean on each and try jumping in unison to the song, but they're messy, and one of them falls on her knees, and another sits down with her legs sprawled in front of her.

"It's like a bad 80s movie with grown-up cool girls." Layla snaps a picture of them. "I kind of love it."

I shake my head. "Those cool girls have grown up and grown boring."

Next to us, Diana sways awkwardly to the music. I'm impressed she's making an effort, but when Nick and Tom hand out shot glasses, she waves hers away.

I shout into her pointy ear. "Live, Diana. For one night, just live a little." I shove a shot glass into her hand and hold mine up. "Cheers, bitches!"

"Cheers!" Nick clinks his glass against Diana's before touching mine.

I don't think Diana has done shots since college, but she presses the glass to her lips and tosses her head back. Her lips pucker, and she looks like she may gag. When she swallows, she makes a horrific face. "What the hell was that?"

I laugh. "Tequila! It'll grow some hair on your chest." I grab Diana's hand. "Let's dance!"

Layla collects our shot glasses and sets them on the bar.

"You're not drinking?" I ask her.

"I'm working, and you have a no-drugs-or-drinking-at-work policy."

Impressive. "You're right. Thank you."

I grab Diana's hand and spin her around. She narrowly avoids knocking into a minotaur, and the man's shout is lost to the thundering music.

I clear a path to the crowded dance floor. Everyone is doing the polite-white-girl bob, but when the music switches to "California Love," I throw my arms in the air and shake my hips. I have zero cares what anyone thinks about me. Maybe it's because I don't live here, or maybe because I'm always in nightclubs, but this is a party, and I'm here for good time.

"Diana!" I shout. "Dance! Have fun!" I press my body against hers and shimmy my shoulders. "C'mon!"

Like a good sport, Diana shimmies back at me and spins in a circle, her skirt flaring around her upper thighs. The next song is Madonna, and I lead Diana off the dance floor. Tom, Layla, Nick, and Kristin are still at the bar.

"Here!" Kristin shoves more shots at us. "Drink up!"

Diana hesitates.

"Don't be a bitch, Diana!" I shout. "Drink." I select a glass and force another into Diana's hand.

Kristin holds up one finger, then two, and finally three. Everyone but Diana tosses back the shots.

"C'mon, Diana!" Kristin yells. "It's a party."

"Fine." She knocks back her shot. "Happy?"

I grin. "Now, it's a party!"

"It's so hot!" Diana fans herself with her hand and pulls her hair off her neck. Kristin styled it into two small buns over her ears and the rest hangs loose down Diana's back. We had to assure Diana that it was appropriate for an elf, and she shouldn't feel foolish.

"That's because there are a hundred bodies crammed into a small space." Nervous energy radiates off Kristin, and I'm sure she's disappointed one of those bodies isn't Joe.

"It's too hot." Diana points at the basement's backdoor. "I need to cool off. Anyone want to come?"

Social smokers crowd around the back door, and a faint hint of pot hits me as we walk past. I lean against the low stone wall dividing the lawn from the patio. Off to our left, Layla appears trapped in conversation with two pervy-looking men.

"Does she need rescuing?" Kristin says.

I wave at Layla, who happily bounces toward us. She whips out her phone from a pocket in her catsuit. "I've taken a ton of videos," she says. "I can't believe this is a house party in the suburbs. Who knew!"

Diana fans herself with her hand. "Is my makeup running?"

Kristin, who has lost her witch hat somewhere, shakes her head. "It's stage makeup. It's meant to stay in place under bright lights."

Diana fidgets with the deep V-neck collar of her sleeveless tunic. "It's not much cooler out here than it was inside." She stares at me. "I don't remember clubs being so hot."

"Oh, they're always like that," Layla says. "That's why I avoid the dance floor during shows. Even if you're not dancing, you get sweaty."

Diana twists her hair over her shoulder. "Do either of you have a ponytail holder? I need to pull my hair up."

"I do!" Layla tugs a scrunchie with little purple hearts off her wrist and hands it to Diana.

"Thanks."

"Are you okay?" Layla peers at Diana's flushed face.

"I'm just hot." Diana pulls her hair into a high ponytail, nearly elbowing the race car driver next to her in the face.

"You're really red," Layla says. "Can I get you water? Something non-alcoholic?"

Diana grits her teeth, a look I know all too well, but I also know Layla is following protocol. When we see anyone who is as red as Diana, our job is to step in and assess them.

"Like I said, I'm hot." Diana points at Kristin who is pounding water. "Kristin's hot, too."

"But she's not flushed bright red like you." Concern fills Layla's eyes. "Let me get you a water."

Diana tosses up her arms. "I always get flushed when I drink. Right, Steph?"

Sweat runs down Diana's face. "Yeah, but you're abnormally red. I think Layla is right; you need water."

Layla tilts her head. "Maybe you should stand by the fridge? Open the freezer door. That's what my mom does when she has menopause."

The word 'menopause' hangs heavily in the tight space. Wisely, neither Kristin nor I want to touch it.

"What?" Diana asks in disbelief.

"Maybe you have menopause." Layla's earnestness is going to get her punched. "My mom always gets flushed and hot when she has menopause. Cool air helps."

Diana stares at us like she expects us to refute Layla's assertion, but both of us burst into laughter.

"First, I'm standing outside," Diana says. "Second, I am not standing in a refrigerator at a party with my neighbors. And third, I'm just hot. That's all."

"Maybe she's right." Kristin giggles in her drunk way. "Maybe you have menopause."

"I do not have menopause!" A few heads turn toward us, and Diana drops her voice to a harsh whisper. "I'm not even peri-menopausal yet!"

Layla blushes. "I'm sorry. You just seem to be about my mom's age, and I thought…"

"You thought wrong." Diana rips the scrunchie from her hair and hands it back to Layla. "I don't need this."

"How old is your mom?" Kristin asks. Her eyes aren't glazed, which means she'll remember this conversation. And that means, I can't let it happen.

Layla screws up her lips like she's afraid of saying the wrong thing. Which she should be. "Like your age, right Steph? Forty-six?"

Kristin blinks. A woman with a riding crop wedges between

us and starts shouting at the gorilla sitting on the wall behind Diana. Kristin pushes her aside so that we're face to face.

My chest constricts, and my throat aches. I don't want to do this now. Not here.

"You know Layla's mom?" Kristin asks.

A buzz builds in my ears, and a chill runs up my spine.

Before I can answer, Layla says, "They were friends like twenty years ago or something."

Kristin's mouth drops open as she makes the connection. "Jess?" she spats. "Jess is her mom?"

"It's irrelevant." I can barely get the words out.

Someone jostles Diana, and she stumbles into me and grabs my arm. "Jess is Layla's mom?"

Despite being on a crowded patio, no one is paying us any attention. It's like we're invisible. Everyone else stands in close groups, laughing and drinking, and not noticing us at all.

Kristin crosses her arms. "What are you doing, Steph? Why did you hire Jess's daughter?"

My lungs knot, and I struggle to inhale. "Since reasoning with drunks is impossible, I am not having this conversation. Not now. Maybe never."

Diana rips off her elf ears and tosses them at me. "Layla. Call an Uber."

"I'm sorry. I don't understand what I did." Layla holds up her hand like a stop sign. "I didn't mean to upset any of you."

Kristin clenches her fists and breathes heavily through her mouth. "It's not you, but you need to leave."

"Steph?" Layla stares at me in confusion.

"Go home, Layla. I'll see you at work on Monday." My friends' angry glares rip through me. "I think maybe you should talk to your mom."

When she disappears into the party, I face my friends. "I didn't know. Not until the other day."

Kristin glares at me. "How could you not see it? She's a mini-Jess."

Twenty years of hidden truth spill from my lips. "Thinking about Jess hurt too much."

13

DIANA

Jess. For years, I've avoided talking about her and until now, I believed Steph had moved on. Jess was forgotten and in the past.

Except now her daughter was just here, hanging out with us, and Steph thought it was unnecessary to tell us anything.

The loud crowd would drown out any profanities I shouted, but no. I'm going to be calm. I'm going to pause.

An uncomfortable silence surrounds us until Kristin spins on her heel and tears into the house. Steph drops her head like she's trying not to cry.

What should I do? They're both upset, but Steph needs to explain why she hired Jess's daughter, and worse, brought her to the party. Did she believe Layla's parentage wouldn't come out, or that Kristin and I wouldn't care?

I stare at my adventurous, funny, and big-hearted friend, and even though I don't understand what her motive is for hiring Jess's daughter, my heart breaks as I watch her blink back tears.

Oh, Steph, what were you thinking?

I touch her back. "Do you need to talk?"

Steph leans against the stacked stone retaining wall. Her nose is already red. "What I really need is to be alone right now. I can't deal with your disappointment or judgement."

I can't tell her I'm scared—not just for Steph, but for Kristin and me too. Having Jess back in our lives, even tangentially, could ruin our friendship with Diana. "I'm going inside. If you need me, find me, okay?"

Steph nods.

The steamy basement is hot from all the bodies crowded inside. The room spins around me, or maybe I spin. It's difficult to tell.

The music changes from 80s rock to something terrible I've heard Emily and Alex listen to. The beat is almost primal, and the tempo matches the confusion swirling inside me.

Nick slides up behind me and runs his hands over my waist and hips. The room spins again. "Hey," I shout. "I need to find Kristin. Steph did something incredibly stupid, and we need to fix it."

"Is it about Layla?" Nick's breath smells like bourbon, and I pull my head away from his.

"Kind of." Around me the room sways, and everything sounds like it's underwater. The strobing lights make me close my eyes, and I unintentionally bobble.

Nick wraps his arm around my waist. "Let's get you some water. You'll hate the morning if you don't hydrate." He forces a water bottle into my hand. Where did this come from? He unscrews the cap. "Drink."

The water feels delicious on my parched throat, and I quickly finish it.

I hand the empty bottle to Nick. "I need to find Kristin."

Nick raises his brows. He doesn't need to say anything; we both have the same thought: if I can't find Kristin, she may be with Joe. All of our neighbors over the age of thirty-five are here, so he must be too.

On the dance floor, a group of women grind on each other, arms swinging wide, making a spectacle of themselves. Discarded pieces of their costumes are strewn around the edges of the dance floor, and every so often, they squeal in unison. I've always wondered what a fraternity party would be like, and now I know.

Tom joins us. "Do you know where Kristin is?" I ask.

"Haven't seen her," Tom says. "Maybe she's upstairs?"

I close my eyes. I can get upstairs. I can do it. "I'll be back."

Nick swats my butt as I walk away, and I stumble into a man near me. I mumble my apology and keep going. If Kristin isn't with Joe, would she have gone home? It's not a long walk. Or maybe she found a quiet place to be alone and think.

I reach the basement stairs and grasp the railing. Tom thinks she's upstairs, so I need to get up there. One step. Two steps. Three steps.

Halfway up, panic blooms in my gut. What if she is with Joe? What then?

I stumble around the near-empty main floor. The non-dancers have gathered in small groups in the kitchen and family room. I move between them, asking if they've seen Kristin.

Somehow, I wind back to the foyer. My ears ring as I part the black foyer curtain and head out the front door. Since everyone has already arrived, it's quieter out here and more private. If anyone walked by and Kristin was with Joe, it was public enough for deniability.

My vision blurs as I scan the front yard and row of cars lining the street.

Nothing.

I turn back toward the house and squint. Kristin and a zombie, who can only be Joe, are semi-hidden in the shadow along the side of the house. Joe leans into her, like he's about to kiss her or maybe he's pulling away from a kiss.

It does not matter.

"Kristin," I say sharply. I'm too far away for them to hear me. Or maybe their ears are ringing from the music too. I shuffle toward them, and neither notices me. Kristin stands with her back against the house and Joe has his hand planted just above her head. My vision is too blurry to make out their features, but Kristin's giggle is unmistakable.

They don't notice me as I creep up.

Kristin reaches out and touches Joe's face.

"Kristin!"

She jumps, and Joe steps away.

"Diana! Hi!" Kristin says breathlessly. "Joe and I were discussing Steph."

"Is that so?"

Joe seems completely unfazed by the current situation. "Kristin is upset."

I glare at him. "Thankfully, she has a real friend right here to talk about it with."

Kristin stares wistfully at Joe like she expects him to say something. Instead, he lifts his chin. "I'll check in with you later, okay?"

I wait until he's around the corner. "What the hell are you doing, Kristin? You're smarter than this."

Kristin's face falls. "We weren't doing anything wrong. I'm upset over Steph, and Joe is a great listener."

"You ran to Joe and not me? Or Tom?" I wish I could believe her, but I can't. "Joe didn't corroborate your story, by the way. In fact, he didn't stick around at all. That says a lot."

"What you saw was two friends in a deep conversation."

"I can't do this right now," I say. I stumble away, my anger increasing as I skirt around the house.

I can't save Kristin from herself, and Steph has unwisely employed Jess's daughter. Add in my agreement to support Alex's disastrous drop-out plan, and my friends and I are a trifecta of bad decisions.

At the patio, I start down the stairs to the basement.

"Oh, hey!" A man says, grabbing my arm. "Let me help you."

The steps shift beneath me. "Okay. Everything is blurry."

He opens the door for me. "That's what happens when you're drunk."

The basement smells like sweat and stale beer, and I push my way through groups of people until I reach Tom and Nick by the bar.

Calm down, I think. *Do not make a scene.* I owe it to Tom to not say anything, but why hasn't he noticed his wife missing? Is he oblivious like Kristin claims?

Tom pushes a shot glass into my hand. "Here you go." He laughs. "You look pissed, Diana."

I face Tom and Nick and hold the glass to my lips. "Bottoms up!"

When I finish choking it down, Nick plucks the empty shot glass from my hand. "You look green."

"I feel green." My stomach gurgles, and I try to ignore it, but the room spins faster, and I cling to Nick.

"You okay?" he asks

"Kristin…"

Nick squeezes my arm. "She's over there. Do you want me to get her?"

"She doesn't need Kristin," Steph says. Where did she come from? "She needs more water, some electrolytes, and ibuprofen. Get her outside, Nick, and I'll get the water."

The room pitches side to side, and I struggle to walk as Nick guides me to the backdoor. Was the dance floor always this big? And where did all these people come from?

"It's too hot," I say, yanking up my tunic until my stomach shows. "Why is it so hot?"

"Sweetheart, let's just get you outside, okay?"

"But it's hot." The blurry figures around me meld together and pulse with the music. My stomach gurgles again and rolls, and my throat seizes. I try clamping my hand over my mouth and running toward the door, but I take a half-step and vomit spews from my mouth and all over the two women nearest me.

14

KRISTIN

I stare at the blank text message. I've been up all night trying to figure out what to say to Diana. After she threw up, Nick and Steph hurried her out of the party, and if she remembers any of it, I'm sure she's so mortified she's forgotten about me and Joe.

Tom's upstairs showering. He slept in, exhausted from the party, while I tossed and turned all night replaying my argument with Steph and trying to figure how to convince Diana her memory is a hangover hallucination.

My stomach is a knotted mess, and it's unclear if it's from my slight hangover, my fights with my friends, or the thrill of kissing Joe.

And what a kiss. I close my eyes, savoring the memory of Joe's lips moving over mine and how his hand ran up my thigh before settling on my lower back. I don't care that it's wrong. It was amazing.

I want Joe to kiss me again… or maybe more… again.

Jesus. I cannot blow up my life like this. I know better. I do.

But how am I supposed to pretend like the kiss didn't happen? How am I supposed to talk to Joe and act normal?

Tom's footsteps on the stairs stop my merry-going thoughts. "Ready?" he asks. "I'm starving."

"Let me put my shoes on." I've put no effort into my outfit and am wearing a ratty T-shirt, PJ bottoms, and messy bun.

Tom, of course, doesn't notice.

The drive to the diner consists of Tom playing his favorite 80s rock, and me staring at my phone waiting for someone—Diana, Steph, even Joe—to text. It's only a ten-minute drive, but by the time Tom parks, I feel like we've taken a cross-country trip with no bathroom breaks.

Tom and I have literally run out of things to talk about. Is this what happens when you've been married for over twenty years? Is this just a normal middle-aged malaise like Diana said, and I just need to push past it?

What does Diana know, really? She and Nick are just as much in love now as they were on their wedding day. They act like a team and probably have tons to talk about.

At least, I'm sure they talk about something other than what takeout to order or movie to watch.

Tom holds the diner door open, and the delicious scent of sweet and fried food surrounds the hostess stand. I only come here with Tom, and I'd never admit it to my friends, but I love chicken and waffles. There's something about the savory gravy mixing with syrup. And the carbs. One meal is about two weeks of my carb allotment, but it is worth it.

The hostess takes two menus from a pile and motions for us to follow her. We pass the soda counter and tables crowded with other patrons until we reach the back corner.

"How's this?" the hostess asks, stopping next to a two-top.

"Great." Tom pulls out his chair.

My stomach gurgles. If I don't get something in me soon to soak up the alcohol, my hangover will only get worse. "I know what I'm having," I say, not looking at the menu. "My stomach is fragile."

Tom studies his menu even though he, too, always has the same thing: the Hunter's Breakfast. In the five years we've come here, he has never changed his order. He flips the menu pages before setting it aside.

"Why do you bother to look?" I ask. "You know you're getting the Hunter's Breakfast."

"What if they have something new?"

"They never have anything new."

Our waitress places two glasses of water on the table and takes our order. Sure enough, Tom gets the Hunter's Breakfast.

I palm my phone. Should I message Diana or wait for her to say something? Because if she remembers, Diana will absolutely say something, but if she doesn't remember, then I'm off the hook. I shouldn't poke the hornet's nest.

Across from me, Tom is engrossed in his phone—reading ESPN most likely.

The burning intensity of Joe's lips pressing against mine pushes to the front of my mind, and all the nerves in my body tingle. Why do I feel excited and scared at the same time?

While other diners chatter around us, Tom and I stare at our phones. Joe hasn't messaged yet, but it's not even eleven. Still, the stress of not knowing where we stand adds to my already queasy gut. What if Joe thinks the kiss was a mistake? What if he wants to never see me again?

What if he wants to take it farther?

The waitress drops my food in front of me. "Let me know if you need anything else."

I need a new life. I need more than breakfasts and dinners with my husband who is checked out. I just need more... engagement.

"Tom," I say, cutting off a piece of chicken and swirling it through the gravy. "What do you want to do today?"

"I don't know." He's propped his phone against the napkin dispenser so he can eat and watch a soccer match at the same time. Years ago, we had a no-TV-at-the-table-or-in-the-bedroom policy, but now, Tom can't even go to a restaurant without needing to be plugged in.

Nausea hits me, and I force myself to swallow a bit of chicken. "I'm not feeling the best," I say. "Maybe a quiet day at home?"

"I'm fine with that," Tom says between bites while keeping his attention on his phone.

"Kristin?"

I swivel my head to the left. Thalia and Joe are being seated next to us, and Thalia looks radiant with her dark hair pulled into a low chignon and a slick of lip gloss. She's always been a pretty woman, but I have never noticed just how beautiful she is. Classic. Refined.

Nothing like me in my ratty clothes and messy hair.

I want to disappear.

"Oh! Hi!" My voice shakes a little. "I'm not feeling the best. You have to forgive me." I fake laugh. "But you look gorgeous!"

"Thank you," Thalia says, taking her seat.

Joe leans over and shakes hands with Tom. Like Thalia, he is polished and not at all hungover.

Am I being punished? "We missed you last night, Thalia."

"It's not my scene." Thalia smiles up at the waitress. "Green tea, please. Joe? Black coffee?"

Joe smiles. "That would be perfect."

I concentrate on not staring at him, but what's running through his head? He isn't acting awkward, and in fact, he's acting like we barely know each other.

Maybe the kiss wasn't amazing for him? Maybe he's realized it was a mistake?

"What game are you watching?" Joe asks Tom.

In her seat, Thalia leans a little closer to me, and the crisp scent of her shampoo fills my nostrils. "Is Nicole enjoying junior year?"

I force excitement into my voice. "She's loving it! Between classes and her sorority, she keeps busy."

"How wonderful!" Thalia says. "When Tyler mentioned that he and Nicole have been seeing a lot of each other, I was excited. I just love her."

I blink. Nicole has been seeing Tyler again? Why hasn't she told me? "Me, too! Tyler is such a great guy."

"I always thought they were well matched." Thalia removes the tea bag from her cup and lies it neatly on the saucer without dripping any water on the table. "Next year, if they're still dating, we'll have to figure out the holidays." Thalia's laugh is high and tinkly. "I know I'm getting ahead of myself, but I'm hopeful."

My brain pounds against my skull. Are Nicole and Tyler that serious?

"Maybe we could do a group celebration." The words come out of my mouth, but I'm hovering over my body, watching the scene play out. Perfect Thalia is updating me on my daughter's dating life, while her husband, who I kissed, is bantering with my husband.

How did I end up here?

The waitress takes Joe and Thalia's order while I pick at my food. Thalia, of course, orders a quinoa bowl with fruit, to go with her green tea.

"Did you guys have a good time last night?" Joe asks, breaking through my spiraling thoughts.

Tom has turned his phone off.

He'll do that for Joe, but not for me.

"It's always a good time, but I can't do it more than once a year," Tom answers and points at me. "She's hungover as usual. Too many tequila shots."

I clench my jaw and smile. "Not too many. I remember the entire evening." I wait for Joe's reaction, but there's nothing. "Did you have fun, Joe?"

He sips his coffee. "It's always weird flying solo to that type of thing, but I had a great time." He locks eyes with Thalia and reaches for her hand, completely ignoring my expectant gaze. "One year, I'll get you to come, sweetheart."

For a relationship on the brink of falling apart, Joe and Thalia are acting awfully happy.

Thalia makes a dismissive motion with her other hand. "I'm well past sloppy drunken parties. Besides, there's usually some sort of horrific fall-out."

My breakfast threatens to come back up. "I think," I say, swallowing the lump in my throat, "some bad decisions were definitely made."

"No doubt," Tom chimes in. "Multiple tequila shots being just the start."

No matter how hard I try, I can't catch Joe's eye, and my unease grows.

Joe regrets everything. He's made it clear, and I have to sit here and pretend I am okay. I pick at my chicken, unable to swallow it. Even my normal hangover Coke isn't helping.

My phone buzzes, and I glance at the screen.

—Hey pretty girl, let's talk later—

I lift my gaze slightly, but Joe is lost in conversation with Thalia. He's literally sitting across from his wife and sending me flirty texts.

Maybe I don't know the whole story? Maybe Thalia and Joe are keeping up appearances?

I'm so confused. Is he sitting with Thalia because he needs to? And is he wishing he were really with me?

15

DIANA

"It could have been worse." Steph picks through my bowl of untouched sliced strawberries until she finds the one she wants and pops it in her mouth. "At least you didn't puke on the hostess."

It is well after one, and I'm curled into the fetal position on the couch. "You're not making me feel any better."

"I'm not sure what will." Steph tosses a strawberry at me, but she misses my face, and it hits the back of my cream sofa leaving a red splotch.

"Stop it! You're going to stain my couch!"

"I'm sure you can afford to have it cleaned." Steph eats another strawberry. "But seriously, you puked at a drunken party. It's not a big deal. It happens."

"It doesn't happen to me." I slowly lift my head. I no longer have a pounding headache, but I need to debloat, detox, and de-everything else because this is miserable. The only good thing is I that I'm so miserable I can't think about Alex right now.

When I dragged myself downstairs this morning, I was surprised to find Steph in my family room, eating cereal and watching Netflix. Apparently, Nick had also forgotten she stayed the night.

"Weren't you supposed to stay at Kristin's?" I ask, as I readjust the blanket covering me.

"You don't remember?" Steph sets the bowl on the arm of the chair. I don't have the energy to correct her.

I rack my brain, trying to remember the events of the night. The last thing I clearly recall—other than puking—is unwisely taking tequila shots. "Did you argue over Layla?" I ask. "Because Steph, I still don't understand why you brought her." I press my face against a throw pillow and try to get the room to stop moving. "Don't get me wrong, she seems lovely, but she didn't belong there."

Steph shakes her head. "Wow. You were drunker than I thought."

"Which is why I spent most of the morning worshipping the porcelain god." I try to sit upright, but it's too difficult. "What happened?"

"Well…." Steph stares at the far corner of the room. "Do you remember being outside?"

A very foggy memory of feeling hot forms. Steph and Kristin were with me, and…

"Did Kristin yell at you?"

Steph sighs. "So, you do remember a little. Do you remember what you saw?"

I furrow my brows, trying to sort through the blurry night. "Not really."

Steph gathers her dark hair and drapes it over her shoulder before focusing her laser gaze on me. I hate when she does this. It feels like she's probing my brain.

"Let's start with what you didn't see." She draws her lips tightly together. "Kristin came into DC the other day and started talking about regrets and all kinds of vague things, but I'm pretty sure she was hinting at having an affair."

"An actual affair?" The ibuprofen I had taken is wearing off, and a sledgehammer pounds my skull. Fuzzy images swim in my mind. "Was she outside with Joe?"

"I think so. You were almost incoherent at that point, and I was trying to keep you from saying anything in front of Tom." She leans forward and plucks another strawberry slice from the bowl. "I was hoping you'd shed some light on what happened."

I was looking for Kristin, but why? I think I went upstairs by myself and maybe outside. I blink. "I think I went out front?"

"I don't know what happened other than you stumbled through the basement door, raging mad."

"Did I see her with Joe?" I stretch out my arm to reach for my phone on the coffee table. "She hasn't texted or called. She should have checked in on me by now, don't you think? Has she texted you?"

"No."

How odd. Something happened that is making Kristin avoid us. "What do you think?"

Steph steeples her fingers together. "Life is too short to be stuck doing something that makes you unhappy." When I try to interject, she lifts a finger and silences me. "That said, even if she doesn't care about Tom's feelings, she needs to consider Nicole's."

"Agreed." I draw in a breath and fight the urge to run for the bathroom. How does anyone think this is worth a not-so-fun night?

"You're becoming more green." Steph takes a long sip of her Diet Coke and places the cup directly on the table with no coaster. "Puking will make you feel better."

In my forty-five years, I have only puked twice from drinking —once the year after we graduated and last night. "I'll be okay. I don't think I have much left in my stomach."

"Which is why you should eat some French fries or some-thing. Strawberries only soak up the booze in sangria."

I grasp my stomach. "Do not mention booze ever again. I can't."

"At least you made an impression," Steph says. "No one will forget you."

My humiliating, drunken behavior clings to me. "I'm done with neighborhood parties. One experience is more than enough."

Steph rolls her eyes. "Trust me; they all have more important things to worry about than you puking. Like if their husbands got a good look at your boobs when you pulled your top off."

"What?!"

She shakes her head. "I'll let Nick take that one."

I bury my face in my hands. "I'm mortified."

"It happens to all of us."

"Not to me."

"Well, now you've joined the club." Steph always say exactly what she thinks, no matter how painful. "But enough of that. Before we get into the Kristin debacle, care to tell me what's going on with Alex? Nick refused to say a word, but you kept crying about how he's making the biggest mistake of his life."

I freeze, and my breath catches. "I said that? Who heard?"

"Only me and Nick."

"Please don't say anything," I beg. "Alex is still figuring things out."

Steph drops her chin and stares up at me through her lashes. "When have I ever betrayed you?"

"Never."

"Right." She points at the door. "Nick went to get McDonald's, by the way."

"I don't eat McDonald's."

"Today you will, if you ever want to feel better."

I narrow my eyes. She's purposely driving the conversation all over the place. First to Kristin coming into the DC and her martial issues, next to my agony over Alex. Plus, she's side-stepping why she and Kristin fought.

The garage door opens, and I close my eyes. Maybe with Nick here, Steph's erratic train of thought will make more sense.

"Hey!" Nick says, holding out two McDonald's bags.

How is he so peppy? Didn't he drink as much as me?

Nick sets the grease-laden bags on the coffee table. Next to them, he places a drink holder with three sodas. "As requested, French fries, chicken nuggets, Big Macs, and Diet Cokes."

It surprisingly sounds delicious, and I force myself to sit up. "Thank you." My mouth waters. "Nothing has ever sounded so good."

Nick laughs. "Thanks, Steph. I gave you strawberries." He retrieves plates from the kitchen while Steph hands me a box and fries. Normally, I insist we eat at the island or table, but today nothing is normal.

"Mind if I eat with you?" Nick asks.

Steph shoves fries in her mouth. "Nope."

When I look up from my food, I catch Nick and Steph exchanging conspiratorial glances.

"What?" I ask, dropping a half-eaten nugget into the box. "What's going on?"

"Just what I told you." Steph shifts her gaze toward the darkened TV.

"If you don't tell her, Steph, I will. She's going to find out." Nick finishes his sandwich and starts in on a box of nuggets. For never eating this kind of food, he certainly appears to be a fan.

"Fine." She inhales sharply and releases a stream of words. "Kristin yelled at me, and you went to find her, and I think you saw her with Joe and then you puked."

Nick raises his eyebrows. "Kristin yelled at you because…"

Like a little kid caught telling a half-truth, Steph squirms. "Because Jess is Layla's mom."

Anxiety clenches my heart. Jess is back?

"Have you spoken to her?" Every word I want to scream stays locked in my throat.

Steph bites her lip. "Only briefly when she dropped off some things for Layla."

Pause, I think. *Pause when unsure or agitated.* Steph doesn't know what Kristin and I did. If she did, she'd say something. "Are you going to see her again?"

Steph shakes her head. "Not that I know of."

"How long have you known about this?" I ask, switching into business mode.

"A few days."

I watch her, noticing that something feels off. Normally happy-go-lucky Steph seems… sad.

"I didn't know when I hired Layla, and I don't think she knows what happened between Jess and me."

Even though my head aches, I am thinking clearly. "Kristin found out, she yelled at you, and she ran off?"

"Yes."

"And you swear you didn't know Layla was Jess's daughter?"

Steph holds up her hand. "I do. I swear I didn't know until the other day."

Pieces of the night start sliding into place. I went to find Kristin to console her. I couldn't find her inside, so I walked out the front door. I dig deeper into my memory. She was on the side of the house with Joe. He had her pinned against the wall. Were they kissing?

"What do you remember?" Nick asks. Like me, he's switched into professional mode.

"Kristin blowing up her life," I say. "And why? Tom isn't wrong. They've made it through the hard part. Being an empty-nester is amazing."

Steph twists her hair into a low bun. "She's not you and Nick, Diana." She tilts her head. "You can't expect her to feel the same way you do about being married."

Nick dumps his empty burger box into a paper bag. "Tom's a solid, family guy."

"He's nice," I add. "And he's given her a wonderful life. Isn't that what she told us she wanted?"

"Is it what she wanted, or did she settle because you were already married, and she didn't want to be left out?" Steph asks.

Tom wasn't my first choice for Kristin, but she was unwavering in her determination to marry him. Since Steph was living in Ibiza back then, I handled all the maid-of-honor duties, and Kristin and I spent months selecting colors, making seating arrangements, looking at flowers and tasting cake—and Tom never got involved or asked questions. He simply gave her his credit card.

Maybe that was a sign of what was to come?

"Tom is a great provider, and that's what she wanted." I shrug. "I don't see the problem."

"He's nice." Steph taps her hand on the arm of the chair twice. "Not everyone wants nice." She snorts. "I never have."

"You're not married."

"Maybe Kristin shouldn't be either."

After Steph leaves, Nick and I settle in to watch a football game. When the kids were home, Nick, Alex, and Emily would lounge around the family room. I would order pizza, wings, poppers, and sodas for them, and I always wondered who would eat all of it, but there were never any leftovers.

Today, I delicately arrange myself on the end of the sectional and place my feet on Nick's lap. He immediately cups my left foot with his hand, and I relax. Thankfully, the second round of ibuprofen is working, and the queasiness from earlier has passed.

"Feeling any better?" Nick asks.

"McDonald's was a good call."

"Good." Nick squeezes my foot. "You've been through a lot this week." He switches the channel to a different game. "And now Kristin and Steph are piling on the drama." He massages my calf. "I know you don't want to hear this, but maybe you need a break from them until you get through your own issues."

I gape at my husband. "You want me to abandon them? Now? When they need me?"

Nick drops my leg and tucks the blanket under my feet. "I want you to put yourself first. You're having panic attacks. You're afraid to discuss anything with your mother. You're worried about Alex." He holds up three fingers. "That's just off the top of my head."

Before I can answer, Emily's ringtone sounds from my phone. I've laid it next to me on the couch and answer immediately. "Hey, honey."

"Mom." Emily's voice cracks. "What were you thinking?"

"About what?" Is she talking about Alex? Does she know about his hare-brained idea?

"The Halloween party! I can't believe you acted like that!"

"Honey," I say, trying make sense of what she knows about the party. "Dad and I had a fun night out. What's wrong with that?"

"It's on Snapchat!"

"Of course it is." I'm not surprised someone posted the party on social media. I must be in the background. Did Emily scour the pictures looking for me?

"Not the party," Emily says tearily. "You!"

My heart races. "Me, what?"

Emily breathes heavily into the phone. "I understand wanting to have fun, Mom, but did you have to get that drunk? Everyone is messaging me about it."

"I'm on social media?" I ask. Nick watches me carefully. "Doing what?"

"Puking on Danny Abrole's mom and taking off your shirt! It's a viral meme!"

I press my hand against my mouth. Oh my god. "What do you mean viral meme?"

A strangled sob comes over the phone. "They're calling you a has-been."

Heat flares across my face. "A has-been?"

"Someone who doesn't know they're past expiration." Emily raises her voice, and Nick leans closer to hear. "Those other moms are insane, but my mom looks like a drunk." She sobs. "I can't believe this is happening."

I'm a meme. A has-been. Vomit pools in the back of my throat. "It's all over Snapchat?"

"And Instagram and TikTok."

The room pitches again, but this time it's from mortification. If I ever want to work again, this is what my clients or employer will see when they google me. Me, drunk at a Halloween party and throwing up on someone.

"Mom," Emily says. "You need to fix this! It's all everyone is talking about—Emily Clarke's drunk mom."

When I don't say anything. Nick takes the phone from me. He speaks to Emily for a few minutes, but I'm not paying attention. There is no way I can fix this. When something goes viral, it's impossible to pull it back.

I stare into the corner of the room. Not only am I being mocked online, but I am being called a has-been.

And it's true. I'm a has-been professionally, and now, I'm apparently a has-been to my daughter, her friends, and the entirety of the internet. Wonderful.

Nick sets my phone down. "Do you have a protocol for things like this?

I shake my head. "Other than wait for it to die down, no." I stare up at him with blurry eyes. "Emily is embarrassed, and any time I'm googled it's going to come up. My only hope is that it'll get buried on search pages. A good search firm will find it though." I collect myself. "I knew I shouldn't have gone. I knew it was a bad idea."

Nick pulls me into an embrace. "Sweetheart, you can't be perfect all the time."

He's wrong. I can be. I should be. I *need* to be.

"There's a trying-to-be-perfect and then there's being a has-been-who-strips-and-pukes-all-over-the-internet." I drag the back of my hand across my cheeks to catch my tears. "Do you think I'm a has-been?"

Nick rubs my back. "You've had some setbacks, but you, Diana Clarke, are amazing. This is just a speed bump."

"I was fired for being out of touch, and now there's this meme." Outside, the near-bare trees sway in the wind. "Emily is irate, and Alex thinks I'm trying to live my life through him." I turn my attention back to Nick and sigh. "What good is being amazing when you're past your expiration date?

"Steph?" Layla sticks her head through the open door. "Can we talk?"

I've spent the past two days avoiding her. I've restocked shelves, busied myself with the kitchen-app fiasco, and took more meetings than I knew possible. I even considered telling Layla to take a few days off, but it's unfair to penalize her for being Jess's daughter.

She has a navy-blue backpack slung over her shoulder. I'm not a name-brand person, but I've traveled enough to spot a high-end backpack and that bag costs more than the meager wages I pay. Jess must have bought it for her.

Is Jess doing that well for herself?

"I was just leaving," I say, even though I had planned on hiding in my office the rest of the day. I push away from my desk and take my jacket off the back of my chair. "You can walk with me."

She follows me down the stairs to the main floor, and we don't speak—which is fine with me.

Around us, the club buzzes. Tuesdays aren't the biggest

nights, but we still pull a decent-sized crowd. Tonight, however, isn't a marquee name, so I'm only using half my normal staff.

When we reach the bar area, Layla stops walking. "Steph?"

"What's going on?" I say, like Saturday night never happened. My hope is that if I ignore it, Layla will forget everything... like Diana did. Problem is, Layla was sober, and she heard everything.

"About Saturday." Layla's voice drifts off. "It was weird for me to be there."

"No. My friends are just crazy. Ignore them."

Layla slips her fingers under her backpack strap. "You're someone I work with. My boss. And I take my job seriously."

Ah. She must have taken Kristin's advice and talked to Jess. "I appreciate that."

"So, I'm saying this at the risk of my job, but I think you should talk to my mom." Her face holds the earnestness of youth. "Please."

"Layla—"

"Steph," Jean-Luc says as he carries two bags of plastic cups around the bar and sets them on the counter. "Sammy is missing again."

What is it with Sammy? "Did you look in the freezer?"

"What?" Jean-Luc stares at me in confusion. "We have a freezer?"

Layla laughs. "No, she means for his body. You put dead bodies in the freezer."

"Sammy is dead?" Horror settles across Jean-Luc's face.

Random shouts and banging echo around the empty club. The walls are painted black, the floor is permanently sticky no matter how often we power wash, and it's always on the noisy side, but there's nowhere I enjoy being more—except right now.

"Sammy isn't dead," I say. "I just want to kill him."

"Oh." Jean-Luc exhales. "I will put him in the freezer for you."

Layla stares at the entrance door before turning back toward me. "Steph?"

"Yes?"

"My mom is outside, and I thought maybe, if you have time, we could grab something to eat at Cooper's before things get crazy here."

I don't want to see Jess. Not now. Not ever.

"I can't." The tension headache that's plagued me all day reappears, and I dig my fingers into the base of my skull behind my ears. "There's too much to do here. Especially with Sammy MIA."

To her credit, Layla doesn't beg. She simply nods and walks away.

She's right. Jess and I should talk, but I'm not ready.

"Jean-Luc," I say, raising my voice over the din of noise around us. "I have some phone calls I need to make. Can you manage until Layla gets back?"

He does his French half-shrug. "Of course."

When I'm in my office with the door closed, I sit on the old brown couch and hunch over my knees. Fat, heavy tears fall on my jeans and dampen my hands. Layla wants to fix something that is unfixable. What Jess did changed my life, and she bailed when I needed my friends the most.

For years, I've hidden from my past and from the truth. I've hidden from myself and my loved ones. Now, the past has barged into my club and wants me to make peace with it.

"Whose purse is this?" The police officer stood next to the bench where Jess and I had left our bags.

Panic filled Jess's olive-green eyes. "Steph?" she whispered. "They can't open that. They can't."

Thirty minutes earlier, we had been plucked out of the crowd and brought to the greenroom. Jess could barely sit still—she loved the band and hoped to hook up with the lead singer. Unfortunately, four police officers had burst into the greenroom shortly after we arrived, and Jess had a purse full of party drugs.

"Ladies? Whose bags are these?"

"That's mine." I pointed at Jess's small black bag.

"I'm going to search it." The officer picked up the bag and set it on the table.

"Why did you do that?" Jess whispered as she clenched my arm. "Steph, you're fucked."

"I know." My heart thundered against my ribs. I had spent the past several months mad whenever Jess ran off with band members like a common groupie. But mostly, I was mad that she couldn't see what was right in front of her—me.

The officer arranged four small baggies on the table and raised his eyebrows. "Looks like we have some weed, ecstasy, and…" he held up the other two bags. "Unknown substances."

One of the other officers walked to me. "It's your bag?"

My legs shook. "Yes."

He spun me around and slapped cuffs on my wrists.

I hoped my grand gesture would make Jess see how important she was to me, and she'd admit the bag was hers as a sign of loyalty.

But she never said a word. Not even when I was led away in handcuffs.

Cooper's is packed, and it isn't hard to spot Layla and Jess at the curved booth near the center of the cozy room. A fireplace roars along the side wall, and the waitstaff bustles about taking drink orders and delivering delicious plates of food. Coopers' isn't a place I'd chose for dinner—it's too expensive— but I've been here enough times on business to know that for a Tuesday, it's hopping.

"Would you like me to show you to the table?" the hostess asks.

I can't believe I'm doing this. "No. I see them."

All I need do is walk across the room, but my Jell-O legs won't move.

"Ma'am, are you okay?" the hostess asks.

"I'm fine, thank you." I step forward and pause. Jess and Layla are caught in conversation and seeing them side by side, it's unbelievable that I never noticed how much Layla looks like Jess. They have the same dark, bouncy hair. The same tall, lean builds. And eyes that are on the olive-green side of hazel.

I shuffle forward, waiting for them to notice me, but they're too lost in conversation. The low lighting creates a dream-like vibe, and it would be a lie if I said I hadn't envisioned meeting Jess again. It was never like this though. Never with her daughter present.

A cranberry-colored scarf is twisted perfectly against Jess's throat and flows into the open neck of her tailored white blouse. Diana would absolutely love her look.

I stop next to their table. Neither look at me. "Hi."

"We're not ready to order," Jess says before Layla touches her arm.

"Mom? It's Steph."

Jess turns her gaze up toward me. There are fine lines around her eyes, and while this version of Jess is soft and elegant, I don't need to squint to see the girl I knew twenty-five years ago.

"Oh!" Her hands flutter to her chest. "Steph, hi, thank you for coming." She speaks rapidly, almost too fast, as if she feels like if she doesn't get all her words out at once, they may never come out. "Join us?"

What am I doing? I should walk away and let the past stay there.

Walking over, I prepared a speech. "Layla," I say, staring down at her. "I want you to know that I will always be objective toward you. You are my best employee, and I want you to know that."

Layla's eyes are rimmed pink, and her nose is slightly red. She glances at Jess. "I'm going to go. You two need to talk."

She pulls her coat off the hook on the side of the booth and takes her backpack off the bench. "I'll see you tomorrow, Steph."

As I watch her walk away, I wish she had stayed. Layla would have been a buffer, and maybe Jess and I could have skirted around some of the tougher things we need to discuss.

"Why don't you sit?" Jess says to me. Her voice is a little deeper than I remember—more gravelly—but it still triggers memories and feelings in me that I thought were long gone. I perch on the edge of the booth, ready to take flight if necessary. "I let Layla pick the restaurant," Jess says. "I come up to DC at least once a month, but we eat erratically given Layla's schedule."

Where does she live?

"Layla's trying to impress you." There's no other reason why a twenty-something would pick an old-school place like this. "The food is good, and it's the typical DC scene. Deals made in the corner booths and all that."

"Layla is a bit of an old soul." The server sets two drinks on the table: a pinot grigio and a whiskey sour. "Do you want Layla's drink?"

"Which is it?"

"The whiskey sour." Jess takes the wine by the stem and takes a small sip. "I'm not a big drinker."

"It's better if I don't," I say, even though pounding a drink would calm my nerves. "I have to work tonight, and I have a no booze or drugs on the job policy." I smile tightly. "I'm sure you understand."

"I do."

My stomach knots once and then again into a double knot. My prepared speech has vanished. "I'm not sure if it's good to see you or not."

Jess's shoulders rise and fall. "I'm happy our paths crossed. You've weighed heavily on my mind for years."

Should I admit that not a day has gone by where I haven't thought about her or that night or any of the rest of it? Once, I considered finding her on social media but decided against it. I didn't want to see her living a perfect life. "Out of guilt?"

"There's that." The server places a cheese board between us. "Layla ordered it," Jess says. "Help yourself."

My stomach is too much of a mess to eat. "Did you know she asked me to see you?"

"No."

My heart drops. "You didn't want to?"

"I wanted to be respectful of your wishes."

The din of the restaurant matches the buzzing in my mind. If she didn't want me to come, I can't do this. I stand. "I'm going. I hope you enjoy the rest of your visit."

"Richmond is a little slower than DC—not that DC is New York or Ibiza."

I focus my attention on the candle burning on the middle of the table. "Richmond is nice."

"It's a nice place to raise kids."

I'm pretty sure Layla is an only child, but honestly, we've never really discussed her personal life. As easy-going as I am with my staff, I remain professional—Halloween party aside.

"Layla is great. You did a nice job with her," I say. Kristin and Diana's curiosity about Layla's age nips at me. "How old is she, anyway?"

Jess folds her hands on the table. A large diamond ring sparkles on her third finger flanked by two diamond bands.

"She's twenty-two. I had her a few months after you left."

I narrow my eyes. "You weren't pregnant when I knew you."

Jess swigs liberally from her wine glass. "The lead singer, Thomas, is her father."

Air rushes out of the room, and I brace myself against the solid booth to avoid falling over. "You married the lead singer of the band from the night you let me get arrested?" I slam my palm against the white-clothed table. "Unbelievable."

"No, I didn't marry him." She drops her head and studies her hands. "Everything happened so quickly, Steph. You said my bag was yours, and I panicked."

"You let them arrest me."

She shakes her head. "You saved me."

"No," I say sharply. "I wanted…"

Jess stares at me expectantly. "What?"

Years of anger and hurt rush out of me. "I wanted you to look at me like you looked at those singers. I wanted you to notice me. To see me. To want me."

"Oh, Steph." Pain crisscrosses Jess's face. "I didn't know. You were always running around with some new guy." She presses her fingertips to her lips. "I didn't know how you felt."

This is what hurts the most: over the course of my life, I have never found anyone, male or female, I loved as much as I loved Jess. I risked going to jail for years for her.

And it never occurred to her that I didn't do it because I was a good friend. She didn't realize that I did it because I loved her.

My insides jitter, and I bite my lip, afraid that if I say anything more, tears will flood my eyes and not stop.

"Steph," Jess says softly. I can't look at her. I can't. "Steph," she says again. "You were my best friend, and when Diana told me to pack my stuff and move out, I shouldn't have listened, but I thought it was what you wanted."

"What?" I knit my brows together. "She made you move out?"

Jess nods. "While you were in jail. Diana gave me no choice. She and Kristin packed all my stuff and left it on the sidewalk." She shakes her head. "They never told you?"

"No." My head swims through old memories. Kristin and Diana said Jess ran away. They told me she didn't ask about me, and I never questioned it. Why would they lie to me? Jess was the one who fled, and Kristin's dad was helping me.

It never occurred to me that my friends had kicked Jess out.

Jess blinks once. Twice. She keeps her eyes shut. "I tried finding you after your court dates, but you were gone." Her eyes flutter open. "When I found out I was pregnant with Layla…

well, life happened." She smiles hesitantly. "But it worked out okay for you, didn't it?"

Had it? Would my life have been different if Jess hadn't been forced out of it?

17

KRISTIN

ing dong.

For two days, I've avoided Diana. I haven't returned her texts or calls even though she's reached out repeatedly. I know the meme thing is upsetting her, but I've been too worried about the Joe conversation we need to have.

But now I'm standing on her front porch, peering through the sidelight windows. Maybe I should have called, but this is too important of a conversation, and I've spent all morning working up the courage to do this.

Please be home. I need to get this over with.

It is only eleven-thirty, but I've already done the grocery shopping, dropped off the dry cleaning, had my nails done, and now I'm walking around the neighborhood trying to keep myself busy so my confusing feelings about Joe stay buried.

Since the diner, he's messaged me non-stop. Nothing flirty. Just little messages of support, and every time my phone dings, my heart flip-flops like it once did when Tom and I were first dating.

I've ignored all his messages—not because I don't want to talk to him, but I need time to think. What if he only kissed me because I pressed the issue and acted desperate? Am I the only one with feelings beyond friendship?

The fact is, Joe is a nice guy. He's been there for me when I couldn't talk to Diana or Steph, and perhaps I mistook his commiseration for flirting. Perhaps I felt something deeper than he did.

However, seeing him with Thalia has made me doubt everything he's told me.

Was he just playing with me? Is his relationship with Thalia better than he led me to believe?

I ring Diana's doorbell again and wait. When there's no answer, I text:

—*I know you're home. I see your car*—

Footsteps stop on the other side of the door before it flings open.

Diana stands framed within the doorway wearing yoga pants and a tank top. I've never seen her dressed so causally in the middle of the day before.

She stares at me with disappointment.

"Hey," I say, trying to sound upbeat. "I was out walking and saw your car and thought I'd pop in." I push past Diana and step into the soaring foyer. I'm not going to give her the opportunity to shut the door on me.

"Where have you been the past couple of days? I've called and texted at least a hundred times." Diana closes the door and stops next to a heavily-polished, round table in the middle of the room with an extravagant flower arrangement.

I hang my head. "That's why I'm here. I wanted to discuss everything in person."

Diana gestures toward the back of her massive house. "Come on. Do you want tea?"

"No, thank you."

While Diana fills the tea kettle for herself, I wander to the bank of windows lining the back of the great room. She has one of the best lots in our development, but she's never hosted a cookout or had anyone over to enjoy her amazing pool.

"You really should invite people over, Diana." I turn toward the kitchen. "You have such a lovely house. I'd have people over all the time if I lived here."

Diana pushes the button on the electric kettle. "I don't like neighborhood parties for a reason." She pads across the gleaming, dark hardwood floor toward the family room and pauses next to the cream sofa. "I want to discuss what's going on with you, but first, please tell me the meme isn't as bad as Emily claims."

The meme of Diana has spread through my various friend groups, and everyone knows who she is now—and not in a positive way. "It's not too bad."

"I'm a crisis expert. Be honest with me." She's not wearing makeup and her hair is in a high ponytail. Even though she is still stunning, the dark circles under her eyes have aged her overnight.

"The neighborhood women are all talking about it." I join her at the sofa and sit on the far end. "They're acting like they've never done anything worse—which is a lie. They have."

The kettle whistles, and Diana strides into the kitchen. "Emily is mortified."

"Does that surprise you?" I ask. "She's never even seen you buzzed, and you go to one party and turn up on social media wasted and puking."

Diana pours the steaming water into her mug. "Obviously, I'm not going to address it online. However, with people I may run into at the grocery store, I feel I need to change the narrative."

This is why she's so good at her job. Diana is objective and thoughtful. "What are you thinking?"

She sits on the chair next to me and crosses her ankles. "I need to go to book club this month. It's low-hanging fruit since they know me."

I want to know what Diana's feeling about what she saw, but I'm thankful that our conversation has meandered in this direction. It means my indiscretion isn't front and center for her. I wipe my slightly sweaty hands on my yoga pants.

Maybe I don't need to do damage control at all. Maybe Diana drank so much—which isn't unlikely given the video evidence—that she doesn't remember anything? I tuck my left foot under my right thigh, and Diana cringes.

"Shoes." Diana points. "You know how I feel about shoes in the house."

I tug my tennis shoes off and drop them on the ground. "Have you read the book?"

Diana nods. "A few years ago."

"You should text Maggie and let her know."

She opens her phone and dashes off a text to Maggie who immediately responds.

"I don't think she's seen the meme," Diana says. "Or she's too polite to mention it."

"She doesn't run with the younger women," I say. "She probably doesn't know about it."

Diana blows on her steaming tea. "True, but I'm sure the other women know."

I've relaxed a little. Diana has made no indication that she remembers anything about Joe, but I need to test what she remembers about the party. "Have you heard from Steph?"

"She stayed the night Saturday and hung out on Sunday." Diana's shoulders round, and she has one arm crossed against her torso like she's holding herself together. "We all need to talk. Not just about you, but also about Jess."

My breath hitches. The Jess-Layla thing is much more important than my kiss with Joe. "Do you think Jess would tell Layla the truth about what we did?"

Diana shrugs. "I don't know, but we've been loyal friends to Steph her entire life. We stood by her side when everything was falling apart." She smiles and tilts her head as if gathering her thoughts. "We did what we did to protect her. If we hadn't, things may not have worked out."

"What are you doing?" I stood in the doorway of Jess's room. Full garbage bags were scattered around the room, and Diana was dumping the contents of a dresser drawer into an empty one.

"I've never liked Jess." Diana shoved a sweater in the garbage bag and tied it off. "Steph wasn't a party girl until Jess got her into it. This is her fault."

Steph was still in jail, and my dad was trying to work his magic, but he didn't have high hopes. "Are you kicking Jess out?"

Diana angrily threw a shirt across the room. "I never want her around Steph again. Or us."

"As for you," Diana's voice brings me back to the present. "I'm not going to sit back and watch you blow up your life. If you want to leave Tom, fine, but do it the right way. None of this sneaking-around stuff."

I hang my head. "It was a mistake, and it won't happen again." And I mean it. I'm done. I have to be. "He doesn't think about me like that."

For a long minute, Diana says nothing, and blood pounds at my temples. "Why do you think that?"

The way Thalia looked at him and their easy rapport comes to mind. "I saw him with Thalia, and I think I mistook our conversations about his marriage."

Diana raises her eyebrows. "He's gaslighting you. He knows you're vulnerable, and he's messing with your head and emotions."

I chew on that for a moment. My friendship with Joe is real. He's been there for me when Tom hasn't been but... it's not adding up. Maybe Diana is right?

"Are you mad at me?" I ask.

"Only if you don't stop." She sets her teacup on a coaster. "Everyone—as evidenced by my colossal drunken escapade— makes mistakes. It's how you come back that matters." She tucks a stray piece of her ponytail behind her ear. "By the way, I'm not the only has-been."

That label is probably the worst part of Diana's meme. First our skinny jeans and side parts were made fun of, but now having fun is not allowed if you're over forty.

"It's just a word," I say. "I wouldn't give it power."

"Says my fellow has-been." Diana waits for me to close my mouth. "You've been moaning about being a retired mom for over two years now. Add in this thing with Joe, and you certainly are acting like someone who believes they're past their expiration date."

Ouch, but not completely wrong. "Is it too much to want to be cool again?"

"I've never been cool, but I've always been relevant." She scoots back on her seat. "That's what hurts the most: I don't feel washed up, but work says I am. My kids act like I am. And the internet... well, I'm the Has-Been poster child."

My shoulders sag. "You can find your way back. You have a career and a strong marriage. I have nothing."

"Are you going to accept being a has-been?" Diana knits her brows together. "You're just going to lie down and wear the label because it's too hard to change?"

"I've spent more than half my life being a mom and wife. What am I if I'm not those things?"

Diana stands, walks to me, and catches my face between her hands. "Hey." She peers into my eyes. "You have always been more than a mom and wife. You're an amazing friend, a flawless event organizer, and a dedicated community volunteer. You have so much to offer the world if you'd just get out of your own way."

My eyes burn, and I do my best to hold back my tears. Diana has always believed in me, even when our lives took different paths. "Maybe I need to burn it all down so I can build it back up?"

"You can pivot without burning it down." Diana releases my

face. "Start with staying away from Joe, and figure out why you're drawn to him—beyond him pretending to understand your marital issues." I start to answer, but she holds up her hand. "This is about more than wanting attention."

I sigh. "Maybe."

She plops down next to me. "I can only help you if you're willing to help yourself."

I nod. As much as I want to believe I can and will stay away from Joe, I know if he has a reasonable explanation for his behavior, it will be hard.

I don't know what to do about that.

18

STEPH

I haven't taken a breath in fourteen hours. I haven't slept. I haven't eaten. But I have polished off two bottles of Malbec and have succeeded at giving myself a raging headache. Fan-fucking-tastic.

I scoop the empty bottles up off the coffee table, gather the corks, opener, and wine glass, and deposit everything onto the kitchen counter. I'll deal with it later.

No matter how much I drink, I can't stop the anger and pain swirling inside me. Diana and Kristin, my best friends, ran Jess off. They never, not once, said anything. Not when I sobbed. Not when I told them I was leaving for Europe. Not when I decided to not come back to DC. Not once.

Why? What did they have to gain from letting me think Jess had abandoned me?

The judge peered down at me from his perch above the courtroom. "You have a very good lawyer, Miss Torres."

My legs trembled as I stood, my hands pressed against the table. Kristin and Diana sat behind me in the courtroom, but Jess was missing. My parents, mortified by my situation, did not come to support me either. It wasn't surprising. We'd always had a rocky relationship.

156

"Mr. Danvers, your client is free to go."

I gasped. Mr. Danvers said I'd get a year's probation minimum, and the only thing I had in my favor is that Jess's ID was in the purse, and I was drunk. The prosecution tried to make a case that I was holding my friend's ID and the purse was in fact mine, but since it wasn't physically on my body, Mr. Danvers claimed I had misidentified it as my own due to being intoxicated.

Kristin leaned over the railing separating us and pulled me into an embrace. "Thank god." She turned and hugged her dad. "Daddy, you're magic."

"You need to complete the paperwork, Stephanie," Mr. Danvers said coldly.

Diana squeezed my hand. "This is an amazing outcome."

My brain struggled to make sense of the turn of events as I glanced around the room. I'd been in jail for a month waiting for my court date, and I hadn't seen my friends. "Where's Jess?"

Diana and Kristin exchanged a look I couldn't place.

"She... she left." Diana squeezed my hand again. "But we're here. We'll always be here."

"What do you mean, left?"

Mr. Danvers snapped his briefcase shut. "Stephanie, follow me."

I kind of understand Kristin's motive. After all, her father is the reason I don't have a record, and she had to beg him to represent me. On our walk to fill out my papers, Mr. Danvers reiterated that he had only helped me as a favor to Kristin, and he also made it very clear that I was to stay away from Kristin.

Kristin and Diana never understand why I had to leave. I didn't tell them about Mr. Danvers's order or my broken heart. I had no direction in life and needed to restart, away from everyone who knew me, and Europe seemed logical since I still had family in Spain.

Autumn sunshine fills my loft. It's probably cool out, but it's the perfect weather for a walk. After I brush my teeth and tame my hair, I dress and sling my work bag over my shoulder.

If I can't get out of my head on the walk to the club, I don't know what I'll do.

LUSH is dark. It's only ten, too early for anyone else to be here. I flip on the overhead lights. We're closed on Mondays, but the crew comes in to deep clean, so, unlike normal, the perpetually sticky floor is swept, the bar shines, and the stage is empty.

The vast floor is standing-room only, but we have balcony seats. Normally, the over-thirty-five crowd buys those and my staff refers to the area as "GS," short for geriatric seating.

I'm ten years past geriatric in their eyes.

When did that happen? One minute, I was a young woman dancing and partying my way through life and somehow, I've skipped straight to middle-aged without noticing. Maybe it's because I haven't had the life milestones other women my age use to count the passage of time: marriage, kids, divorce, re-marriage, kids leaving home. No, I've had the blessing of being able to focus solely on me without any distraction.

I don't regret a thing.

But when did I become… old? I still know all the bands. I can still pull all-nighters. But, when my staff looks at me, they don't see a peer but an old lady who is hanging on. I'm someone who should be in the GS area.

I climb the stairs to the stage and flick on the overhead lights. I place my bag on the ground, sit on the edge of the stage, and stare out at the main floor. I've had the privilege of meeting numerous fascinating people over the course of my career, but the only one who has ever mattered walked through the front door last week, wearing an emerald-green coat and carrying a reusable shopping bag.

The passage of time has caught up with her, too. She looked

polished and poised like Diana, while I'm still wearing black jeans and leather jackets and dressing like Layla.

I run my hand over my face and through my hair. I've built an amazing career for myself, but have I built a life? Beyond Diana, Kristin, and their families, I'm not close to anyone, but that's good enough, isn't it? I'm loved by my chosen family, and I love them.

In Ibiza, I spent two years loving Lucien, a French native caught up in the Ibiza scene like me. We loved madly, passionately, but ultimately, I walked away. Lucien wanted to settle down and move back to France. He begged me to come. We'd get married, he said, on his family's estate outside Bordeaux and live in a small house on the property. Lucian made domestication sound wonderful.

The tarmac rippled under the June heat, and Lucien squeezed my hand. "Are you sure?"

I was destroying my only chance of getting married and having a family. I was letting go of the one person who would give me all the things a twenty-something woman should want.

I turned my face toward Lucien. "I'd be a terrible wife. You know that."

"Then it's good-bye." He brushed his lips over mine.

Confusion welled inside me when he disappeared down the gangway. I pressed my hand against the airport window, but I didn't cry. I was making the right decision. Lucien deserved more than what I could give him.

It took me years and dozens of men—and women—to understand why I couldn't commit.

Jess.

I wasted years hoping she'd find me and tell me she cared about me the way I cared about her. I dreamed of reconciling, of working through our big misunderstanding, and creating a life together.

She, meanwhile, went on with her life. She had Layla, got married, and exchanged her club clothes for a respectable suburban outfit. Her life went on while mine stalled in third gear.

If Diana and Kristin hadn't sent Jess away, my life would be different. I wouldn't have had Ibiza or Lucien or any of it. Jess and I would have had a hard conversation at some point, and it would have freed me from a lifetime of 'what-if.'

I lie back on the stage and close my eyes. The spotlights blare down at me, like they're trying to focus my attention.

Maybe I should thank Diana and Kristin. I'm here because of one decision they made about my life. If they hadn't, I'd probably have some boring desk job and maybe I would have caved and married the first guy who promised financial security. Maybe I would even have kids.

Yes, I should definitely thank them—they saved me from a life of tedious boredom.

At noon, my staff trickles in and I switch into boss-mode. Jean-Luc arrives first and lugs his bicycle toward the staff room.

"Hello!" I say from behind the bar. "I don't think you've ever been the first to work."

His bike helmet is still strapped to his head, and he shrugs in his French way. "No traffic today."

"First time for everything." I hold up a pitcher of simple syrup. "I've started prepping for you."

He eyes me suspiciously. I never work behind the bar unless we're short-handed. Plus, Jean-Luc is obsessed with running the bar his way, and I never intervene since it works. "Have you tasted it?" he asks. "Is it too sweet? Americans like sweet."

"It's fine," I say, setting the pitcher aside. "Go put your stuff away."

He wheels his bike across the door and disappears backstage.

Tonight's performer is a local band, and the crowd will most likely be all college kids. We've only sold out half the floor, and the more expensive GC seats are empty. This kind of crowd doesn't order from the kitchen; they only want beer and to get drunk—which is why I have extra security.

A few more staffers roll in, including Sammy, and they pass me with brief hellos or head nods.

Layla hasn't arrived yet ,which isn't like her. She's usually the first in and the first out.

My heart seizes. Did Jess explain everything to her, and Layla no longer wants to work for me? Would she quit with no notice?

To distract myself, I quarter lemons and drop them into a container. Jean-Luc scoots behind the bar, scrubs his hands, and says, "I can do the rest, Steph."

He wants me out of the way.

The club is now alive with noise and bodies. I've always loved the time before a show. We work hard, but nothing beats pulling off a great night.

My phone buzzes, and I take it from my back pocket.

Layla.

"Hey," I say. "Everything okay?"

She's quiet for a moment. "Is it okay if I come to work?"

"Is it okay?" I ask. Is she worried I'm angry with her because of what happened between Jess and me? "Layla, you are my best worker. I need you here."

She exhales loudly. "Thank you."

If I were sentimental, which I'm not, I'd tell her everything will be okay and not to worry. I'd tell her my feelings about her as my employee haven't changed one bit. If I'm honest, I see so much of myself in her—without all the drugs and drinking.

"You better hurry up. You're late."

"I'm standing outside," she says. "Not late at all."

The front door swings open, and she strides in. I shove my phone back into my pocket and nod at her. "Can you check on Sammy? We're going to need extra kegs tonight, and they need to be easily accessible."

Layla grin is full of youthful optimism. "I'll whip him with a stick if he doesn't get it together."

I laugh and shoo her away. "Go. We've got a ton to do."

As she walks away, a pain of nostalgia hits me. I could have been part of this amazing young woman's life like I was with Nicole, Alex, and Emily. I could have been her fun Aunt Steph.

But you know what? The universe sent Layla into my life now. Into my line of business. And I'm pretty sure it's a sign that I owe it to her to teach her everything I know so she can avoid all the stupid mistakes I made.

I may not have been there when she was a kid, but I can be here now.

19

DIANA

The bottle of Xanax sits on the bathroom counter like a miniature soldier waiting to attack. I've taken it exactly once since Nick picked up the prescription last week, and I have no intention of needing it again. I can handle panic attacks with diet and exercise. I can breathe through them.

And yet, I can't throw the bottle away.

Kristin's visit threw my already-sideways day even more askew. I've been trying to reach Alex since yesterday, but my calls go straight to voicemail and my texts haven't been read. Nick has had the same results. His solution, to wait until our son is ready to speak to us, is not a solution.

Which is why I'm standing in my bathroom, staring at a bottle of Xanax, and wondering if taking one right now, while my pulse races and my heart bangs against my chest, is an okay thing to do.

—Diana, we need to finalize Thanksgiving—

My mom's text pops up again on my phone, reminding me of my failings as a daughter. I've avoided her as much as possible, and I can't put it off much longer.

The phone rings.

"Diana." My mother's tone prepares me for the guilt trip she's about to embark on. "Can't you make time for your mother?"

"Mama, I've been busy with work." I lie because my mom loves when I'm busy at work. It means I'm important and power- ful. However, if she knew about the meme, she'd most likely disown me. "We can discuss Thanksgiving now."

Every year we host, and Nick makes the turkey and most of the side dishes for our family, my parents, Kristin and her family, Steph, and my aunt, uncle and their children and their grandchil- dren. It's a huge undertaking, but it makes my parents happy.

"Papa and I will stay the weekend," Mama says. "Your aunt and uncle will, too."

"That's two guest rooms." My house is large enough to accommodate everyone, but it means I won't get alone time with Alex and Emily.

"Diana. This is not for discussion. Marta and Ed are too old to travel for only one day."

I'd love to say they shouldn't come and that my cousins can host them instead. "Yes, Mama."

I spin the Xanax bottle around on the counter. Mom spent my entire youth warning me about the dangers of strangers with drugs, but she's the one who's driven me to pop pills. I twist off the top and shake one pill onto my palm.

"Tell Nick to put more nutmeg in the pumpkin soup. It was too bland last year."

Nick is an amazing cook, and his soup was far from bland. "Yes, Mama."

"And Diana." Mom waits for me to acknowledge her. "Make sure Emily and Alex are prepared to discuss all the wonderful things they're studying. Marta's granddaughter only got into UVA."

I hate the competition between my mother and her sister. It's a constant game of one-upmanship. "I went to UVA," I say. "It's a fantastic school, and you and Papa were thrilled I went there."

"It's not Princeton or Brown."

God help me if Alex decides to not go back after winter break.

I read the bottle. One pill twice a day. Two at once is basically the same thing. I shake out another pill and pop it in my mouth.

"I am not going to make my cousins feel terrible about their kids not going to an Ivy. Thanksgiving is not a competitive sport." I pop the second Xanax in my mouth and swallow.

Mom huffs. "Nutmeg," she says. "And prepare the twins."

———

The keypad on the front door beeps, and I try to pry my concrete eyelids open. Angry voices boom around me, and snippets of conversation wedge into my consciousness. FireSpot's name is mentioned, but I can't understand what's happening.

The front door slams shut and footsteps thud toward me. Nick always comes through the garage where he parks. So, who is this? Mama? My tongue sticks to the roof of my dry mouth.

"Mama?" I whisper. She has a habit of letting herself in, and it's not surprising she's come over after our conversation. One of the reasons Nick and I chose to live here is that we thought it was close enough to my parents to help them, but far enough away that they couldn't just pop over. We discovered after the fact that my parents consider a forty-minute drive local.

Something heavy drops in the foyer and there are more footsteps, going upstairs, I think.

Mama wouldn't go upstairs.

I swallow to wet my mouth. "Hello."

There's someone in my house, but I'm not at all concerned. In fact, all I want to do is go back to sleep.

"Mom?" Alex's voice calls to me through the haze.

This time, I force my eyelids open.

Alex stands in the doorway with white Beats slung around his neck like a musical turtleneck, blasting some sort of awful rap. "Hey," he says rushing toward me. "Are you okay?"

I am hallucinating. I took too much Xanax, and now my brain is torturing me.

"I'm fine." A mush of sounds jumbles out. "What are you doing home?"

A very real Alex lifts me to sitting. "I'm going to get you water. Wait here."

The FireSpot congressional hearing blasts from the TV, and my mind slowly churns to almost alert. I don't recognize the woman or man representing them.

"I don't know what's wrong with her," Alex says in the kitchen. "Should I call 9-1-1? Maybe she had a stroke?" The refrigerator door opens and closes, and Alex walks into the room with a glass of water. "Okay. I'll keep you posted."

Alex stares me as if I'm an alien. "Can you drink this?"

I nod. The cool water quenches my parched mouth, and I finish the glass all at once.

"Thank you."

Alex crouches down and peers into my eyes. "Do you know where you are?"

I bobble my head. "Honey, I took Xanax. That's all. I'm fine."

Relief washes across Alex's face. "Oh. Good." He shakes his head. "I mean, I'm happy you aren't having a stroke—but Xanax? Is it the meme?"

Music still blasts from Alex's headphone which are now on the coffee table. I point at them, and he taps his phone, turning off the music. Then he turns off the TV.

"What time is it?"

"Almost six. Dad will be home soon." He fumbles with his phone. "I should call and tell him you're okay."

I loll my head against the back of the sofa. My arms and legs are impossibly heavy and holding my body upright is a struggle. Alex speaks quickly into the phone, but I'm not paying attention to his words. All I can think is, Alex shouldn't be here. He should be at school. Or was I in a coma? Is it now Thanksgiving?

"Why are you here?" I manage to mumble.

He runs his hand through his wavy, too-long hair. While Emily is a mini-me, Alex is a solid mix of Nick and me. He has my dark hair and wide eyes, but Nick's straight nose, average height, and thin lips. And like Nick, he is generally evenly tempered. "I withdrew, remember?"

I focus on his face. "What? No. We are discussing it. Nothing is final."

"Mom, I had to withdraw by today for a partial refund. It's done." Alex sits on the coffee table so we face each other. "I know this isn't what you want for me, but it's what I need to do."

I inhale. I should be upset, but I can't touch that emotion. I'm just… oddly calm. "You needed to?"

Alex leans forward and presses his elbows onto the tops of his knees. He steeples his hands together. "I'm not dropping out and doing nothing. Don't worry. I have a plan." He pauses. "Why are you home, anyway? You're never home before seven."

"I'm home because—"

"—of the meme? Because it's not really as bad as Emily says." Alex shrugs. "Or as bad as some other ones—not ones about you. Just other memes."

He's giving me an escape hatch, but I ignore it. "Honey, I was fired." My voice cracks. "JKP fired me."

"Because of the meme?" Alex stares in disbelief. "Can you sue them for that?"

"Because I'm not a good fit, culturally." My tongue loosens its hold on my words. "They fired me before the Halloween party."

"That explains why you got drunk." Alex pulls me into a hug. His once sweaty little boy smell has been replaced by the scent of clean clothes and mountain fresh deodorant. I rest my head against his shoulder and hug him back. "You're too good for them anyway," he says before releasing me. "Is that why you're taking Xanax?"

"I took it once, and I'm never taking it again."

"You shouldn't be embarrassed." Alex sits back on the coffee table. Normally, I'd scold him for sitting there, but today I don't care. "Everyone needs help sometimes."

I can't tell him he's part of my stress. I'm not putting that on him. "Thank you, sweetheart." My brain fog has dissipated slightly. "Why don't you finish getting situated and when Dad gets home, we can discuss your plans over dinner."

"Thanks, Mom." Alex reaches out and squeezes my hand. "I love you."

"I love you more."

Nick picked up Afghani takeout on his way home, and the mouth-watering food is spread across the island. Alex and Nick have heaped piles of kababs and rice on their plates, but I go for the chickpeas, spinach, and shawarma.

A film of Xanax haziness still hangs over me, but at least I'm up and functioning. "This looks delicious," I say, following my family to the breakfast nook. "Thanks for getting it."

"I figured it was easy."

We haven't had a moment alone to discuss Alex's situation, but Nick seemed as surprised as me that Alex followed through with withdrawing.

Alex takes a bite of food, swallows, and says, "I know you want to know my plan. So, here it is: I've accepted a coordinator position with Clean Water Now, and I start Monday."

My heart drops. "Clean Water Now?"

"Yes." Alex says. "They're working on bringing clean water to West Virginia and Appalachia."

Breathe. Breathe. Breathe.

Nick twists his lips into his thinking face. "A nonprofit?"

I bite my lip. "I'm familiar with them. It's run by a young woman, right?"

"Lulu Lucketts," Alex says. "This is her passion project. She's from West Virginia and started it during college."

"What do you know?" Nick asks me.

"She's clashed with Senator Dyson a few times." I shoot Nick a concerned look. "Some people call her an environmental terrorist."

Alex shakes his head. "She a revolutionary—but not in a bad way. She's going up against the status quo, and the old guard doesn't like it. They don't want to save the environment."

"Do you feel the same level of passion?" Nick scoops a forkful of rice and shovels it in his mouth.

Alex swallows. "I do."

I can't tell Alex not to do this. I can't take away his opportunity to follow his passion the way my parents took away mine—even with my not-so-great opinion of Lulu.

"Tell me about this organization," Nick says when we're alone in our bedroom. "Everything."

I stretch out in bed. The drowsiness from the Xanax has not fully receded, and I can't wait to close my eyes. I prop up on my elbow and watch Nick basketball shoot his dirty clothes into the hamper. "Lulu loves protesting outside the Senate and sometimes gets inside. She has been arrested a dozen times for trespassing, and Clean Water Now was linked to attacks on coal plants a few years back."

"Sounds solid." Nick flops next to me. "Should we guide him elsewhere?"

"I don't know. I'm not crazy about this, but it is better than living in the basement playing video games." My eyelids hang heavy. "Plus, his father is an excellent lawyer."

My phone buzzes, and I check it.

—*what do you think about the book?*—Kristin follows it with a bunch of book emojis.

"Who is it?" Nick asks.

"Kristin. She wants my opinion on the book club book." I set my phone down.

Nick tucks his hands behind his head. "You're going this month?"

"Emily is embarrassed and some of the women are gossiping." I roll onto my side. "Everyone has a dumb moment they wish they can forget, and I need to hold my head up."

Nick flashes an encouraging smile. "You shouldn't be embarrassed."

I kiss Nick's cheek. "If it all goes wrong and the ladies run me out of town, I'm never speaking to you again."

His boyish grin makes my heart flutter. "Never?"

"Never until next Monday."

He laughs and rolls me over. His lips hover over mine. "I'll take that risk."

20

STEPH

I kick back my sheets and let the chilly air hit my bare skin. It's late, but I asked Layla to manage the opening routine. It's my way of showing her there are no hard feelings.

As I stare at the steel beams crossing the ceiling, I frown. When I bought my loft, I loved the fifteen-foot-high ceilings and wide-open space, and I thought it was perfect for parties. Now, all I can think of is how expensive it is to heat and cool this place. More than once, I've considered moving into something with more defined spaces, but then my fear of the suburbs kicks in, and I quickly push the thought from my mind.

I never throw parties anymore, and honestly, would it be that awful to move into something less vast? Maybe a condo near LUSH so I can easily walk to work or even something closer to a metro stop?

My phone sits on the side table, face side down, and my chest clenches when I spy it. I've texted Kristin and Diana about random things but asking if they ran Jess off over text is wrong. It's a conversation to have in person or over the phone… and I'm dreading it.

My joggers lay across the end of the bed, and I pull them on, jumping to get them in place. Then I tug a sweatshirt over my head and head toward the kitchen. I need coffee before I can speak to Diana.

As it brews, I mull over what to say to my friends. Should I come right out and confront them? Or should I wait for them to say something? Is there any point in confronting them? What's done is done.

I fill my mug, no milk or sugar, and sit on a barstool. I flick open the last text thread I had with Diana and read. We were discussing Thanksgiving and how Helen is already driving her crazy.

I can do this. I can ask her about what really happened.

I tap her name and put the phone on speaker. It rings once, twice, three times.

"Hey, Steph," Diana says. Her gravelly voice sounds unusually rough.

"Hey," I say. "Up too late last night?"

Diana breathes heavily into the phone. "Not really. I'm just worn out. How are you?"

The heavy grayness pressing against my loft's windows matches my mood. This is my moment… and I say nothing. "I'm okay."

"Kristin came by yesterday," Diana says. "She was trying to figure out what I remembered from the party. Has she spoken to you?"

"Only texts." My heart pounds. "What do you remember?"

"Layla is Jess's daughter, and I caught Kristin making out with Joe."

My mouth drops open. "You saw what?"

"Kristin and Joe on the side of the house, kissing. She says it's done, but I have my doubts."

My ears ring, and my Jess issue is suddenly less important. "What are we going to do? She's self-destructing."

Diana huffs. "What can we do other than counsel her to stop?

Or at least leave her marriage if she's hellbent on finding someone new."

"Nicole will be devastated if this blows up," I say.

"Which is why Kristin needs to stop and make some hard life decisions."

For as long as I can remember, Kristin has embraced domesticity. She prided herself on being the perfect wife and mother. Is she really willing to throw it all away for a guy who's married and possibly toying with her?

I spin my mug from right to left and left to right. "Diana," I say tentatively. "About Layla—"

"Not my business, Steph. If you want to regress twenty-five years, I'm not going to stop you."

The questions I want to ask lodge in my throat.

"Steph? I need to tell you something."

Is she going to confess what she did to Jess? Am I ready to open that up? "What?"

"Alex dropped out." Diana's voice wavers. "He's going to work for this nonprofit that's a borderline front for an environmental terrorist, and I'm freaking out." After a long exhale, she adds, "I have to tell my mom."

Since the day Alex and Emily were born, Diana has mapped out their lives: a top preschool, a move to one of the best school districts in the country, and she's created resumes for those kids that are insane given they are just eighteen. I mean, she had Alex and Emily volunteering at animal shelters when they were six. "They" founded a group that paired school children with shelter pets that the kids read to. It was cute, but so over the top.

"Does he have a plan?"

"He thinks he does," she says. "Nick wants us to let him do it, and honestly, I can't tell him not to—not after what my mom did to me."

I nod even though she can't see me. There will be no discussion of Jess today, and I'm okay with it. My insides stop jittering.

"He could work for me," I offer. "Sweeping floors, washing dishes, grunt work."

"Could he?" Diana sounds unsure. "It might be good for him, but I'm not sure a club is the right place for someone so… structured."

"I need organized people," I say. "But then you'd need to tell Helen he dropped out and is on the same path of debauchery I followed."

Helen has never liked me. In college, when Diana, Kristin, Jess, and I shared a quad, Helen would drive down to UVA and bring food for Diana and Kristin. She'd blatantly ignore me. And on one more than one occasion, I'm positive she told Diana to lose me as a friend. But Diana never did. She stuck with me, and it's the only time she's ever defied Helen.

I blink. Is that why she made Jess move out? Was she worried that she would lose me?

Diana sighs again. "I think Nick is right. We need to ride this out and hope he doesn't get arrested."

"Too bad Mr. Danvers isn't practicing anymore," I say and wait for my words to land.

"He was a miracle worker." There's a faint hesitancy to her voice. "Steph?"

"Yeah?" My pulse speeds up. I'm not ready for this conversation. I'm not ready for twenty-three years of confusion and lying to be exposed.

"Thank you for always being here. Even when you were in Ibiza, I knew you'd always be there for me." She pauses. "I love you, you know that right? That I'd do anything for you?"

My chin quivers. This is her apology, and I'm okay with it. "I love you, too."

This is the thing about lifelong friendships: they're never easy. At least not one-hundred-percent easy. Dumb things are said, feelings get hurt, and bad decisions are made. But through it all, we want what's best for each other. I want what's best for Diana, and she's always wanted what she thought was best for me.

I can respect that.

My coffee is now cold, but I drink it anyway and try to convince myself it's cold brew. It's not. It's disgusting, and I pitch the remainder down the sink. As I run the water and watch the black swirls of coffee expand away from the spray, it occurs to me that Diana and I are like cream and coffee. Sometimes, we swirl around each other, but ultimately, we come together.

As for Kristin, I have some thoughts she needs to hear.

I pick up my phone. Before she can utter a word, I start in on her. "You kissed Joe? What the hell are you doing, Kristin? And don't give me the bullshit story you fed Diana. I know you have no intention of staying away from him. You're one hundred percent having an affair. Do not deny it."

I draw a breath and wait.

She says nothing.

"Seriously!" I yell. "You're not going to say anything?"

"Steph, this is Tom. Kristin and I are driving. You're on Bluetooth."

Bile builds in my throat, and heat rushes through me. "I… ummm… I'll let you two talk."

I hang up, run to my sink, and wretch. What have I done?

21

KRISTIN

"You're having an affair?" Tom jerks the car onto the shoulder. His normally tan skin is ghost white, and he clenches the steering wheel. "With Joe Nillson? That motherfucker?"

The air rushes from my lungs, and my shoulders collapse forward. How do I answer this? "Tom. Sweetheart. No."

"No?" He doesn't look at me and continues to stare out the front window. "Then Steph is making stuff up? What if I called Diana? What would she say?"

I touch his arm, but he yanks it away as if I burned him.

"It's not an affair... it's complicated."

Tom clenches his jaw. "Explain that to me. Explain how being unfaithful is complicated, because it seems to me like you chose to do it. Affairs don't just happen."

Joe did just happen. I wasn't searching for someone else. Joe was just there at the right moment. But how do I explain it? How do I tell Tom that his inattentiveness, his inertia, his indifference is pushing me in this direction?

"Say something!" Tom bashes his hand on the steering wheel. "Say something."

My stomach rolls. "I'm... I'm sorry." The weight of my husband's anger and hurt shocks me. I honestly didn't think Tom cared anymore. "Don't be rash. Give me some time to figure things out."

Tom whips his gaze toward me, and his eyes flash with anger. "Time to decide if you're going to leave me?" He starts the car. "No. You don't get time."

He pulls out into traffic, cutting off a speeding car.

"Where are you going?" I whisper. My throat constricts too much to form a louder sound.

Tom says nothing. He guides the car off the freeway and onto our neighborhood's main road. Every nerve in my body burns, and my muscles tighten as I stare at Tom's ashen face. We were going to lunch. A new place I found. We were starving.

I am no longer hungry.

I'm rooted to the seat, unable to move.

Tom turns in the opposite direction of our house, past the waterfall. He's headed to Diana's. He's going to ask her what she knows.

Images of our life together flood my brain. Good memories. Tom, Nicole, and me at our beach house. Tom helping Nicole with her first steps. The day Nicole graduated from high school. There's been so much good over the years.

"You don't want me anymore," I say softly. "You only want to watch TV and don't want me."

Tom hits the brakes hard at a stop sign. His checks flame red. "Do not make this my fault. Do not."

I can't bear to look at him and turn to stare out the window. I press my forehead against the window and watch the manicured lawns rush past.

"How long?" Tom sounds harsh and colds

Do I tell him the truth, or do I spare him the pain of knowing? "It's not an affair."

"Then what is it? Steph said you kissed Joe."

I choke out my answer. "I was drunk."

Tom stops outside Joe and Thalia's house. "If I knocked on their door and Joe answered, how do you think he'd react to me standing on his porch?"

"Confused." My head swims. "We're not having an affair."

"And if I told Thalia you kissed her husband, how do you think she'd react?"

I shake my head. "Don't do that. There's no reason to upset her."

Tom taps his hand against the steering wheel. "And why would she be upset, Kristin? It was just a drunken kiss, remember?"

I stare at Joe and Thalia's red-brick colonial and the neatly landscaped yard. An American flag hangs off the porch and flutters in the light breeze. It looks like a perfect, magazine-worthy family home.

Tom grabs my phone from the cupholder. "What's your password?"

Panic wells in me, and I press my lips together.

"What is your damn password?"

"3716483." I can barely make the sounds.

Tom scrolls through my list of texts until he finds Joe's. "You two certainly text a lot." He reads a few before tossing my phone at me. It falls to the floor. "You make me sick, K."

I pick the phone up. "Tom, please. Don't tell Thalia."

"She deserves to know what an asshole her husband is." Tom swings his door open and jumps out.

"Please, no." I chase after him as he storms toward their front door. "Don't do this to Thalia. It's nothing. Just a flirtation."

He spins around, anger etched into every inch of his face. Gone is the man who hasn't noticed me in months. In his place is a man that sees me too much. He sees my lies. He sees my struggles. And he sees that if he hadn't overheard Steph's call, I'd make a fool of him.

I grab at his arm and try pulling him back to the car. He yanks me to a stop. "What?" he yells. "You weren't worried about hurting her when you kissed her husband."

"I was drunk!" I shout. "Everyone does stupid stuff when they are drinking!"

"No one sends thousands of texts and has their lips accidentally land on the other person's."

A car turns into the driveway. Thalia sits behind the wheel, looking confused. Her daughter is in the passenger seat.

"Tom, not now. Not with their daughter here." I tug at his hand. "Let's go."

"Is everything okay?" Thalia asks. She motions for her daughter to stay in the car. "Do you need help?"

I hold my breath and wait for Tom to answer, but instead he heads to the car, starts it, and drives off as I try to get in. I fall to my knees.

"Kristin!" Thalia runs to my side and offers me her hand. "Are you okay?"

I stand and dust off my jeans. Thalia's daughter is still in her car. "I'm fine," I say. "Tom is… Well, I need to go."

I start walking toward my house, not looking back. I'm sure she's going to ask Joe what this was about. I don't care what he says. The damage to my life is done.

"Tom?" I call when I arrive home. "Where are you? Can we talk?"

He doesn't answer.

I find him in his office with my iPad on his desk.

"Did you know that all your messages back up here?" He moves his finger over the screen. "They go all the way back, from what I can tell, to when you and Joe started seeing each other."

I lean against the door frame. While I'm not proud of the flirtatious nature of our texts, there's nothing damning. There are no plans to meet up in hotel rooms or sneak away from our spouses. Just flirty banter. "He's just a friend," I say. "That's it. We kissed once—at the party—and I realized it was a mistake. I told Diana as much."

Tom sets my iPad aside. "It's called an emotional affair, Kristin."

Isn't that what Diana and Steph have been telling me?

"You shared things with him that you don't share with me." The hurt permeates Tom's words. "I thought we had something good. Why do you want to throw it away?"

I shake my head. "I don't. I... I just need more." I close my eyes. "You're always saying we made it to the good part of marriage, but this isn't good for me."

"Why? What did I do wrong?"

I open my eyes. "I think we've gone off track. I'm lonely, and I envisioned a more exciting empty nest. Weekends away. Romantic dinners. All the stuff we put off while raising Nicole."

Tom glances away before focusing on my face. "Kristin. If that's what you want, then say something. I'm not a mind reader."

I curl onto his office loveseat. "I have."

"You haven't." He crosses his arms. "You've told me that you miss Nicole. You've said you don't know who you are if you're not being a mom twenty-four-seven, and I've suggested you keep yourself busy."

I pull my knees to my chest and wrap my arms around them. "It's not enough. I need you to notice me. I need you to engage and not watch Netflix all night." My shoulders heave. "When is the last time we had sex? Because I don't remember."

Tom blinks his watery eyes. "I don't know." He uncrosses his arms and rubs his palms together. "Are we too broken?"

That's the question I've been asking for months. "I don't know."

"Me neither."

We decided to sleep on it. To not make rash decisions. To talk some more in the morning.

And now, I want to roll over, away from the minuscule ditch between Tom and me on the bed, but he snores softly with his hand resting on my upper thigh and his head almost touching mine. It's the most intimate we've been in months.

On our wedding night, I promised myself that I would always fall asleep touching my husband, but now, his warm hand reminds me of how far we've drifted apart.

I lie there until every cell in my body screams to move. I slide out from under Tom's hand and roll off the bed. He doesn't stir. A few years ago, I begged him to buy a "princess bed" from Restoration Hardware. The gorgeous oatmeal upholstery and antiqued gray wood caught my eye as soon as I saw it, and Tom didn't give any push back, not even when he saw the insane price tag.

He always gives me what I want except romance and passion. Why are those two things so hard for him?

I slip my feet into my furry slippers and plod quietly across the room toward the door. Tom keeps snoring as I creep into the hallway. Across the landing, Nicole's dark room reminds me that Diana is right. I am very much a has-been. I'm so pathetically lost that I almost had an affair. There's nothing more has-beeny than a retired mom who is trying to recapture the excitement of youth by hooking up with a neighbor.

Downstairs, I settle onto the sunroom couch. The owl who lives in our pine tree screeches and the sun breaks orange and purple across the sky. I rest my cheek on the back of the couch and stare out the window.

I turn my phone on and it dings as messages pour in.

—*What was that about?*—Joe wrote several hours ago.

—*Kristin. What the hell is going on*—

I delete his messages.

I felt like I was fourteen again when I was around Joe, and I acted like it too. It's so stupid. We're both married to great people and have kids. I know Joe says he and Thalia are more like roommates, but that's not how they acted at the diner. In hindsight, even though I said the same about Tom, it doesn't mean I don't love him or the life we've built.

A clarity I haven't felt in ages settles over me. Diana was right; I risked hurting the two people I love unconditionally for a man who… well, I don't know what Joe is. As I sit here, watching the sun rise higher in the sky, I question if any of it was real for Joe. Was he playing me for a thrill and gaslighting me like Diana said?

Did I stupidly almost throw away a perfectly good life?

I walk to the foyer and swing the front door open. Cool November air strikes my face, and I pull my robe tighter. At the porch swing, I push aside the pillows so I can sit. The sun doesn't hit this side of the house until later, but the inky sky has given way to a hazy gray.

Tom and I bought this house because of the porch. I had visions of us sitting on it watching Nicole and our grandchildren play on the lawn. I had wanted a future with Tom. A forever.

When did that stop?

Or has it? Did I ignore what Tom wanted because I was too caught up in myself? Have I been the selfish one?

Until I saw the hurt in Tom's eyes, I'd forgotten that I loved him. I have since the day we met, but after twenty-four years together, things are stale. And maybe, instead of waiting for Tom to seduce me, I should try harder to find ways for us to rebuild our passion.

I tuck my feet under my legs and type "rekindling romance in marriage" into my phone. Pages of articles pop up. Over the next hour, I surf through them and bookmark the most promising until it's time to shower and get ready for the day.

If Tom is willing to work on us, then I am too.

Steph called me in a panic and once I heard what she did, I tried leaping into action to help Kristin, but she rebuffed my efforts.

"I appreciate you wanting to help, but I need to handle this myself, Diana."

That was yesterday, and the only text she's answered was Maggie's group text asking for a headcount for book club. She confirmed, but I have doubts on whether she's going to show or not as I stand on Maggie's tastefully decorated autumn porch.

I don't knock and push the unlocked door open.

"Diana! How are you? We haven't seen you in... what? Six months?" Maggie rushes to greet me as I step inside. Her bobbed hair stops just above her shoulders and is dyed pale blonde to hide the gray. Unlike most women in the neighborhood, Maggie looks her age with a few wrinkles and crow's feet. And like me, she prefers wearing casual dress pants and blouses.

"I know. I'm so sorry. Work has kept me busy." I hold out a bottle of Bordeaux, and Maggie takes it. "How are you?"

Maggie reads the label. She's a wine snob, so I always bring a nice bottle to her house.

"I'm great. Steve and I have been traveling and keeping busy." Maggie retired from the government last year and seems to have slid into her new lifestyle easily.

"That's wonderful." I slip off my wool coat and hang it on the coat tree next to the front door. Voices ring out from the kitchen. "Is everyone in the back?" I ask.

"Yes. I've put out snacks and help yourself to some wine."

I almost didn't come tonight, even though Nick insisted I get out of the house and focus on something other than Alex for a few hours. However, when I saw Kristin's "yes" RSVP, I couldn't let her come alone. Not when she's falling apart.

Maggie's pristine kitchen has white cabinets, white granite countertops, and stainless appliances. I doubt anyone cooks in it.

There are several unfamiliar women gathered around the island. Last year, our numbers were dwindling due to members moving and general attrition, and Maggie posted on our community Facebook page looking for new members. I guess it worked.

Kristin stands alone next to the island. Her falling-out ponytail, track pants, and yoga sweatshirt disguise her skeletal figure. Dark circles ring her pink, swollen eyes.

"Hey," I say quietly when I'm standing next to her. "You okay to be here?"

She leans against the island as if she needs it to hold her up. "I need to keep my brain busy."

"Everyone." Maggie waits for the other women stop chattering. "I know some of you know her, but for those that don't this is Diana Clarke. She's been with us for… five years?"

"I think so."

Everyone stares at me, but one woman pips up. "Diana, hi! How are you feeling?"

Someone giggles. It must be the meme, but what is this? Middle school?

I keep my head up and ignore the giggler. "I'm excited about tonight's book," I say even though I barely remember much about it. Normally, I read and annotate my book club books, but I haven't had the time to go back through it.

"Let's introduce ourselves since so many of us are newish." Maggie turns toward a willowy brunette. "Phoebe?"

Phoebe is the only woman who has touched the food, and she finishes her cheese before wiping her hands on her ankle-length flowing skirt. Unlike all the other women, she has broken the traditional outfit mandate. In fact, she looks a little like a hippy with her layered bracelets and tunic. "Hi, Diana. I'm Phoebe. My kids are in fifth and eighth grades. Boys."

I smile. "Hi! I have boy-girl twins who graduated last year."

Each woman introduces herself until finally, a petite woman steps toward the island and puts her glass of wine down. "Hi, Diana. It's nice to see you again."

I'm usually great about remembering faces and names, but I have no idea who she is. "I'm sorry, I'm terrible with faces."

"Becky Davenport."

Emily and Becky's daughter, Sophia, were friendly until eighth grade when Emily decided she preferred video games and computers over dance and cheerleading. There was drama, or rather, Becky tried to create drama, but Emily and I were not interested.

"Becky!" I fight to hide my surprise. "Did you cut your hair?"

"Doesn't everyone?" She purses her lips in a duck-bill kind of way. "Except you, I guess. You look exactly like you did years ago."

I know she's taking a dig. After five years, this woman should be over it, and yet she's still fuming that Emily didn't want to join the cheerleading team. As if I should have forced my daughter to aspire to popularity instead of being her true self. "I guess I found the fountain of youth."

Maggie claps her hands. "Shall we go to the dining room and get started?" She lifts a tray of mini quiches off the kitchen island that no one except Phoebe will eat. I may not get out much, but I know these women don't do carbs in public. "Would you all mind carrying something out?"

"I've got the wine," a younger blonde says.

Maggie mutters, "Of course you do."

I try not to laugh. Maggie rarely shows her sassy side but when she does, it's funny.

As I reach for a mini quiche, my phone buzzes. I set the platter down. It's my lawyer, Cheryl.

"Hi," I say. "Is everything okay?"

"Hi, Diana. I have some great news. JKP has agreed to waive the non-compete if you agree to not poach current clients."

It's not a terrible offer. I nod my head as I think. "What are your thoughts?"

"It's the best you're going to get."

I cast a glance at the dining room where the women have arranged themselves around the table. "Send me the papers, and I'll sign."

"Great. I'll have it done first thing in the morning."

I pick up the quiche and head into the fussy, over-done dining room. A few of the women have laid copies of the book on the heavily-polished mahogany table. I take my seat next to Kristin, reach into my bag... and realize I left it at home. I quickly open my phone and buy the Kindle copy.

"Are the new women serious readers?" I whisper to Kristin.

"Not really." She pulls at the end of her ponytail. "We've been reading the same kind of literary fiction over and over again since you stopped coming. Maybe you can suggest something new for next month. Spice it up."

"I don't want to spice anything up, Kristin."

"That's Maggie and Phoebe's fault. They only want to read literature," a blonde woman across from me says. She doesn't lower her voice or anything. Just says it loudly with both Maggie and Phoebe sitting there.

No one bats an eye.

"I'm Charlotte, in case you forgot." She smiles at me. "And I agree with Kristin. We need new spice. Did you read the book? It was too long, right?"

"I did read it." I don't add that it's been over two years and I hated it, but since I never give up on a book, I forced myself to suffer through endless pages of detailed description where nothing seemed to happen. "Has anyone ever suggested something different? A beach read, maybe?" Everyone speaks about Phoebe and Maggie like they aren't present, so I might as well also.

Kristin leans closer to me and whispers. "Good luck with that. Maggie and Phoebe are locked in a power struggle over the book selection, and they really dislike each other."

"I think they try to pick books the other will hate, and we all suffer because of it." Charlotte finishes her glass of wine and refills from the bottle in the middle of the table.

"Why do you keep coming?" I ask.

She chuckles. "Entertainment factor."

"Everyone." Phoebe places an unfolded piece of paper on the table. "I took the liberty of printing out the publisher's book club guide." She touches the paper like it's the ancient scroll holding the secrets of the universe. "There are so many meaty topics here."

Maggie scans the table and lands on the open chair next to Charlotte. With her finger, she ticks us off one by one. "Who are we missing?"

Everyone stares at each other, trying to figure out who isn't here.

"Oh!" Phoebe says. "Thalia asked to come, remember?"

Kristin bristles. She fidgets and looks like she wants to run out of the room, and I don't blame her.

"Hey," I whisper. "Do you want to leave?"

Kristin's hands tremble. "It will look bad," she whispers back. "I can't."

"Let's start," Maggie says. "Thalia can catch up if she gets here."

Please let Thalia be a no-show. Please.

Phoebe holds up the paper and reads the first question. She stares at us expectedly, and when no one answers, Charlotte mouths, "Get ready."

"I think the author is making a comment about the crushing burden of higher education debt," Phoebe says. "He's correct, or course."

"No one forces anyone to go to college, Phoebe." Maggie sits opposite of Phoebe at the head of the table with crossed arms. "There are other options."

"Like what?" Phoebe steeples her fingers like a nun reading to give a lecture. "Our young people—especially the underprivileged —deserve top-level educations, access to enrichment programs, and three meals a day. A college degree can be the difference between poverty and living comfortably."

I entwine my hands on my lap and try to calm my racing heart as images of Alex living in a questionable apartment and eating canned food for the rest of his life pop into my mind. Damn it. Are we being too lenient on Alex? Are we encouraging him down a path of ruin?

Charlotte winks at me. "See?"

"We are not a socialist country, Phoebe," Becky says, joining the discussion. "Someone needs to pay for all this."

Next to me, Kristin stares at her lap. The loose hair from her ponytail falls across her face, and her lips are pressed firmly together like she's trying not to cry.

"We should provide opportunities with a no or low barrier to entry." Phoebe stares at Maggie as if she's challenging her.

Well, this is interesting. Normally, we have wine and lightly discuss the book, but in my absence the group has shifted to full-on hostilities and conflicts.

"I'm so sorry I'm late." Thalia breezes into the room. Her

shiny, chestnut-colored hair falls perfectly over her shoulders, and she wears a cute dress and tights with ballet flats. "Joe was late getting home."

Kristin tenses and keeps her gaze down.

"Hi, Kristin," Thalia says taking the seat opposite of her. "How are you?"

Why did she single Kristin out? She knows the other women too.

My friend briefly looks up and gives a grim smile. "Hey, how are you?"

Thalia raises her eyebrows and leans slightly forward. "I've been better."

"Take the swim team, for example." Charlotte guides us back to the book conversation. Apparently, everyone is still fixated on college educations or something. "Should we continue to subsidize the swim team out of our HOA fees?" she asks. "Especially since they collect an additional fee from the swimmers?"

Becky nods. "Charlotte is right. It's ridiculous that they don't pay a use fee to the HOA when they literally close the Meadows pool for hours each week."

A strangled sound comes out of Kristin, and when I glance at her, she's drained of color.

"Everything okay, Kristin?" Thalia says. "Do you need air? Maybe on the side of the house?"

Oh. Thalia knows about Kristin and Joe.

"Thalia," I say. "That's a great idea. Kristin," I push back my chair. "Let's get some air." I pull her to her feet. "C'mon," I whisper. "Don't fight me."

"Are you okay, Kristin?" Maggie asks. "You're unusually pale."

I link my arm through Kristin's and her weight presses against me. "I think she just needs air. We'll be right back."

When we reach the kitchen, a sob tumbles out of Kristin.

"Do not cry," I hiss. "Do not. These women will latch onto

that." I use the sleeve of my sweater to dab her eyes. "What do you want to do? Go home or go back in?"

Kristin lets out a shaky breath. "Advice?"

"If you go home, you can claim to feel unwell. You look like shit." I don't hold back. "If you go back in there, you're baiting Thalia and I have no idea what she'll do."

Kristin nods. "She never comes to book club anymore, so the fact that she's here—"

"—means she's out for blood." I purse my lips. Now is not the time for I told you so. "Go to the car. I'll make our apologies."

"No. I've got to hold my head up. I can't run away."

"I don't think that's wise," I say. "You look sick, so let's lean into it."

Kristin wipes her face with the bottom of her shirt. "Okay. I'll wait in my car."

When I enter the dining room to give our regrets, Phoebe huffs. "That's what we're doing, Maggie. Discussing the larger themes and how they apply to us."

"No," Maggie snaps. "You're discussing the swim team, and that's not why we're here." Maggie turns her attention toward me.

Oh no.

"Diana, what are your thoughts on how the author used the bird?"

"The bird?" What was this? High school again? I'm not even sitting at the table. I wrack my brain. Was there a bird? An important bird?

"Did you read the book, Diana?" Becky asks with undisguised glee.

"Of course, I did. A few years ago, and it was… interesting." I can't leave yet—it will look like I'm ducking out because I didn't read the book. "The bird doesn't care about the swim team," I say to buy a few extra seconds. A few giggles break out from around the table, and I smile. "But the author uses imagery and characters to comment on larger social issues, like Phoebe said." I hope I sound coherent. "Ultimately, the bird is a symbol of things taking flight: our hopes and dreams. They can fly or they can have their wings clipped." I walk to my chair, lift my water glass to my lips and sip. I have no idea what I'm talking about, but it sounds decent.

From her end of the table, Maggie opens to a sticky-tabbed page. "Phoebe, what other questions do you have on that list?"

"Actually, Maggie, Kristin isn't feeling well, and I'm going to take her home." I catch Thalia's eye. "She needs more than a little fresh air, I'm afraid. I think she has that bug going around."

"Oh. That's too bad." Maggie sounds annoyed. "Give her my best."

I grab our coats and hustle to the car. Kristin sits in the passenger seat of her car, slumped over her knees, sobbing. "What have I done?" she cries. "Why didn't I listen to you?"

"Because you're unhappy." Her keys are on the center console, and I start her car. I'll have Nick pick me up from Kristin's and come back to get my car.

Under the streetlight, Kristin's tear-streaked face is a red, blotchy mess. "Am I though? Am I really?"

"Happy people don't look outside their marriage." I pull onto the street. "What do you want, Kristin? Deep down, what do you want?"

She balls herself up on the passenger seat. "I want everything to be like it was. I want Nicole to be tucked into her bed and for Tom to appreciate the meals I make. I want the life I envisioned when we got married."

"But didn't you already have that life?" I reach across the console and touch her arm. "We can't stand still or go backward, and that's good. Imagine if we were stuck at twenty-one, working in entry-level jobs, drinking every night, and not maturing. We'd be miserable."

Kristin sobs harder. "Why can't we freeze ourselves at the perfect moment?"

She's being irrational. "I'm going to take you home. If you want your marriage, you need to be honest with Tom about your feelings. If you want to leave, you need to be honest with yourself."

She turns her tear-stained face toward me. Under the streetlight, she looks more ragged than when we were inside. "I tried talking to Tom."

"And?" I ease her car out of the parking space. "What did Tom say?"

"Nothing," she sobs. "He says nothing."

I can't tell her, but this may be too big of a crisis to come back from.

23

STEPH

It isn't an ask. It's an order.

"Just hurry, Steph." Diana's voice is brisk. "Tom told Nicole, and it's a mess."

"Shit." I grab my keys off my desk. Downstairs, tonight's performance thunders through the building. This is terrible timing, but I have to go. "I'll be there in forty minutes if the traffic isn't bad."

Even though Kristin did this to herself, my heart hurts for her. Yes, Diana and I both warned her, and she ignored our advice. But if it was just a drunken kiss and some flirty texts like Kristin claims, why did Tom tell Nicole? That hardly seems like a solid reason to blow up your family.

I press through the crowd surrounding the bar. "Jean-Luc," I shout, waving him toward me. "I have an emergency." The music envelops us. I point at his walkie-talkie. "Tell Layla to run the floor."

His eyes grow wide. "Is everything okay?"

"It's not about me." I point at the customers crushing against the far end of the bar. Our new bartender, Micki, seems a bit overwhelmed, but she's good and I know she'll be great once she settles in. "Just keep the drinks flowing."

My BMW is parked behind the building. I connect my phone, shift into in reverse, and take off. Melancholy music blasts around me. Normally, I'd listen to something upbeat—not dance music, I hear enough of that at work—but something more pop. My musical tastes are a dirty secret, and my staff would be appalled if they knew I regularly listened to Top 40.

As I cross from Fairfax County into Loudoun, my phone rings.

"Hey," I say. "I'm almost there."

In the background, Kristin sobs. "Can you go to Kristin's instead?" Diana asks. "See if Nicole will speak to you?"

"Nicole's home?"

"Apparently. Tom told her earlier today." Diana drops her voice. "Steph, if he's told Nicole, I'm worried he's going to ask for divorce." She exhales. "I've gone through the texts and they're not damning. I understand why he's acting like this."

I change lanes and speed through the toll booth. "Do you know what Nicole knows?"

"No, but can you get a feel of where she is on all this? She'll open up to you."

I've always doted on Nicole. I'm her fun Aunt Steph—the one who takes her and her friends to concerts. The one who said she'd bail her out of jail. The one who chaperoned her and her two girlfriends on a ten-day trip to Amsterdam and Spain and didn't corrupt them too much.

I am not nurturing. I'm fun.

But I'll be damned if I'm letting her handle this on her own.

"I can't make promises." At our exit, I turn onto the large central road circling the neighborhood. "But just so we're clear, I'm one-hundred percent Team Nicole."

Kristin's house is lit up like she's hosting a party. I park in the driveway, behind Nicole's car plastered with JMU stickers. She's a junior this year, but I can't for the life of me understand what she's studying. It's a weird hybrid of communications and computer science. At least, that's what it sounds like. Honestly, I don't think Kristin understands it either.

I ring the doorbell and wait. No one answers even though both Tom and Nicole's cars are in the driveway. I ring the door-bell again and press my ear to the door. There's a faint noise inside.

Before punching in the door code, I knock. When I open the door, I yell, "Hey, it's me, Steph!"

The TV plays at the back of the house, but no one answers me. I hurry through the foyer, past the pictures of Nicole, Kristin, and Tom lining the hallway, and stop in the entryway of the family room. Tom is passed out on the couch with empty bottles of bourbon scattered on the floor next to him.

"Tom?" I walk over to him, stoop, and pick up a bottle. "Did you drink all this?"

"Maybe," he slurs. "I don't remember. It's been a long couple of days."

I place the bottle on the side table. "Where's Nicole?"

He stares at me like I'm speaking a foreign language. Fortunately, I know how to handle drunks. I walk to the kitchen, grab three of Kristin's fancy bottled waters, and return to Tom. "Sit up. You need to drink this."

I twist off the cap and force the bottle into Tom's hand.

He gulps the first bottle down. "I'm thirsty."

"I bet." I hand him the second bottle. "You're going to feel like shit tomorrow."

"Can't be any worse than now." He shoves the half-drank bottle back at me. "Kristin is a whore."

Whoa. If he's going there, then what has he said to Nicole? Did he call her after he'd been drinking all day?

I help Tom lay back down. "You good, buddy?"

He slurs what sounds like yes and closes his eyes. I steal the one nearly-full bottle of bourbon and put it on the kitchen bar. He's done for the day.

Aside from Tom's snoring, the house is silent. I climb the stairs and pause outside Nicole's closed door. I wait a moment before knocking. "Nicole?"

A beat.

"Steph?" Nicole flings her bedroom door open. Her high-lighted, blonde hair is a mess and her red-rimmed eyes have smeared eyeliner and mascara under them. She wraps her arms around me, and I hug her tightly.

"Can I come in?" I ask. Sad country music plays softly in the background. Like me, Nicole listens to music based on her mood.

She steps aside. "I guess you're here to talk about my parents' marriage?"

The frilly, pink comforter is bunched at the bottom of her bed, and I sit on it. "No, I'm here to check on you."

She flings herself on the bed, stomach side down before rolling over. "I'm scared." Her big, hazel eyes lock in on my face. "Did you know?"

Should I be honest? Maybe? "I know that your mom has been very lonely." I avoid the part about how Nicole leaving for college has set Kristin adrift. "She thought Joe was just a friend."

"I can't believe she was hooking up with Tyler's dad." Nicole's voice hitches. "What is wrong with her?"

"Who's Tyler?" I ask.

"My boyfriend."

Yikes. Kristin failed to mention that wrinkle.

I lay back on the bed so I'm parallel to Nicole and stare at the ceiling. "She wasn't hooking up with Tyler's dad. She kissed him once when she was drunk. That's it."

Nicole props up on her elbow. "Dad said it's been going on for at least six months."

That's also news to me. Has Kristin hid him for months? "I don't know what your dad has told you, but Diana went through their texts and says there's no indication that there was anything more than flirty texts and one kiss." I run my right thumb over my left palm. "If there was an affair, it was purely emotional."

Nicole falls onto her back and closes her eyes. "I feel like she lied to us."

"I do, too." I shouldn't have said that. "What I mean is, your mom has made everything look perfect even though she and your dad are disconnected. They were both lying to themselves and us about the state of their relationship."

"Dad didn't cheat."

Okay. So, in Nicole's book, cheating is flirting with someone who isn't your partner. That's a strict line.

"Honey, I think you should talk to your mom. Hear her side." I pause. "You're not getting the full story."

Nicole shakes her head. "What is there to know? She flirted or whatever with Tyler's dad, kissed him, got caught, and now she's trying to make it look like she did nothing wrong." Nicole's eyes glisten. "But she did. She decided to throw our family away because she was lonely or bored or whatever."

I sit up. "Come here." I pull Nicole upright and wrap my arms around her. "Life isn't black and white, and neither are relationships." Nicole rubs her face against my shoulder. "Sometimes, someone you love hurts you or does something that upsets you. It's your choice to forgive them or not."

Nicole rests her head on my shoulder. "How?"

It's a fair question. "You've got to ask yourself: does one mistake overshadow a lifetime of happy moments? And is it worth giving up on the happiness the future can hold?"

The song changes to a country-pop hit. "Do you like this song?" I ask.

"Yeah."

"Have you ever paid attention to the words?"

Nicole shakes her head.

"It's about how if you have a solid relationship, you can rebuild it when something sends you sideways."

Nicole doesn't say anything, and I kiss her temple. Finally, she asks: "Do I need to choose between my mom and dad?"

"Never. You never have to make that decision."

Nicole buries her face into my armpit, her tears staining my leather jacket. I rub her back. "You know, I'm here for you no matter what, right? I'm always on your side?"

"Thanks, Aunt Steph."

Maybe I don't always have to be fun Aunt Steph. Maybe I can be compassionate Aunt Steph, too.

I wait until I'm at Diana's to tell Kristin that Nicole doesn't want to see her. At least, not yet.

A wildness has invaded Kristin's normally calm personality. She paces across Diana's family room and her eyes flash. "Did you tell her it was nothing?"

"That's the thing, Kristin, it is something to her."

Diana and I sit on the sectional and exchange glances. This is a disaster.

"Kristin, you're going to have to give her time to process," Diana says. "This is a lot. Especially if she believed everything was great between you and Tom."

Kristin curls onto the chair across from Diana and wraps her arms around her knees. "I should have told her first, but I thought Tom and I were going to keep it private and work on things."

I rock my head side to side. "He drank God knows how much bourbon. He probably drunk-called her."

"Or," Diana says solemnly, "you need to prepare for the worst. Tom called Nicole, told her, then got drunk."

Kristin rests her splotchy cheek on her knee. "Why would he do that? Why bring Nicole into it?"

I wait for Diana to answer. She's a pro at breaking bad news. "Have you considered that this is Tom's way of starting a divorce."

Kristin blinks in confusion. "A divorce? No. Why would we get divorced over this?"

Even I understand, and I have zero marriage experience, but I let Diana explain. "If you've been feeling lost in your marriage, Tom probably has too. There's a good chance he's evaluated everything and has decided to move on without you."

"Jesus Christ," Kristin snaps. "You make it so fucking clinical."

"Then how's this?" I say sharply. "He fell out of love with you when you fell out of love with him, and he was comfortable floating along. You were the dumbass that got tangled up with someone else. Does that make you feel better?"

Kristin narrows her eyes at me. "You're the one who told him!"

"No," I say. "I rang you, and I called you out on your behavior. Tom just happened to be there."

Diana holds up her hands. "Stop. This is going to get us nowhere. Kristin, you need a Plan A, B, and C." She waves her finger in the air likes she's circling something. "First, no matter what plan you take, you need to call an attorney first thing tomorrow." Kristin balks, and Diana hushes her. "If—and it's only an 'if' at this point—Tom wants a divorce, he's already retained someone. It's better to be prepared."

A sick feeling builds in my gut. Would Tom do that? He's a decent guy. Wouldn't he be willing to talk things out first? I stare at the windows. I can't see outside because the house lights reflect at me, but I drift off in my thoughts as Diana and Kristin hash things out.

"He's going to poison Nicole against me," Kristin sobs. "He's already started."

Tom is not a bad guy, so why are they jumping to conclusions?

"We need to work fast," Diana says. She scribbles furiously on an iPad. "Especially if you want Nicole on your side."

The anger inside me explodes. "No. You will not manipulate Nicole. She's an adult, and she can make her own decisions." I jab my finger in Kristin's direction. "You need to take some fucking responsibility. You did this. You're the reason your marriage is imploding. And you're the reason Nicole won't speak to you. Own it."

My friends stare at me slack-jawed.

I grab my jacket and drape it over my arm. "Until you do that, Kristin, I've got nothing to say to you." Anger oozes from me. "And if Nicole doesn't want to see you, I'm honoring that."

24

KRISTIN

iana told me to go home. She explained that by leaving, Tom can claim I abandoned him, which may hurt my alimony if we go that route.

I park in front of my house, unable to go inside. There are so many good memories in there, but are Diana and Steph right? Did Tom stop loving me at some point just like I stopped loving him? Were we at an impasse, waiting for the other to fumble?

I don't know.

The light in Nicole's room is still on. I need to go inside and talk to her. I need to own this mess like Steph said.

I heft myself out of my car. Chilly November air whirls around me as I walk toward the front door, and I shiver. What was I thinking wearing flip-flops and a light jacket in this weather? The book club ladies are probably speculating about what's wrong with me, and I wouldn't put it past Becky to have sent out "concerned" texts behind my back.

I honestly don't care anymore if they gossip and speculate. I've spent too much of my life running in circles trying to convince others that my life is perfect. I need to stop caring what other people think and truly put my family's needs first.

I punch in the door code and wait for it to unlock. Steph said Tom had passed out, but I don't hear his snores. Maybe he went to bed? I set my car keys on the foyer console table and place my bag on its hook. Then I tiptoe toward the stairs.

"What are you doing?"

I whip around. Tom stands in the hallway behind me. His hair is a mess, his clothes are askew, and he has a wild, drunk look in his eye. Tom never gets sloppy drunk, and I'm not sure how I'm supposed to react to him. He uses the wall to hold himself up. "You can't be here."

"I live here, and I'm going to talk to Nicole." I start up the stairs.

Tom lunges at me, and I brace to support his weight. "No. You don't live here. Not anymore."

Diana instructed me to keep everything civil and to not give Tom anything that can be used against me, but given his current state, I doubt he'll remember any of this tomorrow.

"You need to sleep," I say. "Let's go to bed." I sling his arm over my shoulder. "C'mon."

"No." Tom turns to deadweight and nearly tips me over. "You're a cheating bitch."

I recoil. In our twenty-five years together, I have never heard Tom call anyone a bitch. Never.

From the top of the stairs comes a strangled gasp.

Nicole stares down at us. Pieces of hair stick to her cheeks, and she glares at me. "I can't believe you'd do this to us!"

"Honey, it's not at all what Dad's told you. I swear."

"Don't." Tom lurches toward the stairs. "You're a liar." He collapses on the third step, and Nicole hurries to his side. He pulls her into a one-arm hug. "You have an hour to pack and leave."

"Leave? Tom, don't be ridiculous." I open my phone and pull up Joe's texts. "Look. It was one kiss and some flirty texts. It wasn't an affair." I shove my phone toward Tom. "Why are you over-reacting?" Diana's suggestion that Tom is also unhappy bubbles up. "Is it because you've been waiting for an out?"

"Stop." Nicole bats away my phone and curls against Tom. "You've been having an affair with my boyfriend's dad." Her mouth is agape. "That's so gross."

"Why didn't you tell me about Tyler? I had to hear it from Thalia that you've been hanging out with him again."

"Would that have stopped you from whatever it is you were doing with his dad?"

I don't answer.

"Exactly. What you want is more important." Nicole's lips twitch. "It always has been."

More important? What is she talking about? "Everything I've ever done is for you, sweetheart. Everything,"

"Really?" She rolls her eyes. "You wouldn't let me drop cheerleading senior year even though I hated it because you were worried I wouldn't be popular." She draws a deep breath. "And you forced me to all those Comic Cons because you thought they were fun."

Shock rolls through me. "What? You loved them. We had so much fun making the costumes and—"

"When I was twelve." She wiggles out of Tom's arms and stands. We're nearly the same height. "Tyler is right. You and his dad deserve each other. You're both control freaks."

My chest constricts, and I stumble against the hall table. Nicole's anger is worse than anything Tom can throw at me. "Can't we talk through this?"

"Don't make this harder, Mom. You've done enough already."

Her words strike the most vulnerable part of my heart. "Nicole. Honey. Just—

"Stop making this difficult, Kristin," Tom says.

This makes no sense. None. Nicole and I have always had a

special mother-daughter relationship. "You're my best friend." I hold out my arms, hoping Nicole will let me hug her. She turns away. "Nicole, honey, you've always been my best friend."

She draws her brows together and shakes her head. "Kylie is my best friend. You are my mom."

The world spins around me.

"You need to leave, Kristin." Tom isn't slurring anymore. In fact, he seems almost sober.

"Go where? This is my home." I fight to stay standing upright.

"I don't care where you go. Go live with Joe. I don't care. We just need you gone."

I hold out my arms again. "Nicole," I plead. "Sweetheart, give me a chance to explain. Please."

She shakes her head. "I never want to talk to you again."

It's 11:30 at night. I have two suitcases piled into my car, and nowhere to go. So, I sit in the driveway, trying to think. I thought I wanted freedom from my marriage. But I don't. At least, not like this. I don't want to destroy my family. I only wanted to feel special and in love again.

I don't text or call Joe. There's no point. I don't want him. I know that now.

A clarity I haven't felt in ages settles over me. I've hurt the two people who loved me unconditionally for what? I rest my head on the steering wheel.

I need to be honest with myself. Tom and I haven't been on the same page in years, and no matter what I did or didn't do with Joe, Tom and I were either going to separate or spend the rest of our marriage living as roommates. Steph's announcement only accelerated the inevitable.

But Nicole... I can't wrap my mind around our diverging

memory of her childhood. She always seemed so happy—but did I ignore her wishes for my own wants?

My chest heaves. Maybe.

Tom's pounds on my car window, and I jump.

When I roll down my window, he says, "You need to leave. You sitting here isn't helping Nicole."

"You're being irrational," I say. "Please. Let's work through this civilly for Nicole's sake."

Tom jabs his finger at me. "You made your decisions. Now you have to live with them."

"I don't understand why you're being like this." I shouldn't engage him when he's been drinking, but I can't help myself.

Tom flips me off. "All these years, I've let you put Nicole before everything else. I let you ignore me and our marriage because you insisted she was more important. I always told myself that when she left home, I'd finally have a wife and not a mother." Years of pent-up resentment spill out of Tom. "But what did you do? You decided you weren't fulfilled or whatever and decided to look elsewhere."

I glare at him. "You checked out the moment we had her. You worked all the time and only showed up for the fun parts." How did I never see this? "When she went to college, you decided you loved watching TV and eating takeout more than spending time with me. This isn't just my fault."

"So, I'm the problem?" He sneers. "Nice try."

"Before you blame me for everything, you need to look in the mirror," I answer.

Tom bangs on the side of the car before shuffling toward the house. I watch as he climbs the stairs and shuts the light green door. When we moved in, we agreed the boring red door had to go, and we both fell in love with a creamy green shade. It complemented the brick siding perfectly, and it seemed like the color a happy family would paint their door.

Were we ever truly happy?

The street is eerily quiet. There's no wind. No birds. Just quiet.

I draw in my breath, count to ten, and release it. Then I start the engine and back down the driveway.

Even though she's mad at me, there's only one place to go: Steph's.

25

DIANA

It's been three weeks since Alex took a leave of absence from Princeton. Three weeks of him getting up every morning, driving to the metro station, and making the long train ride into DC. I wondered if the commute would wear on him, but Alex is the type of kid who sees everything he does through without complaint—Princeton aside.

I used to admire his determination; now, I see it as stubbornness.

"How was work?" I ask Alex. He, Nick, and I are gathered around the island eating dinner. Takeout Asian chicken salad for me and burgers for them. This is what we get when I'm in charge of dinner.

His face lights up. "Really good. We made some progress on Senator Dyson."

"Oh?" Nick looks up from his phone and casts a furtive look at me. I recused myself from working with Dyson when Alex told us his plans.

Alex finishes chewing before speaking. "Lulu finally got him to agree to sit down with her."

Nick and I side-eye each other. Dyson agreeing to sit down

with Lulu is the equivalent of JFK and Stalin being friends—bizarre and unlikely.

"Did she say what the agenda was?" I ask. Last year, Dyson contributed to the Coal Commission through back channels which isn't all bad by itself, but he allegedly also guided congressionally earmarked money away from a solar project in West Virginia to coal. I had a hell of a time sorting it all out.

Alex shakes his head. "No, but I assume it has to do with the West Virginia solar field."

Well, this is curious. Apparently, Nick thinks so too because he sets his phone face down. "Lulu didn't say anything else?"

"No, but I'm a lowly coordinator." He gives his lazy shrug, the one that looks like he may fall asleep if he exerts any more energy. "Still better than Princeton, though."

I finish picking at my salad and put the leftovers in the fridge. "You still need to tell Gigi and Papa." I'm dreading that conversation and haven't pressed Alex to have it. "They need to know soon."

Alex puts more ketchup on his burger. "I know."

"We're not doing it for you," Nick says. He balls up his burger wrapper and drops it in the brown paper bag before wiping the grease off his hands. "So good," he says, patting his stomach. "But I feel sick now."

"Should have had the salad," I tease.

Alex shoves the last bit of burger in his mouth and swallows. "Can I be excused?"

I nod, and he quickly picks up after himself and scurries away.

When I'm positive Alex is out of earshot, I whisper to Nick, "Dyson and Lulu?"

He runs his tongue over his teeth and raises his eyebrows. "I don't see the advantage for Dyson." Nick scowls. "Unless..."

"I'm listening."

Nick draws his brows together. "Is there something to the

solar field? Something you may not have dealt with that Lulu knows?"

I shake my head. "I buried everything."

My husband tilts his head. "Maybe so, but if I was a crisis PR wunderkind, I'd be digging into that instead of managing Kristin's crumbling marriage."

"Her marriage is a lost cause in my opinion." I open the wine fridge and stare at the bottles. "Do you want a glass? I think I might."

"Pick a red." Nick gets the corkscrew and glasses while I try to decide which bottle to open. He sets everything on the island. "What's the latest on the Kristin front, anyway?"

After Tom forced Kristin out, Steph agreed to let her stay in the loft. "She's still at Steph's, and Nicole still refuses to speak to her."

"That's rough."

I nod. Kristin had banked on Tom not remembering their conversation or that he had tossed her out. Unfortunately, Nicole did remember, and she made sure Tom did, too. "At least Kristin can keep an eye on Steph."

Nick uncorks the wine. "I didn't realize she needed babysitting." He sets the bottle on the countertop. "Let it sit for a few minutes."

The day after the Halloween party, I explained the Layla-Jess situation to Nick. Since we were dating when everything happened, he remembers Steph's legal troubles as well as I do. "She shouldn't let Jess back into her life. It will destroy her."

"Babe, that's not your decision." Nick's big, chocolate brown eyes study my face. "You're worried that Jess will tell Steph the truth, aren't you?"

I press my lips together and nod. I forced Jess out of Steph's life and then lied to Steph about it. I didn't bother to get Jess's story, but why would I? My best friend of nearly twelve years was in jail for drug possession and Jess hadn't tried to help her. "If Steph finds out, she'll never speak to me again."

"Sweetheart, this happened—what—twenty-three years ago? You and Steph have made a whole lifetime of memories since then, and Jess hasn't been around." He walks over to me and hugs me tight. "You did what you thought was right. Steph will understand."

My phone dings, and I'm thankful for the interruption—until I see it's my mom. "I should answer."

Nick nods.

"Hi, Mama!" I greet her in English, but she immediately switches languages. I never put her on speaker because it's rude to have a conversation in a language Nick doesn't understand.

"Diana. Have you finished shopping? Thanksgiving is in three days. You need to be prepared."

"Nick and I have everything ready."

Mom snorts. "When do the kids arrive?"

"Emily gets in tomorrow afternoon and Alex is already here." I've practiced my answer.

"Why is Alex home already? Is he missing classes? Princeton's calendar says tomorrow is the last day of classes."

Of course she has the calendar. I switch to English. "His professors canceled tomorrow's classes."

Nick gives me a stern look, but I keep lying. "We flew him home early. I couldn't wait to see him." Nick slugs my arm. "What time will you get here on Thursday?"

"What time is our meal?"

We always eat at four. "Four."

"Papa and I will be there at noon to help."

I don't need my mother's help and neither does Nick. "Wonderful. I can't wait to see you and everyone else."

When I hang up, Nick shakes his head. "I know we told Alex he has to be the one to tell your parents, but Diana, don't make things harder for him."

"You know that she won't blame him." I rest my forearms on the island. "She'll say Alex dropped out because I gave him too much leeway and coddled him too much."

"What do you believe?"

I bite my lip. "I don't know if she's wrong."

Footsteps click-clack on the hardwood floor, and I look up from the drawer I'm digging through. My ferocious mother stands across the room staring at me with her arms crossed. She's tiny, only five-one, and she scares me to death.

"Diana," she barks. "Your guests are waiting. Where are the appetizers and drinks?" She scowls. "The hostess shouldn't be hiding from her company."

It's not easy pretending everything is okay when it is not, but despite my horrible month and panic attacks, I'm not an emotional mess today—at least not outwardly. Alex and Emily are both home which is wonderful. However, the tough conversation Alex needs to have with my parents hangs over our heads.

"Mom, Nick is handling drinks and appetizers." I hold up a stack of gold-flecked placemats. "I needed to get these for the extra table."

She shakes her head. "You're the hostess, not Nick."

"I know." I stand, clutching the stack of placements. Mom added more cousins and their families at the last minute, giving me ten extra mouths to feed. "I wasn't expecting Linda and Sam's families to come. I had to rearrange the tables."

"A good hostess is always ready for anything." Mom frowns again. "You know that."

I nod and follow her to the spice-scented kitchen. Pots boil on the six-burner Viking cooktop; the turkey roasts in the one oven while stuffing bakes in the other. Nick has everything planned to the minute so that the food is served as warm as possible.

"Hey," Nick says from his place at the cooktop. He's wearing a silly, frilly aqua polka-dotted apron, and I love him for it. "Did you find the placemats?"

I hold them up. "I'll set the breakfast table for the kids. I don't think they'll mind if there isn't a tablecloth."

Nick stirs a bubbling pot, and the steam disappears into the overhead hood. "Helen, can you see what people would like to drink? I have a few bottles of prosecco and white chilling. The red wine and spirits are uncorked and ready in the butler's pantry."

Mom scowls. "Diana, why don't you have a bar set up?"

"We do, Mom. In the butler's pantry." I set each placemat at a spot on the breakfast table then I cross the room and grab my everyday silverware from the drawer. The kids don't need fancy stuff. "You should direct people there."

"Very well," Mom says in Hungarian. I hate when she does that. It's just another way she shows how she'll never fully accept Nick as my husband even though we've been married for over twenty years. Nick, to his credit, ignores her slights.

When she's gone, he sets the spoon he's using on the holder and walks toward me. He places his hands on my shoulders and stares down at me. "You okay?"

I shrug. "I wasn't planning on forty for dinner, but it's fine. We'll just have fewer leftovers for Steph."

"I mean, is Helen driving you crazy?"

I shrug again and tilt my head back. "She's my mom. She wants me to be successful in everything I do."

"Dropping ten extra guests on you Thanksgiving morning doesn't exactly support that position."

"They're my cousins. Of course they had to come." I head back to the breakfast table. "Are you on track with dinner?"

"I'm taking the turkey out in ten minutes. Everything else is nearly ready, too." Nick's back at the cooktop, checking on his dishes. Normally, for large gatherings, I have catering, but Nick loves making the Thanksgiving meal. Since my parents didn't grow up celebrating the holiday, they are happy to have him run everything.

I smooth the front of my rust-colored, A-line dress. "Since you're good here, I'll check on our guests." I walk around the island and plant a kiss on Nick's cheek. "Thank you for putting up with my family's craziness."

Nick chuckles. "It's because I love you."

"I love you, too," I say over my shoulder as I pass through the butler's pantry and into the still empty dining room. On the other side, is the great room. Despite its enormous size, the room feels overstuffed. Kids run every which way, and the adults who aren't sitting on sofas, lean against the furniture and sit on my coffee table. I take a deep breath. Who goes to someone's home and sits on their coffee table and the arms of their furniture?

With a fake smile, I take drink orders from my guests, and Mom watches me from across the room.

"Hi, Diana!" my cousin Lainey says with a huge smile. Unlike everyone else, Lainey is dressed like she's going to a cocktail event. "Thanks for the invitation."

"Of course!" Truth be told, I'm not a Lainey fan. I only invited her because Mom said I had to. "How are you?"

Lainey sips from her red wine—no doubt the expensive Spanish red Nick and I brought back from our Barcelona trip. "I'm great!" She holds her wine glass and somehow manages to spin the gigantic diamond on her ring finger at the same time. "Sorry we couldn't make the twins' grad party. We were in the Dominican. You understand, don't you?"

"Of course."

"Really sorry to miss it," her husband Mike says. He played college football, and he's stuck twenty years in the past, relieving his glory days. He spies my other cousin Steven across the room. "Hey, I need to talk to Steve-O. Be right back."

Lainey and Mike are, for reasons I don't understand, my mother's version of the perfect couple. A few years ago, they bought a second home in Deep Creek, and Mom seems to think this is the most amazing, aspirational thing ever. She's been hounding Nick and I to buy one ever since, even though we have zero interest in a second home.

My gaze flits over Lainey's shoulder. Alex stands near the fireplace lost in conversation with Lainey's eldest son, Mason. When they were younger, Alex and Mason were inseparable, going to science camp together and even playing on the same soccer teams. However, once the boys hit middle school, they drifted apart—or more correctly, we all grew busier with life. Now, they only see each other during the holidays.

"Diana?" Lainey says, pouting out her lip. "Are you listening? You seem distracted."

I widen my eyes and smile. "Don't you miss when the boys were small? They were so close."

"We all were." Lainey glances at our sons. "How does Alex like Princeton?"

My job has made me an expert at hiding my true feelings. "He loves it! And how could he not? It's all he's ever wanted."

"Riiight." She says the word slowly, and my brain churns. What does she know? Before I can ask, she changes gears. "Dinner smells delicious! I've always appreciated how Nick loves to cook for us. It's so modern of him."

I'm not sure if it's a dig or not. Yes, my husband loves to cook. It relaxes him—especially after a long day of work. "I'm lucky that I married such a renaissance man."

Nick stands in the doorway between the dining room and great room, and waves at me. "I think dinner may be ready, and Nick needs help." I glance around the room. Kristin still isn't here, but Steph is. Weird, since I thought they'd drive together. "Steph just bought a new BMW," I say to distract Lainey. "You should see it!"

"Oh?" Lainey's never been good at hiding her jealousy. "BMWs are so... which one?"

"I don't know. You should ask her," I say, walking toward Alex and Mason. Mason jerks his head in my direction and both boys clam up. Hmmm.

"Alex," I say. "Can you help Dad and me with dinner?"

"Sure."

I glance around the room one more time. Still no Kristin. Steph said they had planned on driving out together, but Kristin changed her mind at the last minute and said she'd meet Steph here. I hope she's still coming because being alone on Thanksgiving is exactly what she doesn't need.

Alex follows me into the kitchen where Nick has expertly arranged the food onto platters. Bowls of stuffing—Nick's and my mom's—and pumpkin soup with the right amount of cinnamon sit next to the perfectly golden turkey. Nick pulls a dish of Brussel sprouts from the upper oven and sets it on the countertop.

"This looks amazing." I playfully lick my lips.

Nick grins. "Glad you like it." He turns toward Alex. "The sides can go out to the tables. You can start with those. I'll bring the turkey.

Alex exaggerates an inhale. "I'm starving!"

"Start with that." Nick points at the bowl of stuffing.

"Kristin's not here." I lean against the island. "Should we wait?"

Nick shakes his head. "We can't serve cold food because Kristin is late."

"True, but it's Thanksgiving." I take my phone from my dress pocket. "Let me call her."

"We'll wait if she's close."

Alex holds both bowls of stuffing. "Do you want me to wait here?"

"No. Take it out. We'll start in a few." I want to ask Alex what he and Mason were discussing—because the last thing we need is my parents finding out about Alex indirectly.

When he's gone, Nick winks at me. "Don't worry. Even with

Kristin being late and all the last-minute additions, everything is going to be okay."

"We still have to tell my parents Alex withdrew tomorrow." Anxiety nibbles at me. Earlier, I considered taking half a Xanax but decided against it. The last thing I need is to be slightly out of it with my extended family around.

Nick counts the platters of food. "Let's take it one thing at a time."

"Agreed." The smell of cinnamon and cloves and savory meat surrounds us. "Everything smells amazing." I lift the sweet potatoes. "I'll prepare everyone for your grand entrance."

"Sounds good." Nick acts nonchalant, but he loves feeding people. And he especially loves presenting the turkey.

After I place the sweet potatoes in the middle of the decorated table, I head into the great room and look around at everyone. My guest list changes a bit year to year; it's going to be weird not having Nicole and Tom here.

Mason, Emily, and Alex stand with my parents who are talking to Steph and Kristin. Apparently, she finally arrived, and no one told me.

Contentment wells in me. Even though Alex left Princeton, I can't help but feel proud of my family. My parents worked endlessly when they arrived in America. They sacrificed and pushed me. And look at us now, living the American Dream and celebrating Thanksgiving.

"Everyone, dinner is ready," I call out. A few heads swivel toward me, and my announcement gets repeated through the group. I smile at the faces looking back at me. This is what Thanksgiving is all about: gathering with friends and family to express gratitude—even if it entails a little stress along the way.

As everyone files into the dining room, I separate the little kids from the adults and direct everyone to their assigned seats. By mixing up the seating arrangements, I give everyone a chance to catch up. This year, Lainey's kids and my two are seated in the dining room with the adults for the first time.

The main table seats twelve and has been draped in a crisp white tablecloth. Nick, Alex, and two guys we hired off the internet brought the second table we typically keep in the basement up, and I decorated it the same. Between the two, we can fit twenty-four guests which is plenty of room with the breakfast-table seating for the teens and the extra card table Nick set up for the little kids.

As everyone settles into their seats, I return to the kitchen. "We're ready for your grand entrance."

"Do you need help?" Kristen asks from the doorway. For the first time in weeks, she looks pulled together. Her hair is styled in bouncy waves, her makeup is subtle, and she's switched out her yoga clothes for a simple deep green skirt and white blouse.

"We've got it." I sweep my hand up and down. "You look nice."

Kristin smooths her skirt. "I'm trying.

"I know."

Next to the island, Nick removes his silly apron and hoists the turkey to chest height.

"It looks and smells amazing," Kristin says.

Nick beams. "Thank you."

"You could have been a top chef in another life," I joke as we walk toward the dining room. I hold up my hand, signaling Nick to stop. Kristin hurries to her seat. "Everyone," I say loudly, and all heads turn toward me. "Nick has the turkey."

When he enters the room, our guests clap, and Nick playfully dips his head like he's giving little bows over and over again. He settles the half-carved, golden-brown turkey in the middle of the table. It's absolutely magazine-worthy.

"Please," I say to our guests. "Enjoy!"

The table hums to life with people talking and passing dishes. Despite my mother's constant nagging, today has worked out perfectly. The wine and conversation flow nicely throughout dinner, and everyone seems to be getting along. Even my cousins, who typically hang back socially, are talking and laughing with each other.

At one point, Nick stands behind me, bends down, and presses his lips against my ear. "Another success, Mrs. Clarke."

"You did all the cooking," I whisper as his hand travels lower down my back. Maybe it's the wine, but I giggle and Nick nips my ear. Normally, I'd be embarrassed by our PDA, but so what? My husband and I love each other.

Toward the end of the meal, I spy Alex, Emily, and Mason whispering intensely. Mason shakes his head and Emily glares at Alex. From other end of the table, Nick catches my eye and raises his eyebrows.

"Mason, tell everyone about UVA," Lainey says. Something about her tone makes me look up. She's always curious about how her children are doing compared to others, but this feels out of place and forced.

"It's great!" Mason says. "I just started my first year as pre-med."

"UVA is a very nice school," my mother says dismissively in her thick accent. She doesn't seem to care that her sister and brother-in-law are at the table, or that I am a UVA grad.

Lainey scowls. "UVA is an excellent school, Aunt Helen."

I hold my breath, dreading what is coming next.

"It isn't an Ivy League school." Mom smiles at Emily and Alex before staring at Lainey. "Maybe one of your younger two can get into one."

My aunt Marta purses her lips but says nothing. She and Mom compete over everything, with the grandkids' achievements being the most important bragging rights now.

I need to change the topic. Fast. "Lainey? Did Steph show you her car?"

Lainey stares at me like I'm an idiot. "Auntie Helen," she says, "we're working on it. We'll have at least one doctor, a lawyer, and possibly an engineer."

Aunt Marta narrows her eyes at Mom and says in Hungarian, "I have three grandchildren, Helen. You only have… those two."

Neither of my children understand, but Alex squirms in his seat, and Emily smiles at Mom. "Gigi, I love Brown. You were right in helping me choose it!"

Mom nods. "Of course, I was. I know what my family needs."

Emily, like me, always wants my mother's approval, and even a glimmer of acknowledgement is enough to satisfy Emily. "I'm declaring my major at the end of the year."

"And?" my father asks. Unlike Mom, he's quieter, but he's just as involved in all our lives.

"I'm going to focus on biomedical engineering." My daughter waits eagerly for praise, and it breaks my heart. I've chased the same praise all my life, and I know no matter what she does, she'll never get it.

Mom smiles. "It's a very good choice." She leans forward in her chair which is in the middle of the main table. "Alex? Are you still focusing on policy studies?" She isn't thrilled with Alex's former major. "I don't think it's a wise choice. You should do engineering or something that leads to a real career. Maybe pre-med like your cousin. Be a doctor."

We had dozens of arguments with Mom during the application process. Alex wanted to pursue something that would funnel into a legal profession, but Mom thought policy studies was a waste. She wanted pre-law even though Nick explained any major can successfully lead to a law career. She kept saying he was going to end up working for "one of those little nonprofits that make no money."

It was a dig at my post-college work experience even though I ended up doing well.

Across the table, Alex bristles, and his gaze slides toward Mason who shakes his head. My son stares at his folded hands. I want to tell my mother to leave him alone but doing so will just subject Alex to more disappointment from her and draw attention to him.

After a minute, everyone resumes talking, and Alex is forgotten. Then he stands. At first, I think he's clearing plates, but he just stands there looking first at me then at my mom.

"Sweetheart," I say, "are you okay?"

"I'm... I'm not at Princeton." His voice wavers and silence descends over the table.

The blood drains from my head, leaving me dizzy, but I keep my expression calm. "Alex. Not now."

Emily places her hand on Alex's arm and makes pleading eyes at him.

Alex exhales loudly through his nose. His cheeks flush, and he picks at his cuticle—something he does when he's nervous.

My mother turns her steely gaze on me and says, "Diana. What is he talking about? He's not at Princeton?"

Before I can answer, Alex places his hands on the table, hitting his gold-platted fork and flipping it over. "I dropped out a month ago, Gigi."

26

STEPH

The entire party holds its breath, waiting for the punchline. Several heads swivel between Diana and Nick, but instead of her normal calm demeanor, Diana stands trance-like at the end of the table. Then she starts laughing. Softly at first, then louder until she grabs her mid-section and leans forward slightly with a maniacal look dancing in her eyes.

A few guests sputter uncomfortable-sounding chuckles, until the entire party breaks into a roar.

"This is bad," I whisper to Kristin. "Really bad."

A tight smile stretches across Diana's face, but her eyes look crazed. "Alex has such a funny sense of humor! Nick and I always call him our little comedian."

I never, not once, have heard her call Alex a comedian. In fact, Diana often speaks of his seriousness and solid decision-making skills.

Kristin leans closer to me. "What do we do?"

"I don't know."

While everyone laughs, Alex stands frozen, and Emily flicks

her gaze from her parents to her grandparents like she's waiting for a nuclear bomb to explode. She doesn't realize it already has.

"I hope everyone is having a great time!" Diana says in a high tinkly voice. She flutters her hands too much and sounds too pulled together. I know her well enough to know she's frantic. "Dessert will be out in a minute." She walks confidently across the room in her towering heels, takes Alex's hand, and guides him to the end of the table. She holds her head high, and Nick clenches her arm like he's afraid she'll fall. They herd Alex away from the party and into the kitchen. Emily trails behind with her grandparents.

I huddle with Kristin. "Holy shit," I whisper. "I don't think Diana was ready for that."

Kristin is focused on the kitchen doorway. "Not at all."

The laughter is replaced by everyone speaking at once, and I strain to make out individual conversations.

"We need to hold the fort down." Kristin grabs a fork and taps her crystal glass. No one hears her over the din of conversation. "Who's hungry for dessert?" she shouts. When the talking continues, she shouts the question again. This time, the room quiets. "If you'll give us a moment, we'll grab dessert." She smiles as if nothing strange is happening. "I had a peek earlier, and it all looks delicious!"

One of Diana's cousins I vaguely recognize from years past, stares at us. "Kristin," she says, smiling like she won the lottery, "I'm not sure anyone wants dessert."

"Of course, they do, Lainey!" Kristin is a natural with these people. "There's pumpkin pie, a few cakes, and some other things."

Lainey moves closer to Kristin and me and drops her voice. "Do you think Diana and Nick knew? Because I don't. I think Alex has been lying to them."

Gossip about a serious family issue is the last thing I'm going to do.

Kristin deftly pretends nothing unusual has happened. "How's the lake house?"

"The lake house?" Lainey stares at Kristin in confusion. "It's really nice, why?"

"I heard it's lovely." Kristin is an expert at pivoting uncomfortable conversations.

I jerk my head toward the kitchen. "If you'll excuse us, Lainey, we need to get dessert."

It's been at least five minutes since Alex's announcement. Diana would never leave her party for this long unless the world was ending.

"Should we wait for Diana and Nick to come back?" Kristin asks when she catches up to me. "Or send everyone home?"

Mouthwatering desserts line the far counter, but there's no sign of Diana or her family. I walk past the island and into the breakfast room where several children crowd around a boy on a phone. They don't notice us.

"Where are you going?" Kristin asks. "We need to bring dessert out or send everyone home."

"I'm going to find Diana." I head toward the long central hallway running from the front to the back of the massive house. "Are you coming?"

"Steph, this is a family thing. Don't insert yourself." Kristin grabs my arm. "Let's help by making sure the damage with the guests is minimal."

"Diana needs us," I say. "She likes to think she can do everything herself, but she can't. She's part of a team. Our team. And I'm not going to let her face whatever she's facing alone."

Kristin eyes me with trepidation. "I don't know."

"She's been doing it for you."

"This is different." Kristin bites her bottom lip. "I think, in this case, she'd stay out of it."

I frown. "No, she wouldn't. She'd do whatever it took to help us."

"Helping right now is heading back to the party and keeping it going or sending everyone home. That's what Diana would want." Kristin spins back toward the kitchen. "C'mon."

I cross my arms. "I'm not afraid of her."

"Who?"

"Helen." I tilt my head. "She can't continue to bully Diana. Not anymore." When we were kids, the worst punishment Helen handed down to Diana was preventing Kristin and me from seeing her. In fact, when Diana's SAT score didn't come back perfect, Helen locked Diana away for nearly three months to study. It was awful.

"I'm not afraid of Helen." Kristin snorts like my comment is ridiculous, but her stiff posture tells me I'm right.

"Then come with me. You know Helen is tearing Diana apart."

Kristin hesitates. At the far end of the hallway, guests spill into the entryway. They stare at us, and several people speak in hushed tones I can't make out.

"Should we go?" Lainey asks. "I don't think they're coming back."

Kristen laughs nervously. "Did you want dessert?"

Lainey's highlighted, light-brown hair swings over her shoulders. "They're not coming back, and who can blame them? Alex's announcement was a shock."

"Let's all go back to the dining room," Kristin says with too much enthusiasm. I can't believe she's still trying to make the party happen. "Steph and I will bring out dessert."

Lainey rolls her eyes. "The party's over but valiant effort."

"Let them leave," I say so only Kristin can hear. "I doubt Diana and Nick want anyone around."

Kids stream past us as their parents call their names.

"Give Nick and Diana our best," Lainey says to us as she heads toward the front door with her three kids. There's a smugness to her that annoys me, but I let it go.

When everyone has filed out, I stand in the foyer and hold my hands out palm side up. "Now what?"

27

KRISTIN

When I turn around, large portraits of Emily and Alex hang over each wing of the dual staircase, and a massive vase of orange roses sits on the round table dominating the foyer along with a small basket for keys. Diana makes everything look effortless, and sometimes I forget how hard she works at it. Being a mom, running a company, and having a healthy marriage isn't easy.

But having Helen as a mom is even harder.

"We should go, too," I say. Diana hasn't come back which means she's a mess.

The sudden sound of yelling strikes my ears, but I can't make out any the words. It's just shouts and noise.

Steph heads back down the long hallway toward the noise.

"What are you doing?" I ask.

"Diana needs us."

"Steph, please. This is family business. We should go." Steph has a way of inserting herself into everything.

"We are her family." Helen's yelling fills the house, and it's coming from Diana's office. Steph turns that way, and I hurry after her.

No one notices us as we stand in the doorway. They're all too focused on Diana, who sits on her desk chair with her head in her hands. Her parents stand in front of her desk, and Helen's voice is growing louder and louder.

I glance around the room. Nick clenches the back of Diana's chair, and Emily is slumped onto the couch near Steph and me, sobbing. Oddly, Alex is missing.

"Hey," I kneel next to Emily. I try to block out Diana's parents' harsh words. "Why don't you go upstairs? There's no reason for you to witness this."

Emily's dark, wavy hair forms a curtain around her face. She's always been a shy girl and prone to crying, and right now, I bet she's trying to make herself invisible. She keeps her head down and knots her hands in her lap. "Why couldn't Alex wait until tomorrow?"

Steph sits next to Emily and slings her arm around her shoulder. "Was he supposed to?"

"Yes." Emily rubs her nose with her index finger while sniffing. "I told him to finish the semester, but he wouldn't listen. And Mom and Dad have been harboring him here like a fugitive." She stares up at us with watery eyes. "Did you know?"

Steph and I shake our heads.

"He..." Emily pauses and stares at her grandparents and parents. Even though I don't understand what she's yelling, I can tell Helen is livid. She waves her hand in the air, not giving Diana a chance to speak, and her father's stony face is a study in disappointment.

"What did Alex do?" I squat next to the couch so I'm at Emily's level.

"He hasn't told them, but the non-profit he's working for is planning some huge protest outside a Senator's home. I'm worried." Emily presses her lips together. "If he gets arrested..." Emily lifts her head. Dark, wet lashes frame her round hazel eyes. She's a pretty girl like Diana but doesn't know it yet. "He ruined Thanksgiving, and my grandparents are so mad."

Steph squeezes Emily's hand. "Go upstairs, Em, or find Alex. Let us handle this, okay?"

"You sure?"

I know for a fact that like Diana, Emily lives in fear of Helen.

"We've got this," Steph says, pulling Emily to her feet.

Despite the shouts from across the room, I give her a confident smile. "When have we let you down?"

"Never." Emily sniffs. "I'll find Alex."

After she leaves, Steph stares at me then at the scene before us.

"We've done our part," I say. "We got Emily out. Let's go."

Steph pushes her tongue against the side of her mouth and shakes her head. "No. Not when they're treating Diana like a ten-year-old."

Helen spies us and pauses mid-scream. "What," she says, "are you two doing here?"

I want to shrink away, like I did when we were teenagers. I pull on Steph's hand. "Let's go."

"I'm not a timid teenager anymore," Steph says. "I have no problem standing up to Helen." She marches toward the group and stops just short of Helen. "I am taking care of Diana since no one else wants to."

Diana lifts her head. Mascara lines swim down her cheeks, and her nose is red. "Steph, not now," she says. "Wait in the kitchen."

Steph has never been one to listen to reason and walks around the desk. She lifts Diana from the chair by her forearm. "You're done here."

I've witnessed enough Helen ordeals over the years to be used to them, and I learned ages ago to never come between Diana and her mom. But, clearly, Steph has not.

"Where are you going, young lady?" Diana's mother snaps as Steph drags Diana from behind the desk. "Get back here."

"Diana's busy," Steph says, harshly. "She'll call you later if she can."

"What are you doing?" Diana asks as Steph shoves her into the hallway. "My mom is going to kill me. I need to go back in there."

"You're a grown woman," I say, repeating what Steph said earlier. I'll never understand the thrall Diana's parents have over her. I'm close to my mom, but Diana's parental relationship goes beyond closeness. It always has.

"What is your mom going to do?" Steph asks. "Ground you? Make you take an SAT prep class? What?"

We move down the hallway and into the formal sitting room. Diana collapses onto a cream loveseat, and her shoulders sag. "My mom's right. Alex embarrassed us."

"Maybe he couldn't pretend anymore?" Steph says. "Helen and her sister were having a pissing match over the grandkids and maybe it got to him."

"I wasn't ready for it." Diana rolls her neck. "Alex is supposed to be at Princeton. He was going to be a lawyer like Nick, but now he's working for this questionable nonprofit and…"

"Sometimes our dreams for our kids don't align with theirs, and that's okay," I say. I've had three weeks to think about my relationship with Nicole, and she wasn't wrong when she said I forced what I wanted on her. I was so caught up doing what I thought others expected of me that I failed to see what Nicole wanted.

Diana picks a piece of non-existent fuzz off her dress and pretend-drops it on the pale blue area rug. "Where did I go wrong?"

"You did nothing wrong," I say. "Emily said Alex is working and doing something that excites him. College will always be there."

Diana glares at me. "Alex embarrassed me. He upset my parents. He's thrown away everything we've worked for, and now my entire family knows it."

"Diana, listen to yourself," Steph snaps. "You sound like your mom."

"What?" Diana scowls.

"Your mom. She used to talk about you the same way. Everything was about the family image. About you being successful and making the family proud."

"Kids need to be pushed to succeed." Diana squares her shoulders. "It's not in their natural DNA."

"You know that's not true," I say.

Diana stands and adjusts the hem of her dress. "No offense, Kristin, but Nicole is at a state school. You don't know what it's like."

It's a blow, but I stay calm. Diana is just upset. "Maybe not, but I've known you for over thirty years. You want what's best for your children, and Princeton isn't right for Alex. Not right now, but maybe later."

Dishes clang and slam, but there's no more shouting. Nick's probably washing up. He's a stress cleaner, which I've always found funny. Tom can barely place a plate in the dishwasher, but Nick will scrub the house from top to bottom.

"Do you think I'm too hard on them?" Diana asks softly.

Steph exhales. "You're too rigid sometimes and loosening up may be good for you."

Diana dabs along the bottom of her right eye with her fingertip, but a tear rolls down from the opposite eye. "How do I do that? How do I let go?"

"You're going to have to figure it out," Steph says. "Alex and Emily aren't little kids anymore." She pauses. "I'd start with putting some boundaries around your parents."

Diana sinks back onto the sofa. "I'm an unemployed empty-nester whose son is a college dropout." She buries her face in her hands. "I'm such an embarrassment."

Steph walks to Diana and pulls her hands away from her face. She squats down so they're eye to eye. "Diana, you are perfect when you're messy. You always have been."

Diana shakes with sobs.

I join them on the sofa, and Steph and I wrap Diana in a group hug. "We've got you," I say. "We will always have you."

Sometimes, I can get my priorities right.

28

DIANA

This is a disaster.

I set my boar bristle hairbrush down on the vanity and turn slowly around. "Nick," I say as calmly as I can. "We need to talk to Alex."

My husband pops out his contacts and places his glasses on his nose. His normal beaming smile that still makes my knees weak is absent.

"Is this about Alex or you?" Nick strips off his button-up shirt and replaces it with the T-shirt balled on the edge of the soaking tub. "Alex decided to rip off the Band-Aid. It wasn't the right moment, but he did it."

"It's about Alex's future." After talking to Steph and Kristin, I realize I need to distance myself from my mom's expectations, but I still think Alex is making a mistake. "He needs to go back to Princeton. This whole working for Lulu has to stop." I grab my silk robe from the back of the water closet door and wrap it around me. "You agree, don't you?"

I study Nick's face, searching for anything that would give away his thoughts, but all I see is a frown. "No," he says softly. "We need to let him continue working this one out on his own."

I hold my hands out palms up. "He dropped out of Princeton and is working with an environmental terrorist group. How can you be okay with that?"

Nick touches my shoulder. "I think you're biased based on your work with Dyson. Clean Water Now is not a terrorist organization, and they are, in fact, making a positive impact on impoverished communities."

"Are you serious? Did you see how upset my parents are?" All Nick and I have done since he kicked my parents, aunt, and uncle out is talk. Well, I've talked. Nick's listened which is what he normally does. Alex, meanwhile, has barricaded himself in his room while Emily… well, I'm not sure what Emily is doing, but she isn't causing a scene.

Nick sits on the edge of the tub and folds his hands in his lap. His face is soft. Gentle. Like a doctor breaking bad news. "This isn't the end of the world."

"Are you sure? Because it feels like it's all imploding." Steph and Kristin calmed me down enough to think rationally. And thinking rationally, I can understand Alex did what he felt he needed to; and he probably thought it over first. If I know anything about my son, it's that Alex is not impulsive. He analyzes and evaluates everything.

Which means, though it's hard to admit it, I need to trust him. I also have to stand up to my parents to protect my son.

"Sweetheart, sometimes life takes us in unexpected directions." Nick takes off his watch and sets it on top of my jewelry case.

"What are you saying?" I catch my reflection in the mirror. I don't look angry, but hard. Upset. I need to soften my stance. Nick is on my side. I need to remember that.

"This may be his career path."

I raise my eyebrows. "He wants to be a lawyer."

"He decided that in fifth grade! What kid knows what they truly want when they're eleven?"

"Our children."

Nick tilts his head. I know that look. He's done something he doesn't want me to know about.

"What?" I ask.

His face holds no emotion. "Nothing."

My husband may be one of the best litigators in the country, but I can read him so easily. I narrow my eyes and an unimaginable-idea forms in my mind. "Are you okay if he doesn't go to college. Ever?"

"It's not our decision."

The pale gray-and-white floor tiles hypnotize me for a moment. I focus on them, trying to calm the words pounding at my lips. Angry words. Words I can't take back and are better left unsaid.

"Diana?"

"He's going to live in our basement. Or in a camper van." Memories of all the utterly unambitious young people I've worked with fill my mind. "Or whatever it is twenty-somethings do that's the opposite of being a productive member of society."

Nick takes me gently by the shoulders. "Sweetheart, this may seem awful right now, but it isn't. I promise you."

Tears sting my eyes. "He's tossing aside a Princeton education to do what?"

"He's hustling. You see it every day. He gets up, makes that commute, and comes home with excitement," Nick says. "When have you ever felt like that?"

My shoulders are shrugged up next to my ears, and I unroll them. "When I interned at that nonprofit in college, but I got my degree—and my business degree after that."

"Diana, c'mon. Do you really want to force Alex to go to college if it's not what he wants?"

I gape at my husband. "Alex does want it. It's what he's spent the past eighteen years working toward. Letting him quit now will throw away years of academic and extra-curricular excellence."

Nick closes his eyes before opening them and staring into mine. "Alex wants to forge his own path, and I'm one hundred percent behind him."

Alex once asked me if working around the clock was worth it, and I said my hard work is what gave him and Emily their lifestyle. It never occurred to me that he saw my endless hours as a negative. I thought I was demonstrating a strong work ethic.

He's rejecting my way of doing things.

I take off my robe and find a pair of yoga pants and a sweatshirt in the closet and put them on.

"Where are you going?" Nick follows me into our bedroom. "It's nearly midnight." Nick points to the bed. "Let's go to sleep. We can discuss this more tomorrow."

"I need some time alone to process everything," I say. "I'm just going downstairs to my office." I peck his cheek. "Get some sleep. You worked hard today making that delicious meal."

"Diana—"

"I'm fine." I squeeze his hand. "I'll see you in the morning."

When I'm in my office, everything is right. I'm completely in control here. I settle into my black Herman Miller chair and touch the neatly stacked folders to my right. I haven't opened them since being fired, but I have dossiers on dozens of high-level politicians that can't seem to stay out of trouble. Under the terms of my separation agreement, I'm allowed to reach out to several of them.

Senator Dyson is one of them. His project last year was questionable but not illegal—I had JKP's lawyers go over it before we signed the contract. I sort through the stack until I find his file. I keep paper copies of sensitive information because computers are hackable, and I have a lot of dirt on my clients. Technically, I should have handed these over to JKP, but they don't know I have them.

A picture of five-year-old Alex and Emily catches my eye. They had just finished an Easter egg hunt, and Alex has a basket brimming with pastel plastic eggs, while Emily only has a few. But they're both smiling. Both satisfied with their haul.

Looking at it, I realize something: If I'm honest with myself, Alex is happy right now. Happier than I've seen him in years.

I flip Dyson's folder open. Something about his coal deal always struck me as odd, but I could never place a finger on it. I study my notes, searching for an answer.

My phone dings. It's almost one in the morning. Must be Steph.

—Hey! Just checking in—

Steph has always questioned my relationship with my parents —specifically my mom. She and Kristin are not wrong… I'm treating Alex the way my mom treats me. I always thought I had to protect them from my mom, but maybe they needed protection from me too?

*—Can I call you?—*I type. There's something I need to say to her; I can't avoid it any longer.

A series of dots fills my screen. I lean back and wait for the barrage that's sure to come. Instead, my phone rings.

"Hey," I say. My voice is hoarse and scratchy from crying. "I just want to thank you again for everything. I want—"

"Diana, you are my best friend. That's like marriage vows times infinity. I will always have your back—even when I'm mad at you."

I fidget with a pen. Years ago, when Steph was arrested, I thought I was making the right decision when I kicked Jess out. I did it to protect Steph, but now Layla has brought Jess back into our lives. It's only a matter of time before Steph learns the truth.

"I need to tell you something." My voice shakes. "When you were arrested, I—"

"I know."

I let the words hang between us, and Steph says nothing else.

"Do you still want to be my friend?" Tears burn my eyes for the thousandth time today. When I kicked Jess out, I made her swear to never speak to Steph again. I lied and said that Kristin's dad wouldn't bail Steph out or represent her if Jess was still in the picture.

"Would I have risked the wrath of Helen if I didn't want to be your friend?" She chuckles. "She was terrifying."

"Good point."

"I'll check in on you tomorrow, okay?" Steph says.

After we hang up, I use my phone to turn on the Sonos soundbar on the credenza. Then I set my phone aside and settle in for a long night of digging on Dyson. There's something here, I just need to find it.

***

"Mom?" Emily knocks on my office door. "I brought you coffee."

At some point, I stretched out on the office sofa and fell asleep while researching Dyson. I also did some digging on Lulu—otherwise known as Lyndsay Lucketts.

"Thanks, sweetheart." I hold out my hands, and Emily places the coffee in them. I move my feet so she can sit. "How are you today?"

Emily shrugs. "Not as bad as when you were turned into a meme."

"Low threshold, Em."

She shrugs. "Our family is imploding."

I pat her leg. "No, honey, it isn't. It's changing, and that isn't a bad thing." I draw a deep breath. "In fact, I'm making changes right now. JKP fired me, and I'm thinking about starting a new firm."

My late-night Dyson research energized me. Alex may see my endless hours of hard work as a negative, but if fulfills me just like working with Lulu fulfills him.

Shock crosses Emily's face. "You were fired?"

"I was."

"Why?"

I pause for a moment. A few weeks ago, I blamed JKP and those working for me. Now, I see I played a role in my downfall. "I wasn't willing to evolve." I give a small smile. "I've never failed, Em. I've never not been the best, and I asked that of you and Alex, too."

Emily tucks a piece of her dark hair behind her ear. "Mom, you are perfect. You have high standards, but—"

"It's unrealistic," I finish. "It's a burden no one should live under."

Emily exhales loudly. "What about Alex? Or Gigi? What's going to happen?"

I haven't seen Nick since last night, but I'm confident in my answer. "Dad and I will always support you and Alex no matter where your paths lead."

Relief wells in Emily's eyes. "Really?"

Oh no. I can't handle another surprise. "Really."

Her body relaxes. "School is harder than I expected." Emily wrings her hands. "I think I'm going to get a B in calc."

"Were you afraid to tell me?" I ask.

She nods. "I didn't want to disappoint you."

I pull her into a hug with all the love I've never felt from my own mother. "Em, no matter what, you will never disappoint me."

She hugs me back. I close my eyes. I am not a perfect mother, but I'm perfect for my kids and that's all that matters. Not my mom's opinion or anyone else's.

"I love you, sweetheart." I release her.

"I love you too, Mom."

Nick and Alex went out to the Black Friday Sales, something they enjoy doing every year. I'll never understand the appeal of standing in line and fighting with other customers for $99 TVs or weird plushy toys, but it makes them happy. Emily has gone to see Nicole who told her the entire story of Kristin's betrayal, and I'm curious to see what stories Emily comes home with.

My inbox dings, and I scoop my laptop off the coffee table and turn down the TV, which is silly since I'm reading an email, not taking a call.

Can you take a call with Senator Dyson? The email reads. *He has an urgent matter. A call today would be best.*

After Emily went to shower, I gathered my thoughts and jotted off an email to Senator Dyson asking if he needed my services. We had a great working relationship despite my unease around his past projects.

I respond that I'm available all day, and within minutes my phone rings.

"Diana!" The Senator's voice booms. "I had my people try to contact you, but JKP said you had retired."

The official statement that JKP and I agreed upon was that after years of hard work, I had decided I needed an extended break. It saved face for both of us.

"Not fully retired," I say, getting up. I grab my laptop and head to my office where my notes are. "And always available to help an old friend."

The senator laughs. "That's good because I'm in need of a friend with your skills."

"Clean Water Now?" I ask.

"Ah, so you know about the son-of-a-bitch Lulu or whatever her name is."

"I do."

"Goddamn millennial trying to save the planet at the expense of jobs." His voice is filled with fire and annoyance. "Kids today have no concept of the long game. They want immediate gratification for everything."

"Technically, she's Gen Z, but I understand your point."

Senator Dyson laughs heartily. "This is why I like you, Diana. You're a ball-buster." He exhales loudly. "Look, this girl, she's trying to do something real shady with a solar farm. You understand?"

I draw my brows together. Dyson is a coal-and-gas man; he despises renewable energy, but I don't understand what Lulu has to do with a solar farm in West Virginia. "I don't."

"Let's meet for lunch tomorrow. Can you do that? I know it's Saturday, but work never stops."

Work never stops. Not even on a holiday weekend. "Have your assistant send along the info."

"Will do," Senator Dyson says. "It's great to have you on board again, Diana."

"Not on board yet," I say. "Just taking a meeting."

When I hang up, there's no rush of excitement. No sense of achieving anything even with the possibility of landing my first client.

I haven't been able to puzzle out what Dyson's up to, but I'm sure Lulu and Alex are going to be on the receiving end, and I'm not going to let my son run head-first into an ambush.

I fold my hands and stare out the window. "Why would Lulu be interested in a solar farm in West Virginia and what does it have to do with clean water? Or Dyson?"

No matter how hard I try, it doesn't make sense.

29

STEPH

We are always slammed the weekend after Thanksgiving. All three of my venues have shows tonight, but I'm at LUSH again, because we're chronically short-staffed. Sammy, unsurprisingly, quit with no notice and a few people called in with the flu. The stage crew hurries around, lugging equipment, and my staff is prepping for one of our larger events of the year.

"Kristin!" I yell. "Can you help Jean-Luc?"

She nods and hurries off toward the bar. Since she's basically living with me until she and Tom figure things out, I'm making her help at LUSH. I hope she sorts out her issues soon, because even though I love the woman dearly, listening to her cry about Nicole and Tom every day is getting old.

I run through my mental checklist as I walk the perimeter of LUSH. The floor is clean, the Geriatric Section is tidy, the kitchen app is working for once, and—

"Layla?" She's sitting on a metal chair near the stage, slumped forward. "Are you okay?"

She tries lifting her head. "I think I have a fever. I don't feel great."

Shit. "Okay. Can you get to my office? I have some Tylenol and you can stretch out on the sofa."

"Honestly, Steph, I don't know if I can manage the stairs."

Oh. This isn't good. I scan the room. I can't risk exposing any more of my staff, but the roadies…

"Hey," I say to a lanky guy near the bass speaker. "Can you help me get her upstairs? She's hungover."

He jumps off the stage. "Sure."

We maneuver Layla upstairs, and I arrange her on the sofa and toss a blanket over her. I'm used to hungover people, but fevers are out of my realm of experience. As she's swallowing the Tylenol, she starts hacking.

"Are you choking?" I ask.

She stares up at me with large eyes and collapses back onto the sofa. "No, I swallowed it." Her voice is sandpaper rough. "I think I have the flu. That's what everyone else has."

I grimace. "What should I do for you? Are you going to puke?"

Layla rolls her head slowly. "Can you call Mom?"

"Isn't she in Richmond?"

There's a ghostly pallor to Layla's skin, and her eyes are lifeless. "She and Dad came up for Thanksgiving."

"She's here?"

"I left my phone in the staff room." Layla's eyes flutter shut. "Mom's number is 571-555-9067."

"Wait. Not so fast." I grab my phone and type in the first part. "Can you repeat that?"

I wait as the phone rings. And rings. And rings.

"C'mon, Jess. Answer." I hang up and call again.

"Hello?" Jess sounds unsure.

"Jess, hey! It's Steph. I have Layla in my office, and she's really sick. It's the flu or something."

"You're at LUSH?" Jess says without panic. If it were me, I'd be frantic. Especially since Layla looks like she's halfway to dead.

"Yeah. In my office. Tell the door staff you're here to get Layla. I'll call down and let them know."

Layla moans. "Everything hurts."

"Give her some ginger ale," Jess says. "I'll be right there."

I flick off the overhead lights and turn on my desk lamp. "Your mom is on her way."

Layla mumbles unintelligibly. She looks younger than normal and frail, and it scares me that she's this sick. I have no idea what to do for her, so I sit on my desk and watch her chest rise and fall. Her lips are slightly apart, and her breath rattles with each exhale. Is that important? If Jess doesn't get her soon, do I call the doctor? Or the ambulance? We have EMTs on standby for big events. Maybe I should call them?

Every second feels like ten minutes. Finally, Jess knocks on my open door. "Hey, Steph," she says as she walks calmly toward Layla. "I hope we're not putting you out too much."

"I don't do sick people." It comes out more harshly than I intend. "What I mean is, she's really sick. Like sicker than anyone I've ever seen."

Layla flutters her eyes open. "Mom?"

Jess strokes Layla's forehead. "Shhh. I'm here, baby. It's going to be okay." The Jess I knew wasn't gentle. She was all hard edges and good times, and like me, she didn't do sick people. This Jess is so… maternal. "Bobby is out front with the car," she says. "Can you help me get her there?"

"Is she going to be okay?" I don't hide my concern. "Is this something serious?"

"It's influenza. She's going to be down for at least a week." Jess hefts Layla up. "Can you give me a hand?"

Together, we half-carry Layla down the stairs, out the back door, and to Bobby's silver sedan. I had him pull around because I didn't want anyone to see us dragging a near-dead young woman out of the club. Bad press and all that.

Bobby is… not tall. And bald. And has a bit of a paunch. If you put him in a lineup of a hundred men and asked me to find Jess's husband, Bobby would be pick one hundred.

He takes Layla from Jess and me. He's gentle with her as he helps her into the car and buckles her in.

"Let me know how she is," I say to Jess.

Jess eyes are soft. "Don't worry. She'll be okay."

"Are you sure? She looks and sounds like a corpse."

"She'll be fine." Jess climbs into the passenger seat of the Toyota Camry. "She just needs rest and fluids. I'll keep you posted."

I let my gaze linger a little too long on Jess's face. Even though she's aged, she's still beautiful, but I don't feel attraction. "You have my number now."

I stand by the back door, watching, until they turn the corner.

Tuesday, I wake up to the smell of garlic and onions—and the sound of laughter. I roll out of bed, trip on my charging cord, and send my phone flying across the room. Not the best start to the day. I stoop, pick up my phone and seeing that it's not damaged, follow the aromatic smell toward the kitchen.

Diana sits primly on the barstool watching Kristin sauté what I assume is the garlic and onions. A fruit tart, a variety box of pastries, and bottle of champagne sit in front of her, and ingredients cover the rest of the countertop.

"What's going on?"

Diana holds up the champagne bottle. "If you get out some glasses, Sunday brunch!"

I yawn and squint at the clock on the wall oven that is only used to reheat frozen pizzas. "What time is it?"

"Brunch time," Diana says, as if that has actual meaning. She's awfully perky for someone whose world imploded three days ago.

"It's almost one." Kristin turns off the heat and dumps the skillet's contents into a bowl. "I'm making a frittata, and Diana brought all that."

I steal a mini puff pastry confection from the box. "I don't think my kitchen understands what's happening." I take a bite of the sugary goodness. Crumbs fall out of my mouth, and I unsuccessfully try to catch them before they hit the ground. "I don't understand why you're here."

Diana shrugs. "I needed a change of scenery. I've been locked in my office since Friday."

I open the glasses cabinet while Kristin cracks a bunch of eggs into another bowl. "Do you have a whisk?"

I stop pulling out glasses and stare at her. "What do you think?"

"I'll use a fork."

"Good call." I gather the glasses and place them on the peninsula before pulling out the seat next to Diana. "Are we going for nostalgia this morning or are you both here to break terrible news to me?"

When we lived together, we often had Sunday brunch which was the perfect antidote to Saturday night binge-drinking and a few magic pills. Like now, Kristin always cooked, Diana always bought something, and I simply showed up and ate.

Diana laughs. "No bad news. In fact, I may have good news."

I expect her to say Alex has magically re-enrolled at Princeton or found a cure for cancer, but she says, "I'm taking on a new client. I'm starting a new firm."

"Ok, but can we discuss what happened at Thanksgiving? Is Helen still fuming?" I ask.

Kristin pours the egg mixture into a pan. "Tell her."

I raise my eyebrows. "Tell me what?"

"Short list," Diana holds up her fist and raises her pointer finger. "One, yes my mom is still furious." She lifts a second finger. "Two, Nick and I are one hundred percent supporting

Alex." She lifts another finger. "Three, Senator Dyson wanted to retain me."

I hold up my hand. "Wait. You're saying all of this like none of it is a big deal."

She lifts her ring finger. "Four, I turned him down."

I blink. "Why would you turn down a job? All you've been doing is moping about being unemployed."

She puts up her final finger. "Five, I am now representing Clean Water Now, a nonprofit group."

I furrow my brows. "Am I supposed to know what that is?"

Kristin pours an egg mixture over the onions and adds cheese. "It's the nonprofit Alex works for."

"You're working with Alex?" There's being supportive, and then there's this. Three days ago, Diana hated everything about Alex's plan and said he worked for an environmental terrorist.

"I am. Or rather, I'm working with his boss, Lulu—who happens to be an articulate, passionate young woman with an honorable vision."

None of this makes sense.

Kristin shuts the oven door, wipes her hands on a dishtowel, and holds out a champagne glass to Diana who fills it. "Let's toast Diana."

Diana hands me a full glass.

"Can you please explain the sudden change of heart?" I ask.

"Let's toast first!" Kristin extends her glass toward us, and we clink glasses.

It's like I've fallen into an alternate universe where someone deleted my friends' issues. Kristin isn't crying for the first time in weeks, and Diana seems downright happy.

Diana takes a tiny sip of champagne. "I met with Senator Dyson. I asked him to be surface-only with me since my gut told me something was off. He basically implied he wanted me to position Lulu as an environmental terrorist stealing jobs from hard-working miners. She supports the development of a large solar field that has the capability to fuel hundreds of thousands of homes, and he's adamantly against it."

"I thought she did clean water?"

"She does." Diana plucks a strawberry off the tart and bites. After she swallows, she adds. "Which made me dig deeper. The solar field will make coal in the area unnecessary which in turn will aid in the water clean-up efforts—which is what Lulu wants."

"And Dyson?" I ask.

"He's heavily invested in coal but bought his way onto the board of the solar company by proxy under the guise of 'progress.' In actuality, he's trying to the kill the deal."

"Umm… okay?" I don't fully understand, but Diana seems excited. The frittata smells amazing, and my mouth waters. "Is it almost done?"

"Ten more minutes," Kristin says.

Diana widens her eyes. "Don't you see? Dyson is setting Lulu and Clean Water Now up. He's going to make them seem like crazy environmentalists who put their agenda before jobs when the solar field will, in fact, create jobs. They have a plan to retrain the coal workers. It's solid."

"Why are you involved?"

She grins. "I'm going to turn Lulu, aka Lyndsay Lucketts, into a respectable political powerhouse. I'm going to position her to be the voice of reason and for the people by focusing on our failing power grids."

"And water figures in how?"

"She'll rebrand but keep clean water a main goal."

There's a rap on my front door. We all exchange looks.

"Are you expecting someone?" Kristin asks.

I shake my head. "No. It must be a neighbor. The doorman doesn't let anyone up with calling."

I step around the peninsula and walk the short distance across the living room to the front door. I don't have a peep hole or side windows, so I swing it open expecting to see a neighbor upset over Diana parking in the garage or something.

There's a woman in her early thirties wearing a sheriff's uniform. She holds a stack of papers in her hand. "Kristin Carter?"

"No." I blink before a buzzing consumes my mind. Did something happen to Nicole?

Kristin rushes past me. "My daughter," she gasps. "Is my daughter okay?"

The sheriff nods. "I assume so, ma'am." She holds out the papers. "You're being served with divorce papers."

"What?" she says calmly. "What are you talking about?"

The sheriff holds out the packet. "Take them, ma'am." She has a clipboard, too. "Please sign here."

Kristin's hands shake as she signs her name and hands the pen and clipboard to the sheriff.

"Is that all?" she asks.

"Yes, ma'am."

I slam the door. Diana already has Kristin in a tight hug.

"Tom wants a divorce." Kristin sounds disconnected from her words. "He decided this without discussing it with me."

"You haven't considered it?" Diana leads Kristin toward the sofa.

"Not... not really," she says quietly. "I thought, maybe, we could work it all out and keep the family together for Nicole's sake."

I sit across from her. "What would be the point?" The oven buzzer sounds, and Diana hustles to the kitchen. "You're unhappy, Kristin. You've been unhappy for a long time."

She wraps her arms around herself and whispers, "I'm scared."

30

KRISTIN

While Diana cleans the kitchen, Steph sets me up on the sofa and hands me the bottle of champagne. "Normally, I'm not an advocate of drowning sorrows in a bottle, but I think this is a special situation."

The stack of divorce—divorce!—papers sits on the coffee table, an unwelcomed reminder of how off-track my life has gone. How did Tom and I get to this point so fast? Just two months ago, we were eating takeout while watching Netflix, and Tom had said we were at the good stage of marriage.

It wasn't bad, and it was admittedly bland—but divorce?

Steph sits on a floor cushion in front of the fireplace. "Kristin?"

"Yeah?"

She chews on her bottom lip for a second. "I'm going to throw this out there." She glances away. "Do you think Tom has someone else?"

I can't lie, it has occurred to me. "I don't know. He's being so rash, and it's not like him." I've tried not to think about it, because it hurts to believe Tom has been looking elsewhere. "I can't understand how he'd do it, though. Unless..." Saying it out loud makes it feel real. "Maybe someone at the office. He keeps going in even though he doesn't have to."

Diana joins us. "Do you want me to dig?"

Do I want to know if Tom was unfaithful? Will that change anything? He will still want a divorce, but maybe Nicole will forgive me. Maybe if he's done worse than me, she'll talk to me again.

Just the abstract thought of Tom with someone else, pains me. If it's true, was our life together a lie? "No. I don't need to know."

"You sure?" Steph says. "It could make things different."

I wedge the bottle of champagne between my knee and the arm of the sofa. "How awful am I compared to Tom? Honest answer?"

"What you did isn't horrible, but you did hurt people." Diana is on the chair across from me with her ankles crossed. "On a scale of ten, I'd put it at about a 7.25."

"I'd say 6.5," Steph offers. "Honestly, it was only flirting and one kiss." She nibbles a pastry and crumbs fall on her lap. "Was it wrong? Yes. Did it break your vows? Hell if I know, but it doesn't seem like something to end your marriage over."

Diana sips her champagne. At this rate, she's going to polish off the bottle on her own. "What scares you the most?" she asks.

Without hesitation, I answer, "Being alone." For most of my life, I've never been alone. I've always had Nicole or Tom around, and the thought of being by myself terrifies me.

"I'm alone." Steph drinks straight from her own champagne bottle. "And it's wonderful. I can do whatever I want, whenever I want."

Steph has never mentioned being lonely and when Diana and I insist she'll be alone in her senior years, she always waves us off. She's braver than me. The thought of being untethered from everyone doesn't feel like freedom; it feels dangerous.

"Staying because you're scared is settling for the status quo."

Diana sets her empty glass down and motions for Steph to handle her the bottle. To my surprise, Diana refills her glass again—out of the bottle Steph was drinking from.

Steph stretches before lying down on the floor. She tucks a pillow under her head and stares at the ceiling. "Have you heard from Joe?"

"Other than the messages he sent the first day, he hasn't reached out."

Steph turns to look at me. "He isn't such a good friend then, is he? And it says volumes about how he viewed your so-called friendship."

Part of my heart clings to a narrative where Joe was caught off guard by Tom's accusations, and once things die down, he'll reach out. My brain knows it's ridiculous, but a tiny part of me wants it to be true. I want to have ruined my family for a reason beyond my own hormones.

"This isn't what you want to hear, but it's what you need to hear," Diana says. How is she still coherent? She never drinks this much. "Joe has most likely done this before."

If she had slapped me, it would hurt less. My eyes smart. I have wondered. Joe knew how to smoothly duck out of things with Thalia, and he always made sure no one saw us together.

"Joe was grooming you," Diana says. "Doesn't excuse what you did, but I hope you don't see him as a viable alternate to Tom."

My phone lays on the sofa next to me, and I pick it up. "Tom and I haven't spoken since he forced me out. I guess it's time."

"You haven't talked at all?" Steph asks. "Not even a text?"

"No."

She and Diana exchange a look.

"What?" I ask.

"Don't call," Diana says. "You can control the conversation easier with a text."

"Okay."

I tap out a careful message telling Tom that I've received the papers and ask if we can meet to discuss. I end with, *I hope we can handle this respectfully.* I share it with Steph and Diana who both approve.

I hit send and wait for a response.

After two hours, when none comes, his answer is clear.

On Wednesday morning, my house is quiet like I expected. Nicole has gone back to school for finals, and Tom most likely went into the office and took Henry with him. It's weirdly uncomfortable standing in the foyer of my home. Am I trespassing? Is it okay for me to be here?

I sent Tom the text yesterday, and he still hasn't responded. I had hoped he needed time to craft his answer, but it's been more than twenty-four hours. His silence is his answer.

Since I've been living out of my suitcase for weeks, I decided to drive home and pick up some more clothes. Tom can't fault me for that.

As I move through the rooms that I carefully decorated, the sense of being an outsider hangs over me. Everything is the same, but different. There's a dish on the counter and an unfolded throw blanket on the sofa, but other than that it looks just like it did the day Tom made me leave. It looks perfectly normal.

Except... there are no Christmas decorations. There's no tree or laughing stuffed Santa on the family room chair. There's no garland.

It's like the happiness has been sucked from the house.

Memories of Christmases past float through my mind. Every year, Tom, Nicole, and I decorate our tree and house the Saturday after Thanksgiving. I put on Christmas music while Nicole and I make sugar cookies and Tom lugs bins of decorations from the basement. I've always loved those days. We laugh and reminiscence about Nicole's past Christmases.

But today, the house is barren and cold.

I should decorate. Maybe if I do, Nicole will remember how wonderful things were.

Two hours later, I've successfully set up our ten-foot artificial tree and spiraled garland around the banisters. As I'm taking a break, drinking a cup of tea, the garage door opens.

Okay. You can do this. You can have this conversation.

The family room is a mess of bins, bows, and boxes of ornaments.

This was not a good idea.

Tom wanted me to leave and here I am decorating for a holiday we'll spend apart for the first time in twenty-five years.

As the door between the garage and mudroom swings open, panic hits me. I need to leave, but he's caught me in the family room and there's nothing to do but have an uncomfortable interaction. I keep my gaze forward, so that I can't see him when he enters the kitchen.

"Mom? What are you doing?"

I turn around too fast and spill tea on my yoga pants. "Nicole? Honey, why aren't you at school?"

"I finished my exams yesterday, and I didn't want to leave Dad alone for too long." She sets her bag on the kitchen island and stares at the scene around me. "You came home to decorate for Christmas?"

"I needed to pick up some things and saw no one had decorated yet." I head into the family room. "Come. Sit down. Let's talk."

She shuffles toward me like she's torn between running away and asking for a hug. "How did you get the tree up yourself?"

A small bit of hope grows in my heart. "Not without a lot of cussing."

Nicole stands near the sofa. "That's why Dad always does it."

This is the most she's spoken to me in weeks. "How are you doing, sweetheart?"

She clenches her jaw. "I..." Her voice wobbles. "I don't understand why you did it. You seemed happy, and Dad gave you everything you wanted."

Is this Tom's narrative? That he provided and I was ungrateful. Stay calm. Stay absolutely calm.

"Mom?"

I try to gather my thoughts. How do I explain this? "I thought Joe was a friend, and Dad and I were not bad, but not great either." I reach for her hand, and she doesn't pull away. "I crossed a line with Joe, and I regret it deeply."

She inhales shakily. "Was it an affair? Dad says it was, but Tyler's parents haven't split up, and his dad denies it."

Well, now I know. Thalia and Joe are rolling on like normal while I'm over here with a shattered life.

"Mom? Was it an affair?"

Hearing the words from Nicole makes my heart seize. I want to explain that while Tom and I love each other, we aren't *in* love with each other. "Sweetheart," I say, "we flirted with each other and went out to lunches and for drinks, and we kissed once when I was drunk." Steph's words pop into my head. Nicole's reaction is valid and legitimate, and I can't minimize it. "You need to decide if that's an affair to you."

"It sounds like an affair to me." She yanks her hand away. "You kissed someone other than Dad. That's cheating."

"I understand, but it's more complicated than that," I say. "I didn't want to see what was happening until it happened, and I didn't mean for it to go as far as it did. I wasn't searching for someone else. The whole thing just happened."

"Your lips didn't just happen to land on his," Nicole snaps. "You texted for months. It's pretty obvious where it was all going."

My stomach rolls. "I'm... I'm sorry, sweetheart." The weight of my daughter's anger and disappointment cripples me. "I don't know what else to say."

"Why don't you fix it?" Red blotches dot Nicole's normally flawless complexion. "Apologize to Dad and come home." She gestures at the explosion of Christmas around us. "Have you come home? Is that why you're decorating?" There's a hint of hope in her voice.

What should I tell her? That Tom won't talk to me? "I came home to get some clean clothes and see if Dad will talk to me." I press my lips together to hold back the choice words I have for Tom's behavior. "He isn't returning my texts or calls."

Nicole side-eyes me. "Dad said you won't talk to him."

"Unbelievable."

"What's unbelievable?" Nicole asks.

I make pleading eyes at her. "You heard him tell me to leave. You know he is being the difficult one."

Nicole paces in front of the TV. "You didn't have to leave. You could have stayed and fought for us, but you left because it was easier." She starts toward the stairs.

"Where are you going?" I ask. "We're not done talking."

Nicole ignores me and runs up the stairs.

I stand rooted to the floor, unable to move. Decorating for a Christmas that will never happen was a mistake. Tom has no intention of reconciling. He's made his final decision, and he's doing his best to turn Nicole against me.

Was he always so manipulative?

Anger boils inside me. How dare he lie to Nicole and dump this mess entirely on me.

I march upstairs and fling Nicole's door open. She's curled on her bed staring at her phone.

"Your father served me with divorce papers yesterday. Has he told you that?"

Nicole drops her phone. "What?"

"He had them sent to Steph's. If he wanted to try to fix

things, he would have given us time to work through things, but he didn't." Fury builds in my chest. Tom will not disparage me to Nicole. He will not walk away from this as the unscathed hero. "I think, instead of fixating on one kiss I shared with Tyler's dad, you should ask Dad why he goes into the office all the time when he doesn't have to." I lean against the door jamb. "Ask him why he was so quick to file for divorce."

Nicole stares at me slack jawed. "What are you saying?"

"Your father has ignored me and has treated me like his mother and roommate for years." I struggle to keep my voice steady. "He doesn't want a wife. At least not the one he has."

Nicole's face drains of color, and she squeezes into a ball. "Stop!"

I don't. "I was the one who has always been here for you, Nicole. Dad showed up when it was convenient, and he did the same in our marriage."

A long, strangled sound chokes out of Nicole. "You're wrong." She clenches a pillow to her chest. "You're both wrong. You love each other."

"No, baby." I sit on the bed next to her and rub her back. "Daddy and I haven't loved each other for a long time, but I'm just now realizing it."

31

DIANA

"Diana, where is Alex? I told him to be here at 4:30." Mom waves the frying pan she holds in her right hand. "It's after five. Call him."

"Mom, I told you, he's at work. He'll be home around six." I had had exactly eight minutes from the time Alex texted that Mom was on her way over to when she arrived. "What are you making?"

Mom places the pan on the cooktop and walks into the butler's pantry. "Noodles."

"Noodles?" I rearrange myself on the island stool. I'm stalling until Nick gets home. "What kind of noodles?" It's been three weeks, and we still haven't discussed Alex's announcement, but that's clearly why she's here. Mom is going to bulldoze the situation to get the outcome she wants.

"Whatever kind you have the ingredients for," Mom calls. "When did you last grocery shop? All you have is garbage."

My jaw clenches. "I shopped before Thanksgiving and haven't had time to go again, but there are plenty of fresh fruits and veggies and some frozen chicken and fish."

Nick and I agreed that there would be no discussion with my

parents about Alex's life choices. We are supporting him, and that's the end of it. Unfortunately, I lack a backbone when it comes to Mom, and I'm afraid to tell her.

Mom emerges carrying two onions, a head of garlic, and a box of noodles. "Is Nick still doing the cooking?" When I nod, Mom clucks. "It's shameful that you push feeding your family off on your husband."

"Nick loves cooking, and I hate it. You know that." I half-heartedly read an old email to look busy. Only fifteen minutes until Nick is home. I can do this. "Why break something that works?"

"Pfff." She takes a cutting board from the cabinet and drops it on the counter with a thud. "Doesn't Alex live here now, too?

Anxiety gnaws at my heart. "For now."

Mom chops and waves the chef knife after each slice. "He's too young to understand what he's done."

My phone buzzes, and Kristin's name flashes across the screen. I hold up a finger. "Give me a minute, Mom. I need to grab this." I rush to my office and close the door. "Hey. What's up?"

"Nicole." There's a shuffling noise, and I can't make out what else Kristin says.

"Is Nicole okay?" The anxiety I felt minutes ago turns to worry. "Did something happen?"

Kristin exhales loudly into the phone. "I came home to get a few things and stupidly decided to decorate for Christmas."

"Why?"

"I thought it would help things, but it didn't."

I scrunch my brows. "What does this have to do with Nicole?"

"She came home, and… Oh, Diana! I was terrible." Her voice fades in and out, and I can barely understand her. "I told her that we haven't loved each other in years."

"Are you in the car?"

"Yes. I'm driving back to Steph's." She sounds clearer now. "I think I made everything worse."

Nick appears on the other side of the office's glass French doors, and I hold up my finger. "Kristin, I'm so sorry. I can't talk right now. I need to deal with my mother."

Kristin clears her throat. "Has Helen done something else?"

"She's here."

"Oh," Kristin says. "Go. I'm sorry I bothered you."

"I'll call you later."

Nick waits just outside my office door. "My knight," I say. "I wouldn't have survived much longer on my own."

"Call with Lulu?" He asks and plants a kiss on my forehead. Since taking Lulu on as a client, I've immersed myself in the project—partly because it excites me, but mostly because I want to protect Alex from whatever Dyson is plotting.

"Kristin. Sounds like she saw Nicole and things didn't go smoothly."

Nick unbuttons the top two buttons of his dress shirt. "Not surprising." He jerks his head in the direction of the kitchen. "Ready?"

"No." I've dreaded this moment since Nick kicked my parents out Thanksgiving Day. I've kept all texts with Mom civil while avoiding her questions. And now, she's here, demanding answers in person. I should have taken her calls instead; it would have been easier. "Give me a second, okay?"

"Okay."

The spice-scented house smells like my childhood, but it isn't a pleasant memory.

Growing up, Mom controlled everything: whom I was friends with, what classes I took, which activities I was allowed to partic-ipate in (yes to chess, no to cheerleading). She micromanaged my life until I married Nick—and even then, she tried.

Who am I kidding? She still tells me what to do, and I've let her do it to my kids.

Mom's annoyed voice assaults me. "That is not how you do it, Nick."

"Helen, I know how to cook," Nick answers. "No one in my family has died from starvation."

Blood pounds in my ears as I head toward the kitchen. "Hey, sweetheart," I say to Nick and smile the best I can. "What are you two making?"

"Noodles." Nick set his chef's knife down and gives me the look—the one that says it's time to rip off the Band-Aid.

I wish there was more time, but we agreed to do this before Alex gets home. He did his part in telling my parents—even though I disagree with how he did it—and now, it's my and Nick's job to stand up to my mother.

"Helen, Diana and I need to talk to you about Alex."

Mom stops chopping. "I've already told Diana. He's going back to Princeton in January."

"Mom, let's go to the family room and sit down." I gesture toward the sofas. "It's easier if you and Nick aren't distracted with cooking."

Mom's eyes narrow. "An ambush?"

"No, Helen," Nick says, turning off the cooktop and moving the pans to the cool burners. "A discussion."

"There is nothing to discuss. You are his parents. He will go back to Princeton."

"Mom," I say. "Come sit down, please. We need to talk."

She reluctantly sets her knife down, wipes her hands on a dish towel, and joins us in the family room. Nick and I choose the chairs, leaving only the couch for Mom. She sits on the edge so that her feet touch the ground. She's a tiny, frightening fireball.

Nick nods his head, and his eyes flick toward me. I tense. I appreciate Nick taking the lead, and I would love to run out of the room and avoid this conversation, but I need do this.

Nick's face transforms from the kind, loving man I know to

the litigator so many fear. "Alex will not be going back to Princeton," he says evenly.

"Of course he will!" Mom crosses her arms. "You need to make him."

Forty-five years of anger builds inside me. "He may not be going to college at all," I snap. "And Nick and I support his decision."

Mom scowls. "You are letting him ruin his life."

Are we? If Alex doesn't follow the plan Mom and I have carefully planned for him, will he become a basement-dweller? Will he be doomed to a life of mediocre jobs and unable to support a family?

No.

Letting Alex make decisions about his own life—no matter how much I disagree with him—will make him happy. And isn't that the goal of raising children to adults? To make them good people who are happy?

The words I've waited years to say erupt from me. "Mama, all my life I've done what you've wanted, and I've never been allowed to follow my own dreams."

Mom stands, her hands on her hips. "Look at what you have! Look at this life I've given you!"

"You've given me?" I can feel red blotches forming on my chest. "I sacrificed a normal college experience because I didn't want to disappoint you. I let you tell me how to raise my kids, because you convinced me I couldn't do it." I ball my hands into fists and release them. "By your standards, none of this has been me—it's been all you."

Nick knows better than to intervene. He's been asking me to have this conversation for years.

"Exactly." Mom slaps her palms together. "Mothers know best. If I hadn't pushed you, you'd be working at some low-paying job and most likely married to a firefighter or some nonsense." She stomps her foot. "Children need to be pushed. They don't know what they want."

Her words, so similar to what I said to Steph and Kristin, are thrown back at me, and I cringe. "Mom! I'm forty-five. I know what I want, and I'm going to let Alex do things his way. I trust Nick and I have raised an amazing young man who is fully capable of making decisions about the life he wants."

"This is a mistake!" Mom heads to the kitchen as if the conversation is over. "You will regret this."

We follow her.

"Helen, Alex is our son, and this is happening." Nick has shifted into his no-nonsense mode. "This stands for Emily, also. She is free to major in whatever she wants—which happens to be history, by the way."

Oh—Nick is taking no prisoners. I study him carefully. His eyes are hard and his jaw set. I have only seen him like this on a handful of occasions, but I know it means the topic is not open for negotiation.

Mom turns on the stove burner. "You are a disappointment, Diana, and Alex is also. I can't believe this is how you thank Papa and me for all we've done."

Am I being ungrateful? My insides trembled. "Speak English, Mom. Nick doesn't understand you."

"No. I will not. You understand and that's good enough." She angrily pushes the now cold noodles around the pan. "You are risking both of my grandchildren's futures."

"You care more about what Aunt Marta thinks than Alex and Emily's happiness!"

Mom frowns. "You've never known what you are doing. This is just one more example."

The words land with a sharp blow, and I recoil as my breath leaves my body. I hold my tears back. Yes, I've been unsure as a mother, but the realization that others see it too, cuts deep.

"Enough." Nick wraps his arm around my waist and pulls me

to him. "Helen, I don't know what you said, but you need to apologize."

"I will not. Diana needs to hear the truth." Mom crosses her arms. "People will judge you by your children and grandchildren. They will look at our family and see failure."

Rage spills from me. "You know what, Mom? Neither my children nor I are failures. We are happy. We love each other. We support each other." I tuck myself into Nick's side. "That isn't failure. It's success." I reach across the island and pick up a spatula. "Now, if you'll excuse me, I'm going to make noodles for my family!"

Nick lets go of me and walks to Mom. He whispers something, and I don't care that I can't hear him; I'm too focused on not throwing the spatula across the room. Nick escorts her to the foyer, and after the front door shut, I pound my fist against the countertop.

"Fuuuckkk!"

"You handled it well," Nick says, stopping on the other side of the island. "But if you don't mind, I'd like to make dinner." He flashes a goofy smile at me. "You're not the best cook."

I relinquish the spatula. "But I am a good mom?"

"Sweetheart, you are exactly the mom our kids need, and that's all that matters." He tosses the already chopped peppers into a separate pan. "Don't let anyone make you feel differently."

I pull out a barstool and sit. "Mom's mad."

"She'll get over it, and if she doesn't, that's on her—not you." Tears I've held inside for years roll down my cheeks, and Nick stares at me. "Did I upset you?"

With each tear, my body feels lighter like I'm emptying my pockets of stones. One stone for each time I was told I was disappointment or failure. One stone for when I wasn't the best at something. Years of stones from living in fear of making the wrong decision and ruining my children.

My eyes meet Nick's. "No. You didn't upset me." I swallow

the lump in my throat. "I feel... free? Like I've been carrying around all this stuff I accepted as normal and was passing onto the kids." I pop my elbows onto the counter and lean forward with my chin on my fist. "Lighter. Freer. But scared too."

Mom will never be out of my life. I can't do that. I love her despite everything, but I can have boundaries, and I can stop forcing my vision of my kids' lives on them.

THREE MONTHS LATER

32

STEPH

The first thing I notice about Nishiyama's is how sparse it is. Tables are tucked around the edges of the room with a large, open sushi kitchen running through the middle. Chefs in crisp uniforms diligently slice fish and make rolls in the slick stainless-steel kitchen.

It's not the type of place I usually go because I prefer low-key and cheap, and Nishiyama's looks very, very expensive.

"How can I help you?" a petite, red-headed hostess asks with a smile.

Patrons speak in hushed tones, their words lost to the sound of the chefs chopping and shouting orders. Despite the sterile appearance of the room, the low lighting somehow manages to make it intimate and cozy. My gaze skips over a dozen or so diners, searching for Jess, but either she's not here yet or she's hidden on the other side of the kitchen.

"I'm meeting Jessica Stevens."

The hostess taps her iPad, and her glasses slide down her nose before she pushes them up with a fingertip. "Yes. Ms. Stevens is already seated. Please, let me show you to your table."

"Thank you."

As we walk over the polished concrete floors, I try not to slip in the one pair of heels I own. What was I thinking wearing heals? Yes, Nishiyama's is upscale, and my normal black jeans and T-shirt wouldn't fly—but heels?

The hostess and I round the kitchen. Chefs line this side too, giving a view of their talents. I'm so focused on watching them that I don't see Jess sitting at a two-person table just behind the central kitchen until we stop next to the table. There's a glass of water sitting in front of her.

"Hi, Steph! How are you?" Jess smiles widely. Unlike Saturday when she picked up Layla, she's bubbly.

"Can I take your coat?" the hostess asks, holding out her hand.

"Um. Hi, Jess." I shrug out of my wool coat and give it to the hostess. "Thank you," I say. She walks away as I pull out my padded chair.

Jess tilts her head, that smile of hers—the one that always got us in trouble—twitches higher if that's possible. "First, thank you for helping Layla."

"Is she feeling better?"

Jess nods. "Not a hundred percent, but she should be okay to work this weekend." She glances away before focusing on my face. "I know her working with you is awkward, but I appreciate how you take care of her."

I shrug. "I wasn't going to let her go home alone like that. I'm not heartless."

"I know."

An awkward silence punctuates the space between us.

"So, Bobby—'

"—I'm sorry, I—"

"—Sorry?"

"I've been thinking a lot about what we shared the last time we met for dinner." Jess stares at the tabletop for a second like she's trying to gather her thoughts. "About how you didn't know about what Diana and Kristin did… and how you felt about me." She creeps her fingers toward me and stops, like she's waiting for me to meet her halfway. I don't move, but she leaves her hand there.

For decades, I've envisioned a moment where Jess comes back into my life. One where we meet again, and nothing has changed. I've thought hard about what I would say if this moment ever arose.

"What do you want, Jess?"

She pulls her hand back. "To be friends again."

The waiter appears next to us. "Ladies, have you made your selections?"

"Unfortunately, no." Jess touches the menus laying on the table. "Can you give us ten minutes?"

"Of course."

When the waiter leaves, Jess picks up the menus and hands one to me. "Do you have any favorites?"

The selection isn't large, but it overwhelms me. I only eat sushi with Diana and Kristin and can never remember what's sushi and what's sashimi. "Honestly," I say, "whenever I have sushi, my friends order. I just eat what they pick."

"Would you like me to order?" Jess's eyes are kind, not at all judging, and it eases the tension pressing against my ribs.

"Do you mind? I'll eat anything."

"Me, too." Jess grins. "What's the most bizarre thing you've eaten?"

I pause, trying to decide between fried crickets in Thailand or sea slugs. "That's a tough question. I travel a lot. But maybe fried crickets?"

"Bull testicles," Jess offers. "Not entirely exotic, I know, but not high on my list of things to ever try again."

"Same." I chuckle. This relaxed version of Jess is nice. Or maybe it's nice to not have to think about the Kristin or Diana dramas that have consumed my life lately.

The waiter returns, and Jess taps the menu with a scarlet-red manicured nail. She rattles off a dozen items, before saying, "Is that a good amount for two?"

"I think so." The waiter tucks his iPad into the waist of his apron. His eyes widen. "I'm so sorry," he says looking down at me. "Would you like something to drink?"

"A glass of your favorite beer." Beer seems to go well with sushi. At least I hope it does.

"I'll be right back."

"Are you happy?" Jess's dark, wavy hair falls perfectly over her shoulders. It's longer than Diana's even and just as glossy.

"Happy?" No one ever asks me that. Am I happy? "Content," I say, "is probably a better word. I love what I do, and I love my friends." I half-smile. "But I don't think I've been truly happy in years."

Why am I telling her this? I don't even tell Diana and Kristin. Maybe because they've spent the past twenty years trying to make me more like them: come home, Steph. Find a nice guy, Steph. Have a big house and fill it with kids. You'll have regrets if you don't.

But the only regret I have is sitting in front of me, listening to me.

An elaborate boat of sushi—or is it sashimi—over ice arrives, and the waiter places it between us. Jess smacks her lips together. "This looks amazing."

"Can I get you anything else?" he asks.

Jess studies the boat. "I think this is everything for now." She has an easy way about her, a kindness that I'd forgotten about. After the waiter leaves, she asks, "Is being content enough for you?" she asks.

"I thought so?"

Jess uses chopsticks to lift a piece of fish from the ice boat. "Thought?"

How much is too much to share? I'm just going to say it.

"I thought I was until I found out Layla is your daughter. I thought I was happy floating through life unattached to anything aside from work, but I'm not." I swallow hard and will myself to continue. "I don't need a life partner or kids, like Diana and Kristin say I do."

Jess finishes chewing her food and sets her chopsticks down. "What do you need?"

"Peace." The word comes out before I think.

"Peace?" Jess stares at me in confusion.

My heart pounds. "All these years, Jess, I thought you abandoned me. I thought you didn't care what happened to me, and you told me that wasn't so."

"It wasn't." She blinks hard. "I swear it wasn't."

"I believe you." I have no appetite, but I sip my drink. "Finding out about Layla... it shocked me, but it flipped a switch in me. I've spent all these years hurting and being mad over how you abandoned me, but when I look at Layla..."

Jess's moist eyes glisten in the candlelight.

"I know I made the right decision all those years ago." I may not be making sense, but I need to say this: "You created this amazing young woman because you had the opportunity, and I had an amazing life because everything took a horrific left turn." I settle against the back of my chair. "Meeting Layla and finding you again... it's helped me see that I need to let go of how I think things should have been and focus on how amazing things are right now."

Tears slide down Jess's cheeks, and she wipes them away. "You think Layla is amazing?"

"She really is."

"And you don't hate me?"

I shake my head. "I don't hate Diana or Kristin either. They did what they did—no matter how misguided—because they love me."

"They do." Jess dabs her eyes with her napkin. This time when Jess walks her fingertips across the table, I take her hand. "Can we be friends again?" she asks.

I smile at her. "That would make me happy."

***

During the rest of our meal, Jess and I share our favorite authors —she devours romance novels and I like Stephan King. She tells me how she became a whisky collector after endless years working with male executives even though she doesn't drink it herself, and I admit my love of wine is primarily from being too lazy to learn about anything else.

It's weird being with this more grown-up version of Jess, and every so often I catch a glimmer of the young woman I used to know—the one who was fearless, who wanted to travel the world, and who didn't know how she was going to pay her bills, but knew she'd figure it out.

"My treat," Jess says when the waiter places the bill on the table.

I'm buzzed from the beer and feel loopy. "Let's split it."

"My treat for helping Layla." Jessica hands the waiter her card before turning her attention back to me. "I appreciate you taking Layla under your wing. She may not realize it, but I do, and she's lucky. Not all young women find a mentor like you—if at all."

I lift my hands in protest. "I'm not really a mentor. I just think she has potential."

"I'll be honest, when she told me she wanted to drop out of college and work in a night club, I lost my mind."

"Understandable." After my legal issues, my own parents have more or less ignored me, so everything I know about adult parental relationships is based on Kristin's and Diana's.

The waiter returns with Jess's card, and she signs.

As we walk toward the exit, Jessica leans in close to me and the scent of her light floral perfume fills my nose. "Tonight was fun. Bobby and I don't get out often."

I shrug. "I spend most of my time in clubs, and it isn't as fun as we thought it was back in the day."

"Still, it's better than the suburban malaise engulfing me." Jess's Uber pulls up to the curb. "I'll be in town between Christmas and New Year's with Bobby. Can we do this again?"

"I'd like that."

It's well after eleven when I get home—early for me—and Kristin is gone. She hasn't texted, so I have no idea when she'll be back. Since I'm not in the detective business, I don't call her. As long as she's quiet when she gets home, I don't care when she comes and goes.

I throw my coat over the leather armchair and kick my heels off next to the couch. Normally, I'd change into joggers and a T-shirt and get comfy, but tonight I stretch my legs out on the sofa and drape a blanket over myself.

If Jess is going to be part of my life again, I need to address it with Kristin and Diana and share what truly happened the night I was arrested. It's a conversation I've avoided for twenty-three years—and one we all thought was in the past.

Neither of them know my past feelings for Jess, and I think that's best. Maybe it would explain why I made the decision I did, but it's also something I have to work through without them in my head.

When I told Jess I needed peace, I meant it; and tonight gave me that. The chapter of past "what-ifs" has closed, and I accept how things are. For too many years—decades, really—I let my pain prevent me from fully moving forward.

The sound of a key in the door pulls me from my thoughts. Kristin stumbles in.

"I'm on the sofa," I say, sitting up.

Kristin places her bag on the floor near the door. "Hey," she says. Her red-rimmed eyes aren't unusual anymore. "I didn't realize you had tonight off."

"I did." I shift on the couch so I can face her when she sits down. "I had dinner with a friend."

Kristin isn't paying attention. Her shoulders roll forward and her blonde hair hangs limply around her face. "I saw Nicole."

I was prepared for a tough conversation about Jess, and this catches me by surprise. "Oh. Where?"

"At the house." Kristin balls her hands in her lap. "I went home to grab some more clothes and random things." She splays her fingers wide like an explosion. "I should have just left, but I decided to start decorating for Christmas."

"Why would you do that?" Kristin loves Christmas but decorating a home that her soon-to-be ex-husband occupies seems odd.

She shakes her head. "I don't know, but Nicole surprised me. I thought she'd gone back to school." Kristin drags her foot across the floor in a tiny arc. "Steph, I told her too much about Tom and me."

"Seems like he's done the same about you."

Kristin shakes her head. "I implied he may be cheating." She covers her face with her hands. "What is wrong with me? Like, seriously. What the hell is wrong with me?"

I motion for her to come sit next to me and when she does, I wrap my arm over her shoulder. Kristin covers her face. Neither of us move. I let her cry because, honestly, I don't know what else to do.

After a few minutes, she lifts her head and wipes the back of her hand across her face. "I'm drowning, Steph. I've lost my family, I have no job, and I spend most of my days lying on the couch watching Bravo." Her chin crumples. "I wish I could be more like you. You know exactly who you are."

I raise my eyebrows. All I've ever heard is that my lifestyle is stunted. That I spend too much in night clubs. That I'm going to wake up one day and realize I've pissed away my child-bearing years.

But now isn't the time to bring up Kristin's about-face or discuss Jess. Maybe tomorrow if Diana is around. I'll get it all over at once.

"Trust me, I don't have much figured out," I say. I spent years in constant motion, searching for something that lurked just beyond the edge of my reach. I understand now that my entire adult existence was spent searching for the one thing that eluded me: peace.

Kristin sighs. "You have a life that isn't solely dependent upon another person for your identity." She lifts her head. "I was Tom's wife and Nicole's mom. Now what am I?"

"You are an amazing friend." I elbow her lightly, trying to change her mood. "And you'll always be Nicole's mom. No one can take that from you."

"Nicole is a mess, and I think she now hates both Tom and me." Kristin rolls out her neck. "She grabbed her things and went to Tyler's. I'm sure Thalia and Joe love that."

Nicole has always been a little dramatic, so I'm not surprised by her reaction at all. "Give her time. She'll come around."

"I don't know, Steph." Kristin tips over on the sofa and buries her face in the throw pillows. "What if this is all there is for me? What if I'm supposed to be a lonely spinster?"

"I don't believe that, and neither should you." I pick up the TV remote. "Should we binge watch something terrible to get your mind off all this?"

Kristin nods.

I flip through previews until we find something we both agree on. For an hour, we lose ourselves in a supposed bad-detective drama that feels more like a comedy. When I hear Kristin softly snoring, I cover her with the blanket and head to my room.

The only life Kristin knows is ending, but my life is just beginning.

33

DIANA

Lyndsay Lucketts came prepared. Her yellow legal pad is filled with notes and every time the media trainer makes corrections, she immediately does it.

"Lulu," I say. "You know the talking points, but we need to create a story around each one. The more relatable we can make your position—and you—the better the chance of winning over senators. Especially since you're going up against one of their own."

"Can you give us a few minutes?" She asks the bare-bones team she brought with her. Not one is a day over twenty-eight, but every single one is passionate about their cause. Alex stands up and clutches a notebook covered in his loopy scrawl.

When we're working, I keep everything professional with Alex, but I struggle with not gushing over him. He was right—Princeton wasn't for him. I have never seen him this energized about anything. Yes, he spent his entire childhood succeeding at whatever was thrown at him, but he never had this kind of light in his eyes.

Nick and I have asked him to consider going part-time to the local community college and eventually getting a business degree—something Lulu suggested also. She herself has a master's in public policy, and Alex hasn't dismissed the idea, but for the time-being, he feels his place is working for Clean Water Now, and I support him.

After everyone files out, Lulu asks me, "What's our best chance at success? I don't want to mess this up."

I pause. "Do you believe in this cause?"

"Yes."

"Do you believe you can make positive impact on the world both professionally and personally with this hearing?"

"I do."

"Why?"

Lulu bites her lip.

"Don't look unsure," I say. "Biting your lip looks like you've been caught off-guard."

She squares her shoulders and lifts her chin. "If I can change one mind, that's one person who can change another mind, and a snowball rolling downhill can become an avalanche."

"You've got this." My heart swells. "Let's bring everyone back in and work on your narrative."

The alarm on my phone sounds. A reminder about my coffee date with Steph and Kristin pops up, but Lulu needs at least two more hours of training. In the past, I would have made an excuse and not shown up for coffee, but that's not who I am anymore. I don't live to work. I'm finding balance.

"Ainsley?" I say to my head of crisis PR. "Can you take it from here? I have a meeting."

"Of course." Like me, Ainsley wears dress pants, a button-up blouse, heels, and tasteful jewelry. When I hired her, I worried about her age and short resume, but now that we're in the trenches, I appreciate her dedication. Like Lulu, Ainsley is young, hungry, and ready to change the world.

"Great. Send me a wrap-up tonight, okay?"

She scribbles on her notepad. "Do you want to see the footage too? Lulu is doing great, but maybe you have some suggestions?"

A year ago, I would have micro-managed Ainsley to death, but I've learned sometimes it's best to let my employees have agency of their projects. "No," I say. "I trust you, and we can work out any bumps tomorrow."

Lulu testifies on Thursday at a congressional hearing, and I have no concern about her ability to be articulate, level, and factual.

I gather my things. "I need to step away," I say to the room. "But I'm leaving you in Ainsley's capable hands."

As I turn to leave, Alex smiles at me. Like Nick, he's mentioned how much happier I seem now that I'm focusing on creating balance in my life.

And you know what? I am.

I may not have a son at Princeton or a job that pays me high six-figures, but I have a husband I adore and who loves me, amazing, independent kids, and friends who stand by me no matter what.

My life is full.

34

STEPH

"I'll be in town next weekend. Maybe the four of us can have dinner?" Jess says over my car's Bluetooth as I pull into the spot next to Kristin's SUV. I'm late, but traffic was awful.

Plus, I overslept, but Kristin and Diana don't need to know that.

"I'll float the idea." I shift into park. "I'll text you later and let you know."

"Sounds good."

Kristin and Diana have been supportive of my rekindled friendship with Jess, but they haven't seen her yet even though she comes up regularly to see Layla. They are tucked against a window table, and Diana waves across the crowded shop when she spies me. "We were beginning to wonder if you'd forgotten about us."

I toss my keys on the table. "Traffic."

"And oversleeping?" Kristin teases. After living with me for two months, she unfortunately knows my bad habits and sins.

I shrug. "Maybe…"

"I'll get the drinks," Kristin says. "What do you want?"

"Double espresso," I say. "Layla had the weekend off, and I'm wiped out." I slump in my chair. I've been giving Layla more responsibilities around LUSH, and she's excelling. "I'm getting ancient. Five a.m. shifts kill me."

"Uh-uh. None of that." Diana wags a finger at me. She turns to Kristin. "A Skinny Bitch."

Kristin gawks. "Who are you and what have you done with our Diana?"

"You mean stick-up-her-butt Diana?" Diana says with a laugh. "She's in here somewhere, waiting for her mother to appear and piss her off."

Diana and Helen are at an impasse. Helen has threatened to disown Diana, but we all know she won't. Diana and her family are all she has, and Diana isn't budging on her positions.

Honestly, the whole thing should have happened years ago, but at least it happened.

While Kristin waits in line, Diana studies me with a look of suspicion.

"What?" I hate when she does this. It's like she can read my thoughts.

"I heard you talking to Jess." She raises her eyebrows. "Never have private conversations over Bluetooth."

"How? You were inside."

"I was tied up at work and only beat you in by a minute." She folds her hands on the tabletop. "I'm open to it—having dinner with Jess."

Kristin sets our drinks on the table. "Dinner with Jess?"

She's the one who I am most afraid to ask, but here it goes. "Yeah. Um. She'd like the four of us to go out when she's in town next."

"Sure."

That's not what I expected. "Sure?"

Kristin blows on her Skinny Bitch. "If everything happened

the way that you say, and Diana and I did what we did based on wrong info, then, yes, I'll meet with her."

I blink away my shock. "Really?"

"Really." Diana touches my arm. "She's important to you and that makes her important to us." Her hand moves to mine, and she grasps it. "We did what we thought was best for you instead of letting you make those decisions for yourself."

Something I've waited decades to say forces it way to my lips. "You know, back then, I liked her more than as a friend."

Kristin chuckles. "You think we don't know?"

"Ms. Obvious. You were always mooning around over her." Diana reaches into her bag and checks her phone before setting it face down. Some things never change. "The important question is: how do you feel about her now?"

"She's my friend. An older, more mature version of my friend." I wiggle my eyebrows. "An older vintage, just like you two, and I have no romantic feelings toward her."

"Are you calling us old?" Kristin shrieks playfully. "Are you calling us Has-Beens?"

Diana winces. "That word. Emily still hasn't forgiven me for that debacle."

I hold out my coffee mug. "Not Has-Beens. We're Begin-Agains."

"Begin-Agains," Diana repeats. "I like that."

"Me too," Kristin says.

"To the Begin-Agains," I say, and we clink mugs.

ALSO BY MIA HAYES

The Waterford Novels

The Secrets We Keep

All the Broken Pieces

Picture Perfect Lies

Memoir

Always Yours, Bee

ABOUT THE AUTHOR

Mia is a notorious eavesdropper who lives in Northern Virginia, outside Washington DC, with her husband, sons, two cats, and Harlow the Cavapoo.

She drinks too much green tea, loves traveling, and has mastered the art of procrastination cleaning.

9 781736 307335